Good Grief

a novel
by Nick Gregorio

Listen along on Spotify while you read!

(scan code on Spotify app)

www.maudlinhouse.net
www.twitter.com/maudlinhouse

Good Grief
Copyright © 2017 by Nick Gregorio

ISBN 10: 0-9994723-0-5
ISBN 13 : 978-0-9994723-0-9

For MT II.

Part 1

1

Tony hasn't been to work since he found his brother dead with a needle in his arm sitting cross-legged on a twin bed in their parents' house.

Now, standing in the staff lot, Tony smokes in full view of the students. He stares at the front of the building, the glass doors swinging open, closed as the kids go inside. Before Nate's death, he would be more discreet. Before all the burnt sick time. He would drive around the block, smoke one or several cigarettes depending on how the kids were behaving. Or how far Principal Adler had jammed his head up his ass.

But now he stands thirty, forty steps away from the doors. His peacoat open. His satchel hanging from his shoulder, across his chest, crumpling his lapels. He smokes his cigarette without using his hands.

It takes a bit for Tony to notice the students reacting to the gossip he's creating. In packs, they stop, point, whisper, and move along. It'll jump homeroom to homeroom, then department to department. Then Tony will be asked to stop by Adler's office.

But then there's the February cold. The difference in color and consistency between the smoke he exhales and his breath. The apartment a couple of cigarettes away. The primetime reruns he's missing. And sleep.

Then there's the vibrating phone in his pocket. The vibrating phone he ignores.

Tony reaches into his coat pocket for his cigarettes. They rattle in the pack, only a couple left. He lights his third smoke with the cherry of his second. Realizes he's not alone after flicking a butt behind him.

"These are new shoes," Chris says.

"Shit, sorry. Didn't see you there."

"No? How you doing?"

"Good, man. You?"

"That's not the answer I was expecting, but alright. I'm good. Give me one."

Tony hands Chris his pack, his lighter, says, "Thought you quit."

"I did. But I miss looking as cool as you." Chris's words collapse into a series of hacks.

"If we were still in high school we'd be cleaning up right now."

"We are still in high school."

They stand and smoke. They don't talk. Chris checks his cell phone one, twice, three times. Tony leaves this in his pocket.

When they were students together, they would come to this lot and smoke during football games on weekends. They had honed a punk rock, fuck authority predilection just interesting enough for girls who went to the games with friends of friends who knew a guy on the bench to break away with them. They'd pass around a Discman loaded with *Bad Religion* or *NoFX* or *Suicide Machines* CDs. They'd share cigarettes with the girls, act badass, spit lines from *Catcher in the Rye*. Semi-acned and suburb-pissed, they'd scoff, laugh whenever the girls said they had to get back, say those particular girls weren't hot enough for them anyway.

Tony felt Karen Kelly up for the first time just feet away from where he and Chris stand now. If he had thought then that he'd wind up teaching here, he would have laughed out loud, gotten his hand caught in Karen's underwire.

"Didn't you get your hand caught in Karen's underwire over there?" Chris says.

"Sure did."

"Christ, she's still gorgeous," Chris says.

"Seriously."

"You know how lucky you were, right?"

"Then? No. Now, yes."

"Never told me you still talk to her."

"Didn't think it was anything to talk about."

When Tony found Nate's body, he called his father, then 911. Then he called Karen. She got off the phone before he could say anything other than his brother was dead. He knew what that meant. She was at the house just after the EMTs rolled out Nate's body covered in a sheet.

"Surprised she was at the service," Chris says.

"Why? You saw her with my parents."

"I just remember Nate being shitty—shit. I'm sorry."

Tony shakes his head, drags from his smoke, slaps Chris on the shoulder. He tells him not to worry about it, says, "He was shitty."

More silence.

Tony can count the times silence has happened to them over the course of their friendship. Once, twice. Maybe.

His phone vibrates again. This time he checks it.

It's not who he was hoping it would be. Again.

"Adler thinks you're coming back too soon," Chris says.

"Yeah, well." Tony drops his butt, mashes it into the blacktop under his shoe. "Dad told me the same thing."

"Think your dad might have a point this time, man."

Tony hears the homeroom bell ring walking backward through the parking lot, laughs. "My brother's dead," he says. "I'll deal with it how I want."

Leaving Chris behind, Tony turns, walks, and shoves his way through the glass doors into a steady stream of panicked students. They lingered too long in the cafeteria, at their lockers. He hears their excuses as he passes classrooms on the way to his own. All boring truths, no creativity, nothing as good as what he used to come up with. These kids don't have the leverage he had either. If a teacher didn't eat the bullshit Tony was spewing as a student, he'd remind them who his brother was. Who his father was.

Entering the newest building added at the tail end of Tony's original stay, he passes the Wall of Fame—a trophy case filled with awards and photos of the school's highest achievers. Photos of Nate holding oars with his crew, or a football helmet under his arm. Groups of students with plaques in hand stand smiling next to board members. Framed in engraved gold are leadership groups, student committees, class presidential cabinets.

And Nathan D'Angelo Jr. is present more than anyone in over seventy-five years of photographed school history.

***

As I Lay Dying on Tony's desk. Addie Bundren's eyes closed on the cover. Her head turned to the side, as bored by Tony's lecture as his students.

Some of his sophomores have their faces cupped in their hands, or smushed into their fists. Some have their heads down. Someone's snoring.

Tony drops himself into his chair behind his own desk, stares across the room. Once, forever ago, he sat in this classroom drinking from a water bottle filled with vodka and orange juice. He was sent home that day before lunch, drunk as hell.

Tony pulls his phone from his pocket, keeps it under his desk, texts Karen. Something stupid. Cute. He sends a smiley face, feels his face turn red. Then his gut sinks. From the texts from earlier he left unopened, keeps unopened. From the texts he just sent.

The class is lost for the period. Tony knows it. It's not pre-lunch drowsiness, it's him. The lull in his lesson was too long, the PowerPoint on Faulkner was too textbook—as in, copied from the textbook.

He stands, lifts the book from his desk, slams Addie down face first. The metal frame under the flakeboard surface rings, bounces off the painted concrete block walls.

The students lift their heads, rub their eyes. Tony says, "Leave."

The kids pack their books. Tony tells them not to pass Mr. Adler's office. "Go to the caf, the library, anywhere but the main hall."

Tony nods to his students as they go, tells them to have a good day, tells them not to get caught in the halls, tells them they'll fail the class if they get caught. He smiles, tries to make it a joke.

The kids flow out of the classroom, some say goodbye. Most just leave.

He flinches from his phone vibrating in his pocket. He doesn't wait for the class to empty.

Another text.

Not from Karen.

He lets this one go too.

There's a pen on a desk. Paper on the floor. A crumpled milk carton stuffed between the wall and the radiator. And the weight in Tony's chest.

He walks the room, picks up the garbage, tosses it in the trash.

His nose stops working, stops taking in air.

He shuts off the projector, closes his laptop, rolls up the vinyl screen.

He has to breathe with his mouth, but it all gets caught up behind his sternum.

Palms on the desk, bent at the hip, Tony's body turns on him.

He runs his eyes over his desk, over the paths in the fake woodgrain. Stretched-out age rings forming faces, mountains, patterns no one notices until forced to.

Now, his eyes water, his mouth dries, his knees shake.

When they were kids, Nate would hide, tackle Tony, sit on his chest, tell him to say uncle.

Tony pushes off the desk, puffs out his chest, breathes.

Principal Adler knocks on the open door, says hello.

And Tony, red-faced and slobbering, smiles, waves.

Adler says, "Have time to talk in my office?"

Tony nods until he's alone.

Then he sits on the floor until he can breathe again.

***

In the principal's office, Adler asks Tony how he's doing, why he decided to come back so soon, how his family's holding up.

Tony says, "I'm good, thanks for asking," despite Adler's all-business folded hands on the desk, tapping out arrhythmic thumb beats.

And, "Felt like a little normal could help," ignoring the portrait of the school's founder on the wall staring down at him, through him.

And, "Family's okay, we're getting by," holding back a laugh at the shift in Adler's globular face.

"Anthony, you can be honest with me."

"I am. Really."

Adler tells him he saw what happened after the memorial, talks about how Tony acted with Nate's friend—Jason, was it. "And you seemed to be having some sort of an attack just now?"

"That was nothing."

"Nothing?"

Tony's phone buzzes in his pocket, a call. Loud enough to stop Adler from blathering. "Can we stop for a second?" Tony says.

"Sure."

"I have to take this." Tony stands, his phone already to his ear.

His mother knows where he is. She's called twice already. Left a voicemail during morning announcements. She told him to stop ignoring his father about getting back to work so soon. Said he should take all the time he needs. Said he should listen to his father. Kept saying Family. And Unit. And Support.

Tony smiles to dull the edge to his voice, says hello.

"Why haven't you called me back, Anthony?"

"I'm at work, Mom."

"Then how are you calling me now?"

"I had a panic attack and got called down to the principal's office."

"What?"

"I'm joking. That was a joke."

"Why do your jokes always have to be so damn nasty?"

Tony closes his eyes, pinches the bridge of his nose, peeks his head into Adler's office and mouths that he'll be just a minute longer. "What can I do for you, Mom?"

"I found some of Nathan's old records. You might like some of them."

"I'll bet most of those records are mine and he died before he could sell them."

Tony's mother says nothing.

He says, "That came out wrong."

And, "I didn't mean to say it that way."

Then she hangs up on him.

Alone, in the hall outside Adler's office, Tony covers his mouth with his hand. His eyes close, tear up. Then he shifts the sound coming from his chest to a chuckle, then a laugh.

This had all happened before. Too many times to remember how many times. His mother hanging up on him. Standing in the main hall waiting for Adler to call him back inside. Only now Nate won't stroll down the corridor with his friends—teammates, whatever—to mock him, tell him how dead he is when he gets home.

Tony walks back into the office wiping his eyes. He thinks he says, "Sorry about that, where were we?"

Wants to say, "Are we done here?"

Probably says, "What's up?"

Principal Adler goes on a tangent regarding death and dying, the loss of family, coping with it. And Tony zones out. His mind drifts to Karen, what she's doing. To whether his mother is crying. To what his father has to say about all this—he hasn't talked about much aside from thinking about going on some hunting trip since seeing Nate on the bed.

Nate being cremated. *Raiders of the Lost Ark*, gooey, bloody.

What people would say if they knew how little Tony was shocked, Nate being dead.

Adler says, "So, why don't you head on home. Come in tomorrow if you feel up to it."

Tony unclenches his teeth, wipes his eyes again, says, "What?"

"Tony, it's okay. We miss him, too. We'll see you tomorrow."

Tony checks his phone. A text from Karen. She's working from home the rest of the day.

"Tony?" Adler says.

Tony says, "Hmm? Oh, sorry. Yeah. Yeah, see you in the morning."

***

Karen clunks a coffee in front of Tony. She sits down across the table from him, blows at the steam frothing over the edge of her mug.

They stare at each other.

Tony clears his throat.

Karen tucks a rope of hair behind her ear.

Tony says, "How's your day?"

"Good. How was the first day back?"

"Well, I mean, I'm here, so…"

Karen laughs a little, polite, says, "Right. Sorry."

"I like your house. It's nice. Glad I finally get to see it."

"Thanks. Sugar? You want sugar for your coffee?"

Tony knows Karen knows that he takes his coffee black. But he stands when she does.

They accost each other between the table and the counter.

Then her pants are on the floor. Her shirt's around her neck. Her bra hangs open. Then she's sitting on the counter next to the sink and Tony's shirttails keep getting in the way.

He pulls her to the floor after his belt buckle starts clanking too loud against the stainless steel dishwasher. She falls onto him, does all the work until she says the hardwood hurts her knees.

They move to the family room, she bends over the arm of the couch.

They stumble up the stairs pulling off what little left they have on.

Karen says, "Guest room."

They clobber through the door into a room with a small bed, a bare dresser, and nothing on the walls. Then they collapse onto the mattress.

Afterward, Karen says, "That was good."

"Just good?"

"No, I mean, like, it was good in the sense that it was us, and it was easy, and it was fun. And…it was just, I don't know, good."

"Hemingway good?"

"Yeah, Hemingway good."

Tony sits up, puts his feet on the floor.

Karen says, "You don't have to go yet. We've got time."

"I have to."

Karen sits up, kisses Tony's shoulder, says, "Ever think about this being us? Capital U us?"

"So sentimental."

Karen throws a pillow. Tony catches it. They laugh until they stop. Fast enough for Tony to know neither of them were really laughing.

"You texted me smiley faces this morning," Karen says. "I'm pretty sure you hate that stuff."

"So?"

"So? Don't tell me this doesn't make you sentimental too."

"I'm not sure it matters."

"Why?"

"Come on. You know why. It's why I don't text after six. It's why you don't respond until late morning."

Karen doesn't say anything. She gets out of bed first, walks naked along the trail of clothes leading down the stairs, picking up what's hers, leaving Tony's stuff behind.

Tony gets dressed in the powder room downstairs. He fixes his hair, washes his face with hand soap, rubs Karen's smell off his lips.

He finishes, finds Karen waiting for him by the front door holding a Pyrex bowl covered with a tinfoil lid. "For me," he says.

"Not everything's about you," she says smiling, handing over the bowl. "It's not much, but I think your parents will like it."

"Could just pop over yourself." Tony cocks an eyebrow, waits for Karen to say her friendship with his parents isn't that weird. Waits for her to tell him to grow up.

But all she says is, "Can't. I'm in the office tomorrow."

He tries again, says, "What about tonight?"

"Sam's already uncomfortable with the whole situation."

Tony looks at the floor, says, "Seriously—"

"Family friends was one thing, Tony. Family friends revealed as an ex-boyfriend's parents, that's something else."

Tony says, "This is something else."

"It's a different something else. Who's getting sentimental now?"

They kiss, push themselves into one another.

Then they say goodbye, goodnight.

And before Tony leaves he has to ignore the portrait on the wall. Karen dressed in white, smiling, standing next to Sam.

***

It's dark when Tony pulls into his neighborhood.

He drove around too long. Practiced all the things he knows he should have said to Karen to himself for too long.

Looking for a parking spot, he says, "Look, we can't do this, okay? I'm sorry, but we just can't."

Says, "This was just a reaction. A bad one. I'm not upset it happened, but it can't happen anymore."

Says, "Think of this as a bookend. Like, an epilogue to the capital U us."

The pressure in his chest doesn't let him turn his body to parallel park when he finds an open space. He has to use his mirrors.

He doesn't bother with his nose, goes right to using his mouth to breathe, shifts the car to park.

Eyes closed, breathing in short gasps, he listens to the sounds from the old car. Every clink, grind, hum until he catches his breath.

He lifts the bowl Karen gave him from the passenger seat. Then he puts it back down, leaves it.

He's farther from the apartment than he thought. Has enough of a walk for his mind to go to Karen and Sam smiling. To the texts that didn't stop coming until he shut off his phone.

His mother, his father, despondent.

Their reactions if he'd died in place of his brother.

The kid standing in front of the door to the apartment.

Tony turns his head left, right. He turns around, looks for anyone else on the street.

The kid waves, shifting his weight back and forth between his heels and the balls of his feet. Like Tony used to when his mother picked him and Nate up from elementary school, when his father's car pulled into the driveway, when Nate passed the house with a group of friends in tow.

Tony waves back, keeps walking.

But then there's the mask tied around the kid's head, the green plastic nose. There's the foam turtle shell velcroed at the shoulders and sides, the green sweatshirt. And the nunchucks tucked into a brown leather belt buckled around the waist of green sweatpants.

The kid says, "Finally."

Tony stops. He turns, checks behind him for someone, anyone the kid could be talking to.

The kid laughs, points, says, "I'm talking to you, dummy."

Tony chokes out a laugh, says, "Little late for Halloween. Or early. Whatever."

"So? I like Ninja Turtles."

"Your parents around?"

The kid says, "Nope," draws out the O.

"What's your name?"

"I'm Mikey," he holds out his hand for a shake.

"I can't lie," Tony says. "You're freaking me out a little."

"Why?"

"Ever see *Child's Play*?"

"No. Well, yeah. If you saw it, I did too, I guess."

"What's that supposed to mean?"

Mikey shrugs, says, "I don't know. I just got here."

Tony's eyes water. He blinks, can't remember the last time. "From—from where? Exactly?"

"Remember when you had to cover your eyes during the scary parts in the first Turtles movie?"

Tony backs away.

Mikey says, "Don't freak out, dude. Don't freak out."

Tony turns, sprints down the street. He banks right at the corner, has to flail his arms to keep his balance. Then he's huffing, puffing, sweating, pumping his arms, listening to his shoes slapping the sidewalk, trying to ignore the high-pitched whine coming from his throat every time he exhales.

Then Mikey jumps into view at the corner ahead, yells hi-yah, twirls his orange plastic nunchucks.

Tony yelps, turns, runs back the way he came. Back toward home.

But Mikey is there, in front of the door again.

"This is fun," Mikey says, laughing.

"What the fuck, man? What are you?"

"What do you think I am?"

"Am I losing it? Am I losing my shit?"

"Mom says it's bad to curse. She makes me put a quarter in the Swear Jar when I say a bad word."

Tony leans against the wall next to his door, slumps his shoulders, puts his hands on his knees.

"What's wrong?" Mikey says.

"You're not real. I'm talking to myself."

"You were just doing that in the car."

Tony says grabs his keys, says, "Holy shit." His hands shake too much from the cold, maybe the panic. It takes one, two, three tries to get the key into the lock.

Behind him, Mikey says, "Hold on, I'm sorry. I didn't mean to—"

Tony's inside and slams the door before Mikey can finish his sentence.

His eyes closed, his back against the door, Tony jumps, curses when Maura says, "Jesus, Tony. You scared the shit out of me."

"What? Sorry."

Maura stands, hand on her chest, phone in her hand. She says, "Are you okay?"

"Huh? Yeah. Why?"

"I've been texting all day. What's wrong? Did something happen?

You're sweating." She walks through the kitchen, tears some paper towels from the roll on the counter.

Tony says, "Sorry," catching his breath. "My phone died."

She dabs Tony's forehead, kisses him, says, "You've got to keep that thing charged, dude. Come on."

"Sorry. Again."

She takes a step back, looks him over, says, "Are you alright? You look sick."

Tony forces a smile, kisses her cheek, says, "Think I might be coming down with something, yeah."

2

Tony can still smell Karen.

She's in his nostrils. On his lips. Embedded in his fingerprints.

The takeout Chinese doesn't help. Neither does the beer, or the coffee. She's there, a cloud of shampoo, perfume, and sweat hanging over Tony's head.

He watches every move Maura makes, every time she inhales through her nose.

If he can talk with an invisible boy, she can smell another woman on his breath. Or in his hair. Or under his nails.

When she reaches for his coffee mug, asks if he wants a refill, he leans back in his chair away from her. When they sit on the couch to watch television he slides to the side until his back strains, until he realizes he's halfway lying. And when she asks him questions about his day, he looks her in the eye when she speaks, but turns away and gives his answers to the TV.

He cranes his neck, looks behind her. He looks out the windows. He checks, double checks the dark corners of the apartment.

Maura says, "What are you looking for?"

He almost says, "Little kid, Ninja Turtles costume," but he says, "Hmm? Nothing."

Maura puts the back of her hand to Tony's forehead, says, "How are you feeling?"

"Off."

"Mentally off or physically off?

"How do I seem?"

"Like you've got a head full of scrambled eggs. I probably should've taken your parents' side about work today."

"Do me a favor?"

Maura raises her eyebrows, smiles a little.

"Never take my parents' side about anything," Tony says. "Ever."

She laughs, says, "I'll do my best." Then she leans in, kisses him on the mouth.

Tony pulls away from her, fast. He knows the look on her face, the angle her head's cocked. But he gets up anyway, tries to make up for it by telling her he'll take care of the dishes.

When he turns on the water Maura turns up the volume on the television.

Tony scrubs, stares at the colors and formations of food caked on the plates and silverware to keep himself from looking for Mikey. But everything becomes familiar. The splotches, reminders.

The orange bandana wrapped around Mikey's eyes.

The blotchy birthmark underneath Karen's bellybutton.

The color of Nate's dead skin.

Maura says his name, asks him if he's listening.

Tony says, "Yeah," smiles.

She says, "Isn't that funny?"

He laughs. It's weak. "Yeah, totally."

After the dishes Tony sits at the opposite end of the couch, keeps his distance from Maura. He picks up the Stephen King novel sitting on the coffee table, stares at the words. Looks at the television. Goes back to the book, then to Maura while she sends emails from her phone. He turns a page or two every so often. He repeats the circuit from book, to TV, to Maura until she says she's tired, says she has a long day coming up tomorrow.

She stands up, says goodnight.

Tony watches Maura wipe down the countertop, push in the chairs at the table a bit more than they already were. She's waiting for him to say something, anything. She says goodnight again like it's a question.

Tony turns his head, smiles, says, "Night."

He peels himself from the couch when the bedroom door closes. He pours whiskey into a tall glass, opens and closes the freezer once, twice, but leaves the whiskey neat.

He takes big gulps of his drink in the kitchen, checks under the table.

He walks through the living room, opens the closet door, pushes jackets aside, looks into the darkest parts of the space.

Then he finishes his glass watching reruns of *Full House*, flinching whenever he thinks he maybe saw something from the corner of his eye.

Not even whiskey kills the Karen smell. But it does make him doze off during a scene where Uncle Jesse makes some profound life statement.

Friends is on when Tony sits up straight failing to pull air into his lungs. He sucks back like he's choking. He tries to cough out whatever lodged itself in his throat, but nothing comes up. He sits, takes short, noisy breaths hoping they'll be enough to keep him from passing out.

Then Mikey summersault into the room. He stands, smiles, waves, and sits on the floor in front of the TV the way Nate was sitting when Tony found him.

Tony pushes himself into the couch as far as he'll go. He watches Mikey, eyes wide, mouth open.

Mikey rolls over to lie on his stomach, props his face up in his hands, kicks when he laughs.

Tony covers his eyes with his hand, counts to three, lets the hand fall to his side.

Mikey looks over his shoulder from his spot on the floor. He says, "What?"

"Nothing."

"Calm now?"

"What?"

Mikey pokes a finger underneath the orange fabric above his

temple, scratches, says, "Feel better?"

Tony gets up, goes into the kitchen, pours himself more whiskey, tries to ignore Mikey through the whole process.

He sips from his glass, turns, and Mikey's gone.

He whispers hello.

"Hi."

He jumps, spills whiskey onto the floor.

Maura says, "Sorry. I didn't mean to scare you."

Wiping the floor with a dishrag, Tony says, "It's okay. I thought you were asleep."

"I tried to sleep." Maura pads into the room. "Couldn't."

"Why?"

Maura pokes Tony in the chest, says, "Because I'm worried about you. Today was so weird, Tony. Not hearing from you, you being...I don't know, whatever you have to be right now."

Tony takes a big pull of whiskey. He gulps, winces, says, "Sorry for today. I'm not..."

"Handling all this too well?"

"Yeah."

"I don't think you're supposed to handle any of this well. I think today probably happened the only way it could've."

Another mouthful of whiskey, another burning swallow. "I could've done some things differently."

"Maybe. But I shouldn't have gotten upset that you didn't."

They move to the couch. Tony flops into the butt-print he left. Maura sits down next to him, curls her legs up, pulls her shirt over her knees.

Tony finishes his drink. All there is to smell is whiskey under his nose now. Nothing else. No one else.

"I don't know how to help you," Maura says. "And that sucks."

"I think the faster I get back into my old routine the better I'll be. I think—"

Maura puts her hands on his cheeks, pulls his face close. "You do what you need to, Tony. But don't forget that I can do whatever you need me to. Like, if you want to go on a record shop binge, I'll take you. If you want a Blizzard for lunch, I'll go to Dairy Queen. I don't care. I just feel like I should be doing something."

Tony laughs, pulls away from her, says, "When I was a kid

my Dad would take me and Nate to Dairy Queen." His breath catches in his throat, but he keeps going. "They used to have these chocolate covered pretzel Blizzards that—"

Then it's Mikey, somewhere behind him. "They were so good."

Tony doesn't turn. But his eyes strain, jammed into the left corners of their sockets.

Maura says, "What's the matter?"

"Hmm?"

Mikey steps into view, says, "They were like the pretzels from the candy store. But with ice cream. Remember?" He laughs, sits on the floor.

Maura says, "Tony?"

"Yeah?" Tony shakes his head, turns himself so he can't see Mikey. "Sorry."

"How much have you had to drink?"

"Just two glasses."

"You're drunk."

"I might be. A little."

She kisses him, asks him if he knows she loves him.

"Yeah," he says. "I do know that."

"I don't know what you saw. I can't imagine it. But if you want to get drunk on a weeknight, I'll get drunk with you. Okay?"

"Okay."

Tony can't bring himself to see if Mikey's watching TV, or spinning his nunchucks, or fiddling with his mask. So he kisses Maura hard, open-mouthed.

He wraps his arms around her. And she climbs into his lap.

***

The day Tony found his brother dead he got a call from his father just after eighth period. The phone rattled the change in his pocket. He let the call go.

Until the change rattled again.

And again.

His father didn't let Tony finish his hello, started nattering on about Nate being off from work, about Nate not answering the phone.

Tony said he was sure Nate was fine.

"You need to stop by the house."

"What? Why?"

His father didn't answer.

Tony walked past the main office, Principal Adler's office tucked in the back with the door open. He cursed, tried to hide his phone, tucked it between his head and shoulder.

But Adler raised his arm from behind his desk, stuck out a stubby pointer finger, got up and walked toward the glass partition between the office and the hall.

Tony pretended not to see him, picked up his pace, made a face he hoped gave people the impression he had somewhere to be.

Over the phone Tony's father said, "Because he's your brother."

"What?"

"You asked why you should check on Nathan. I goddamn answered."

Tony heard his name bounce down the hall.

"Fine. Yes, okay. I'll go right over."

Nothing from his father again.

"Hello?"

"You're going to need to get over...whatever the hell you think he's done to you, Anthony."

Tony rolled his eyes, said, "I know." He made a face, said, "Sorry."

Adler called down the hallway again, said, "Mr. D'Angelo," emphasizing syllables that created a melody Tony hadn't heard since he was featured in the school newspaper as School's Easiest Teacher.

Tony said, "Got to go." He ended the call, dropped the phone into his pocket, turned on his heel and smiled wide, fake, and stupid. "Yes, Mr. Adler?"

"Do I have to remind you about our cell phone policy?" Adler balled his fists, put them on his hips.

"Sir?"

"You were on your cell phone. If we expect our students to follow the rules we have to as well."

"Oh. Yeah. Sorry. It was my dad. He's not doing so well lately. I had to take his call, you know? He wants me to visit."

Adler's face went white. Redness crawled its way up from under his collar. His hands fell to his sides. "I'm sorry to hear that. I'll have to give him a call. He's a good man."

"He is. And I'm just trying to do the right thing. We're not all that sure how much longer we'll have with him."

"Jesus. I'm—I'm sorry. I had no idea. How's Nathan taking it? With, you know, everything?"

"Going to go check in on him now, actually. Have a good night."

"I thought you were—"

Tony turned, walked out the door. If he'd heard the end of Adler's sentence he would have ignored it. But he hadn't, so he didn't. Crossing the lot, texting, Tony put on a show for Adler regardless. He contorted his face, wrinkled up his forehead, flattened his lips together. He made the potential of his father's imminent fake death look like it hurt more than the cold.

He waited to laugh until he got in the car.

His parents' house was far enough away to cue up his iPod. Misfits' "Walk Among Us". He drummed to the beat on the steering wheel with his thumbs, sang along to Danzig's crooning, lit a smoke, banged his head.

He lit another when he pulled up to the house. He parked in the driveway, smoked until he burnt his numb fingertips on the butt.

Between the car and the front door he retweeted an announcement about a new Lawrence Arms record, favorited a tweet by Greg Graffin, then almost tripped over the porch step.

His house key didn't work.

It got stuck in the lock twice before he said fuck it.

His father had mentioned changing the locks to keep out any of Nate's old acquaintances—Nate had been generous with the keys...and with anything in the house worth selling—but Tony hadn't been told they'd gone and done it. He wasn't given a replacement.

It didn't matter. It was another reason to bail out on Sunday dinner.

No one picked up the house phone. He heard the phone ringing inside. When it cut out, his mother's voice greeted him in his ear, told him to leave a message after the beep.

Tony called again.

A third time.

After that he pounded on the door with the butt of his hand.

He called his brother's name. Said, "Open up, dude." Then, "Open the goddamn door."

Tony had to search through his contacts for his brother's number. He called, a robot told him the number was no longer in service. He said, "Motherfucker."

He called the house again, waited for the answering machine, said, "Nate, it's me. Pick up."

After a beat, "You're freaking Dad out, dude. Pick up."

He waited, said, "Okay, call me back."

He walked around to the side door, passed a ladder his father left outside. A classic Nathan Senior move. Leaving physical evidence for his wife to notice that he was, at some point, going to take down the Christmas lights. Or clean the gutters. Or replace the missing shingles.

Tony walked around back, didn't bother with the gate. He hopped the wooden fence, the rotting wood crackling under his weight.

The French door was locked.

Tony's phone was back at his ear, he was running back toward the gate.

"Nate," he said. "It's me. Pick up."

Letting himself out of the backyard he said, "Fucking pick up, Nate."

Trying his bad key at the side door, "Nate."

He didn't see his parents' neighbor peek her head outside. But he heard her when she told him to keep his voice down, to watch his language.

Tony told her to get the fuck back in her fucking house.

"Nate. You need to pick up right now. Pick up."

Tony grabbed the ladder, dragged it across the driveway, dented his car swinging it vertical.

He called the house again after he got the ladder leaning on the house, propped just underneath Nate's bedroom window.

Tony said, "Now you're freaking me out."

Said, "Where are you?"

Said, "Why are you doing this again?"

Every rung Tony climbed, he cursed. Every second that passed without a return phone call, his breathing became heavier, more erratic, turned to hot bursts of steam in the air. Standing a story up, Tony heard his breath. Heard every wheeze from deep in his chest.

He pressed the butts of his hands to the glass, looked inside.

Nate was on his bed, sitting like he used to when they were kids in reading circles at the library. How kids were told to sit in kindergarten.

The television was on, daytime TV.

Tony laughed. Then knocked.

Nate didn't move. His head was slumped, staring at something he was holding in his folded hands resting in his lap.

Tony knocked on the window, said, "Nate."

He thought he saw Nate move, wanted to see his brother move. He knocked again.

But Nate was still. His eyes were open, white. His jaw rested on his chest, lips parted. His skin was colorless. Not white, not gray. He was without color.

Tony knocked on the window again, said, "Nate."

Then there was the needle in Nate's arm. The syringe hanging from where the metal was poked into the skin at the pit of his elbow.

Tony lost his grip on the ladder and fell.

He landed in an overgrown bush his father never got around to trimming this past fall.

Tony tried to regulate his breathing, lying in the bush. He checked every point of pain with his hands. For compound fractures, for branches poking through his body. No blood, no torn skin. He was fine, but he stayed lying in the bush. He had to concentrate to breathe.

The sound of rattling change.

Tony dug into his pockets for his phone.

It was Nate calling him back. The needle, he'd imagined it.

Tony didn't say anything, pressed the phone to his ear.

"Hello?" his father said over the line.

Tony tried to speak.

"Tony?"

Hyperventilating, Tony said, "Nate."

"Where is he?"

"Here."

"Put him on the phone."

"Can't."

"What? Why not?"

"Nate."

"What's the matter with you?"

Tony drew in as much of a breath as he could. He yelled into the phone, his father needed to come home.

There was nothing on the line. He couldn't even hear his father breathing.

"Come home—Dad. You—need to come—home."

Then he threw up in the bush that broke his fall.

***

Maura's asleep on top of the covers where she collapsed after they'd finished.

Face to face, Tony can smell her breath. He listens to her breathe. Listens to the one or two word sentences she mutters as she dreams. He never realized she talked in her sleep until after Nate died. Never knew she snored.

Now she's doing both. She's gone for the night. There's nothing short of a fire that'll wake her up. Even if there were an actual fire Tony wonders if she'd wake up. Or be burned to death in her sleep.

He curses at himself for that.

Tells himself he should see somebody about that.

Then he almost laughs. Almost. He should see somebody for something else.

Death does funny things to people.

He gets out of bed, puts on a pair of shorts and a shirt. Drops his phone into his pocket. He peeks around the corners of the apartment, tiptoeing through the place, hoping Mikey's not still watching TV.

Tony says the kid's name, rolls his eyes, slaps his palm to his forehead.

He checks his phone.

Nothing.

He texts Karen, waits.

No response.

He texts Chris.

More nothing.

Tony watches the tail end of Nick at Nite until it switches over from bad 90s sitcoms to *Spongebob Squarepants*. Eyelids heavy, but not heavy enough to stay closed, he stares out the window until sunlight leaks into the apartment. Until the alarm on his phone squawks and echoes through the empty room. Until his mother calls, asks him to stop by the house.

3

Tony uses Nate's key to unlock his parents' front door.

It sticks a bit.

He tucks Karen's bowl in the crook of his elbow, rams his shoulder into the door, stumbles into the house.

His mother asks what happened from the kitchen.

His father says Jesus from the top of stairs.

And Tony curses, kicks the door closed.

Tony's father tromps down the stairs, says, "Did Mom tell you about the trip?"

Tony opens his mouth, doesn't get a word out.

His father talks about things he always wanted to do with his sons, mentions Nate's name first. He talks about a ranch in Wyoming. The type of terrain he'll be on. How big the elk can get. He says there's nothing better than being out in the wilderness. "Nothing better than proving to yourself you can survive alone."

Tony raises his voice, says, "Good to see you, too, Pop."

"What? Oh, you too. Sorry, I'm just excited. Anyway, I've always wanted to go back there."

The only way Tony can respond is by raising his eyebrows, smiling without teeth.

His father says, "Did I ever tell you about the most heartbreaking thing that ever happened to me?"

One of Tony's eyebrows stays up. But his grin slacks, his chest tightens.

"Mountain goat," Tony's father says. "Standing broadside on a cliff? Perfect shot. Perfect. And you know me, I never get the perfect shot. Never works out for me like that."

"I know, Dad, you—"

"Or Nathan." Tony's father goes silent, stares, says, "Always had the worst luck."

Tony wants to say, "Nate would miss on purpose and blame me for distracting him."

And, "Nate would fake sick so he could smoke pot in the cabin all day while you dragged me around the woods all pissed off."

And, "Nate sold most of your hunting shit for drug money."

But he says nothing instead, grinds his teeth, breathes through flared nostrils.

"Anyway," Tony's father says. "So I get him in my sights, right? He's not moving, just standing there looking out across a gorge, like there was nothing on that mountain that he was afraid of, you know?"

Tony grunts, says, "Uh huh."

"I pull the trigger. The sound echoes up and down the cliffs. Sounds like thunder. And that son of a bitch just lays down dead."

"Dad—"

"I turn to look back at my guide. I'm thrilled, you know? But the guide's pointing over my shoulder."

"Dad—"

"I look back. The goat's legs are up in the air, they're rolling clockwise toward the ledge. Then his weight takes him. He rolls right off the cliff into the gorge. Had to be a hundred and fifty foot drop."

Tony stares, has to use his mouth to breathe. Deep, belabored.

"Pretty cool, huh?"

"Yep. Pretty cool."

They stand, stare at each other, silent until Tony's father says he's going to head back upstairs to research rates for flights.

Tony says, "Okay."

His father says, "Alright then," and leaves Tony alone in the living room.

Then it's footsteps on the patch of noisy floorboards overhead. The patch Nate had taught Tony to avoid when sneaking around. The patch his father had taught them both to avoid when their mother slept in on Sundays.

It's his father's mumbling echoing down the stairs that Tony knows is meant to be heard for no other reason than wanting to be heard. Knows because he does it himself. Knows because Nate did it too.

Then it's Mikey behind Tony, saying, "Can you help me? I just need you to retie my mask."

Tony leaves the room, walks fast. Doesn't look back, doesn't say anything.

Mikey says, "Please? Hello?"

In the kitchen, Tony kisses his mother on the top of the head. He asks her how she's doing, apologizes for what he said yesterday. He hands over the bowl, says, "Brought this for you."

His mother says, "Karen?"

"How'd you guess."

"She's got good taste in kitchenware."

"Wasn't really a question."

Tony's mother pats him on the stubbled cheek, cocks her head to the side. "How are you? You look sick."

"Not sleeping."

"No, it's not that."

"Mom, you know what it is, come on."

"It's not that either. Want something? How about Dad's trip? Sounds nice, doesn't it?"

Tony shakes his head, pours himself a mug of oily coffee. He says, "You're going to let him go, then?"

Tony's mother, Karen's bowl in her hands, stares past him, off somewhere else. Through the walls, out over the neighborhood.

Tony says, "Mom," loud enough she flinches.

She says, "Want something?"

"I'm good."

"How's Maura?"

"Good. Mom, why are you still letting Dad go?"

His mother laughs, says, "Letting Dad go?" She pulls the tinfoil off Karen's bowl, smiles. "Have you ever had Karen's macaroni and cheese?"

"Have you?"

"It's delicious." She turns, puts the bowl in the refrigerator.

Tony opens his mouth, silent screams with his eyes wide and his hands curled into claws on both sides on his face. Then he takes a breath. "Dad shouldn't be going on a trip," he says. "He shouldn't be leaving you alone."

His mother says, "I don't want him to go. But maybe he has to." She puts a pan on the stove, drops a clump of margarine into it. "Maybe you should go with him."

Tony laughs. Hard. He asks if that's why she called him here. He says he hasn't been hunting since Nate made varsity everything. Says it was always the two of them talking about how big that buck was that time they let one get away. Says, "Without Nate it'll be two assholes sitting in the woods, staring at each other with nothing to say."

His mother stares into the pan, at the margarine flattening into yellow sludge.

Tony says, "I—I just mean." He runs his hand through his hair. "If Dad goes alone you won't be here all by yourself."

"You're never around much anyway, Anthony."

Tony stops himself from speaking, from saying something he knows isn't true.

His phone goes off in his pocket. He ignores it.

At the stove, Tony's mother cracks an egg, drops it into the sizzling pan, says, "What am I supposed to say to him? He gets his mind set on these things, and—"

"I don't know, Mom. Say, Nathan, I don't think this is the right time to plan a trip to go traipsing around Wyoming? And maybe... maybe..." Nothing else comes to mind. He balls his hands into fists, squeezes until his nails dig into his palms.

Tony's mother pokes the egg with a spatula, says nothing.

When Tony turns away from her he yelps.

His mother says, "What the hell, Anthony. You scared me."

Mikey, standing on the kitchen table, spins his nunchucks in both hands, says, "I'm getting good at this, right?"

Tony apologizes to his mother, makes up some bullshit about a really big, hairy spider that he thought he maybe saw in his periphery. And when Mikey says, "Hey. Look. I'm good, right? Please look," Tony doesn't turn to look, refuses to fucking look.

His mother stares into the frying pan. She's stopped poking with the spatula, lets the egg bubble, begin to burn.

Tony has to call her once, twice before she snaps back to attention again, scooping up the egg, flipping it over. "You should go with your father."

"Mom—"

"I'm just saying that it may give you two the opportunity—"

"Mom, stop."

"—to be friends. You're always so angry—"

Tony yells her name, slams his fist on the counter.

She jumps, drops the spatula into the pan.

Tony tells her he's not going on any fucking hunting trip. Says, "And you shouldn't let Dad go either."

From behind Tony, his father says, "I didn't invite you."

Tony spins himself around, doesn't flinch at Mikey still standing on the table.

Tony's mother says, "Nathan."

Tony says, "Dad."

Mikey says, "Uh-oh."

"And I don't need permission to do anything," Tony's father says. "Go to work, Anthony."

Tony curses, looks at the clock on the microwave.

"Any reason you're here so early anyway?" his father says, voice flat. Face a mask, stiff, not moving with his words.

Tony watches his mother staring at the stove again. He says, "Nope," and leaves the room.

On his way out, Tony hears his father ask what's for breakfast. He stops at the front door, stands, hand wrapped around the doorknob, waits for her to respond.

She says, "Hmm?"

His father repeats himself.

Tony slams the door behind him once, twice, three times before he gets it to close right.

***

Once his parents were home, the EMTs and the police already in the house, and Karen on her way, Tony called Maura. He told her he found Nate.

He said, "He's dead."

Said, "No, don't worry about it. We have to go to the hospital, anyway. I'll just see you when I get home."

It was a string of questions after that, reassurances, all the things Tony was expecting from her. All the things he didn't want her to hear. So he screamed at her, told her that didn't want her to fucking see him like that. Told her to please give him some fucking space.

Then he apologized.

Over the phone, Maura said, "It's okay. I'm just trying to help."

"I know, I—"

A body shaped lump under a sheet rolled past on a gurney. Karen's car pulled up, stopped in front of the house.

"—I have to go."

He heard Maura say she loved him, that if he needed her to call.

"Okay."

Tony watched Karen walk up the driveway. She covered her mouth with her hand as the stretcher rolled past, as it was hoisted into the ambulance.

Karen ignored the police, let herself in like she used to. Back when Tony's mother insisted she never knock. When Tony's father told her to stop by whenever she wanted. When Nate stopped noticing her being there. When she was comfortable enough to walk right up to Tony's room without asking, to do homework, or listen to music—as long as they kept the door open.

She went to Tony's father first, hugged him, kissed his cheek, told him how sorry she was.

One of the officers called her Miss, but Tony's father said, "Family."

She moved to Tony, squeezed her body into him.

He smelled her again, felt her again. Held her hand again, ran his thumb over the cluster of freckles between her thumb and pointer finger.

She cried when she saw Tony's mother sitting on the couch, staring at nothing on the wall across the room.

But Tony's face stayed dry.

He tried thinking of Nate's mouth hanging open, the needle hanging from his arm, the whites of his eyes, the irises rolled up and staring at his brain.

Nothing worked.

He watched his mother's face turn red on Karen's shoulder. Watched his father's eyes well up. Watched Karen comfort his family.

He had hugged his mother, but had nothing to say.

Patting his father's back, he had said nothing other than sorry.

He left, went out to the patio, let Karen do what she had always done better than him since they were teenagers.

Outside he texted Maura, apologized for yelling, for hanging up so fast. He left Karen out of the messages.

She texted back, said she loved him.

He typed, Me too, sent it away. Then he smoked cigarettes, wondered what the next step with Nate's body would be. Drain his blood. Pull his organs. Leave him overnight in a refrigerator with a Y on his chest in stitches.

Then breathing got difficult.

He didn't hear the door open, flinched when Karen touched his shoulder.

She said she was so, so sorry, sat down next to him on the patio.

Tony didn't say anything, handed her his cigarette. When she smoked it, he cocked an eyebrow.

She said, "What?"

"What, what?"

She shrugged, said, "It's been a while."

"Since we've seen each other, or since the last time you smoked?"

"You pick." She took another drag from the cigarette, handed it back to Tony, said, "Police say they need to ask you some questions."

Once Tony told the police the circumstances in which he found his brother, they thanked him for the cooperation. They said his parents were planning on going to the hospital and he was more than welcome to go with them. "Sometimes people need to see the process through. It helps them," they said.

Tony said uh-huh.

Bundled in their coats, his parents came to him after the police were out the door.

His father called him bud, asked him how he was. His father had never called him bud.

His mother called him sweetie, said something else, but choked on her words.

Tony asked what he should do now.

"Stay," his father said.

He and Karen watched his parents' car curve down and around the bend in the road, turn onto Papermill. Then out of sight. Just brake lights behind the tree line.

Tony said, "What do I do now?"

Karen took his hand, squeezed it twice, said, "Drink."

Tony listens to a voicemail from Chris asking him where he is, telling him that first period has already started, that they sent his class to the library, that he should pick them up when he gets in.

"And call the office," Chris says. "They think you died or something, man." There's a pause, then, "Oh, shit, man. I didn't mean to say that. Sorry."

Tony deletes the message.

Then Tony's father calls.

Tony taps the ignore button.

A voicemail notification later Tony puts his phone on speaker. As if being forced into the words, Tony's father says, "Anthony, I apologize for what I said. If you want to come along, feel free. Call me ba—"

The tinny voice on Tony's phone says the message is deleted.

From the backseat, "Can you slow down? Raph drives like this."

Tony twists around, sees Mikey, and screams high and loud. Almost drives off the road. Then it's foul language and questions. Answers and kid laughter.

Tony says, "Why are you happening?"

Mikey says, "I don't know, I'm nine."

A text from Maura spins Tony's phone around a cup holder.

He picks it up, types a message telling her he hopes she has a great day, too.

Then he looks into the rearview mirror, back to the road, then into the rearview mirror.

Mikey says, "What?"

"What do you mean, what? I'm crazy and you're staring at me."

"No I'm not."

"Yes you are."

"Nuh-uh."

"I'm pretty certain imaginary friends—or hallucinations, whatever—aren't supposed to antagonize the people who imagine them."

"Well you made me up. I'm just trying to help."

"How? How is talking to an imaginary friend helping?"

"You're not talking to anyone else. You just get all red and sound like you have something stuck in your throat."

A car slows ahead, angles to the left. No turn signal. Just brake lights and a rear bumper getting larger through the windshield. Tony slams the butt of his palm onto the steering wheel, blares the horn. He jerks the car into the right lane and presses a middle-fingered fist to the window.

His phone vibrates.

He ignores the call.

"So what?" Tony says. "So what if I'm not talking to anyone else? There's nothing to say."

Mikey laughs. And Tony asks him what's funny.

"You."

"Me?"

"Yeah. You're a big dummy."

Tony curses, turns on his iPod. *Descendents* on shuffle, "Jean is Dead" playing from a bank of several thousand songs.

Tony unplugs his iPod, tosses it aside. Static snows through the speakers.

Mikey says, "You should be nicer to your parents."

"Is this how it's going to be?"

"Huh?"

"A running commentary from a preadolescent Ninja Turtle?

Tony turns onto Cheltenham. The car fishtails on black ice.

An SUV tearing down the street lays on its horn. Tony rights his car and calls the SUV driver a rotten motherfucker.

Mikey says, "That was your fau—"

"Because if that's how it's going to be," Tony says. "I'll get you electroshocked away."

The cell phone rattles in the cup holder again.

Mikey asks him if he's going to answer it.

"It's the car. It shakes on hills."

"You know you're lying to yourself when you lie to me, right? I figured that out. And I'm nine."

"You said that already, shut up," Tony says, steering the shaking car into the school's parking lot.

Devoid of human life, the lot confirms how late he already knows he is. And checking his phone, seeing a missed text from Chris, a missed call from the main office, he says, "I'll tell them I'm having a rough morning. Tell me I'm lying about that."

He turns, looks into the backseat, sees nothing but garbage on the seats and cigarette burns in the upholstery.

Tony drags himself from his car into the cold. He walks inside with his shoulders slumped, eyes to the floor, into the front office. He tells the women sitting behind desks he's sorry. Tells them he had car issues. And phone issues.

Sandy tells him to just make sure he calls in next time, smiling.

Ginny tells him she understands after all he's been through.

Sue tells him Principal Adler's waiting for him in his office.

And now, Adler folds his hands on his desk, cocks his head to the side, raises his eyebrows in frowns of hair, asks Tony how he's doing.

Tony says he's good. "Fine," he says.

Adler motions to the Keurig across the room, asks Tony if he wants a coffee. He says, "You look exhausted."

"Rough night last night."

"Anthony, I—"

"I've been having trouble sleeping."

"I really don't think you should be here."

"What?"

"Most people use all the bereavement leave available to them when something like this happens. You're forcing yourself into a situation you're clearly not ready for. I'm no psychologist but

I'm sure you could be doing more damage to yourself than you think you're preventing."

Tony hyperventilates, tries turning it into a rhythmic cough, a hack for every cut-short breath. Through his fit, his fist covering his mouth, he tells Adler that maybe he'll make himself that coffee. He stands, turns, feels himself go red. His shoulders shake, his eyes water, his mouth hangs open.

The sounds from the machine, the coffee gurgling into the Styrofoam cup, calms him. He wipes his eyes with a napkin. The corners of his mouth caked in gummy saliva.

He brings the coffee to his face, he takes a sip, sucks air back hard. And then he's choking, coughing the hot liquid from his throat.

Adler asks him if he's okay.

Tony says, "Wrong pipe. Sorry."

He wipes his mouth. Has to pick clumps of fibrous paper from his stubble underneath the portrait of the school's founder. He spent so much time as a student under that picture that he'd worked out a plan with Chris to break into the school and carve off the old bastard's face and draw an asshole in the blank space.

Tony turns, finds his seat again with Adler staring him in the eyes, the founder boring holes into the back of his skull. "You were saying?"

"I can't force you to make a decision one way or another. If I were you I'd go home, take another week. But, truthfully, you've never really been one for following direction."

Tony smiles a little.

"Do you remember the conversation we had? Before everything happened?"

Tony had come in late, hungover. Unshowered. It wasn't the first time. The third. Maybe the fourth. Of course the incidents were spread out over several months. A year. Tony made sure of that. "Frequency only matters if there's a pattern," he'd said to Chris, pulling his fingers from and leaving a dollar between a stripper's squeezed-together tits.

But Chris had made it to work on time, every time. Tony was the one who ended up in Adler's office. Listening to lectures on responsibility. On professionalism.

Self-respect.

Conduct.

Tony had faked sick to get himself excused—burped something up from deep in his gut—then actually got sick.

But now, having watched his mother sleepwalk while using a stove, having listened to an imaginary friend berate him, he says, "Yes, sir. I remember."

Adler says, "You've been through some serious trauma, but I have to protect the best interests of this school and its students while I try to look out for yours as well."

Tony nods.

"You're a good guy. People like you."

Tony shrugs.

"But I have to view your case as a full body of work. Just like I would with anyone else who's struggling. Understand?"

Tony stares. Wants to ask if this whole thing is a setup, an opportunity to get rid of him. Wants to use FUCK in as many creative ways he can come up with in thirty seconds. Wants to splash his lukewarm coffee into Adler's face.

"It's nothing personal. Your track record was shaky at best before Nathan passed, and your behavior since you've come back, despite the circumstances, has sort of forced my hand. I can't force you do anything, but unfortunately I have to do what's expected of me."

Dillinger Four replaces Adler's speech. "Define 'Learning Disorder'" from Verses God.

Adler says, "I have no doubt you'll be able to come back from this."

Listen up, sit up straight, that's the only way you'll get a break.

"This'll be no more than a wake-up call. Just try to aim higher, Anthony."

Aim so low that you can't miss your mark.

"I'm not the one who can change your mind about anything that's happened before, or how you're planning on handling things moving forward."

Tony drums his fingers to the beat of the song in his head on his kneecap.

"That comes from you. Know what I mean? Anthony?"

"Yes, sir?"

"Do you agree?"

"Yes, sir."

Adler describes how the probationary period will work, how long it will last, and what's expected of Tony during that time. And after. He says, "Again, if I could handle this any other way, I would. Truly."

Tony nods, smiles, says okay.

They stand together, Adler reaching a hand out. Tony takes it, shakes it, and wipes the man's sweat onto his khakis.

Adler tells him to stop on by anytime. Even if it's not for a probation meeting.

"I'll do my best," Tony says.

Leaving Adler's office he passes Sandy, Ginny, and Sue. Waves. They smile, wave back at him.

He tells them all to have a nice day. And before the office door closes behind him, he hears Ginny say, "Poor thing."

4

Maura orders a cheeseburger with a fried egg on top. With bacon, extra crispy. And a Miller Lite despite the fancier options.

Tony says, "I'll have the same." He doesn't smile or say thank you. He lets the waitress pick his menu off the table where he leaves it. He says, "Oh, sorry," but she's already gone.

The restaurant's filling up, and Tony looks at everything but Maura. The cluster of balloons near the door reserved for birthdays. The giant plastic bird welcoming customers. The random placement of assorted Americana bolted to the walls. The open kitchen, the flames from the grills.

He says, "Hmm?"

Maura says, "What are you thinking?" She smiles, reaches her hand across the table. Tony looks for freckles, a fleshy connect-the-dots, but finds nothing but lines etched into Maura's palm.

He puts his hand in hers. Says, "You first."

Maura talks about work.

The project she's working on.

Something Tony doesn't hear.

His eyes drift over her shoulder. Out the plate glass window. Down the road.

Maura squeezes his hand, brings him back, says, "Hope you don't mind coming out tonight. I thought we could use a break from takeout."

Tony says, "No. Yeah, no. I like this place."

They were introduced here. Couple years ago, in a group. They were set up. Chris, a couple of mutual friends. Tony was told that Maura was a lot of fun. Really funny, too. And smart. He couldn't imagine what she was told about him.

Tony tried to be aloof but cool, but that translated into ignoring Maura most of the night, talking to the people he knew. But Maura kept asking questions. She'd asked, "What's your favorite band?"

Asked, "Who's your favorite writer?"

Asked, "What do you do for fun?"

And Tony told her, gave her answers for every question. But never asked anything in return. He let her do all the talking.

Until everyone had gone home. Until he and Maura were standing by their cars, saying nothing important, laughing because of the beer.

She told him he was sort of awkward. Sort of detached.

And he said something stupid like, "How's this for awkward?" wrapped his arm around the small of her back and kissed her.

Their foreheads pressed together, beer breath in each other's nostrils, Maura asked him, "Do you do this with all the girls you meet at chain restaurants?"

He said no. Said, "Haven't met a girl recently who wanted to know so much a—"

Maura said she didn't care. She put her hand on the back of his head, pulled his lips to hers.

Now, holding her hand, Tony sips from a tall glass of beer that was left for him without a word from the waitress. And Maura asks him questions.

"How do you feel being back at work?" she says.

"Good. Everyone's been really nice."

"You know I can tell when you're lying, right? You're an easy read."

"What? I'm not lying. What do I have to lie about?"

"Come on. Tell me what's going on."

"Nothing. Nothing's going on."

Sitting to Tony's right, Mikey says he wants pizza, readjusts the orange mask on his face. He fidgets with the front of the foam turtle shell, pulls at it every time it rides up to his chin. He says, "Tell her."

Maura says, "What?"

Tony says, "What, what?"

"You look like you have a hanger stuffed in the back of your shirt."

Mikey says, "Go ahead. Tell her. You'll feel better."

Tony takes a breath, says, "I was put on probation."

Maura clenches her teeth, purses her lips, but resets her face before she speaks. Soft, approachable. "You didn't have to lie to me about that."

"It's embarrassing."

"When was this?"

"Couple days ago."

"Did they say why?"

"Erratic behavior. Before and after Nate. To tell the truth, I think they're trying to set me up."

"Tony, come on. You're not the most focused teacher in the world."

"Well, maybe they could cut me a break for my brother being dead."

"You've used a lot of breaks there, though, haven't you?"

"Can we talk about something else?"

Maura smiles, cocks her head to the right, says, "You can fix this. That's the last thing I'll say."

Before Nate's death, whenever Tony had a bad day, or whenever Maura's day was less good than the previous one, she would say, "There's always tomorrow."

Or, "You can't appreciate a sunny day without the rain."

Or, "Happiness is a choice, not a result."

And Tony would roll his eyes, scoff, laugh at her.

She'd call him a pessimist. An elitist. A crotchety old coot.

Then post the most absurd positive cliché she could find on his Facebook wall with a flowery backdrop and a fancy font.

Now, Tony says, "You don't need to change your moods for me."

"What?"

Mikey says, "Stop."

"You know what I mean," Tony says. "You can just be mad at me sometimes. You don't always have to be so happy. You can still get pissed even though I'm...I don't know. I don't need to be treated like glass."

Mikey stops adjusting his costume, stares at Maura. The whites of his eyes fill the almond-shaped eyeholes cut into his mask. His mouth hangs slack under the green dome of plastic covering his nose.

"You've seen me pissed, Tony," Maura says.

"That's not what I mean. You're human, not a robot. But I saw your face. You were mad when I told you about work."

"You think I'm faking, then? To spare your feelings?"

"No. No, that's ridiculous."

"Now I'm ridiculous?"

The last time Maura yelled at Tony was before Nate, before Karen. He'd closed a bar with Chris, slept off his drink in the car until birds woke him up, drove home half shitty.

She doesn't sound like she did then now. Not quite. But her voice is loud enough for the parents in booths around them to ready themselves to cover their children's ears should the expletives begin to fly.

Mikey taps Tony on the shoulder, makes him flinch.

Maura asks what the hell that was.

"What what was?"

Mikey says, "Say you're sorry."

Maura asks Tony what the flinch was about, says, "You jumped out of your seat."

Tony says, "Sorry?"

Mikey blows a raspberry, says, "That stunk."

Across the table Maura tucks a loose bundle of hair behind her ear, takes a breath, licks her lips, says she'll be back. She slides out of the booth, heads toward the restrooms.

The tables around Tony's booth go back to normal, the canned music from the stereo gets lost beneath conversations. Laughter. Someone saying, "Excuse me?"

Tony says, "Hmm?"

The waitress asks if he wants another beer.

"Yes," he says. He's sure he thanks her this time.

"Mhm. Think she'd like another, too?"

"Probably."

Tony responds to a text from Chris asking to grab a beer later with a yes in all caps, a half-dozen exclamation points. He begins another text, finds Mikey in Maura's seat, puts his phone away.

"It's okay that you're acting weird," Mikey says. "It's okay that people act funny after bad stuff happens."

Tony says nothing, looks to the women's room door, back to Mikey.

And back to the door.

"But you don't need to pretend," Mikey says. "Like me."

Tony contorts his face, squints his eyes, curls his upper lip. He mouths, "What?"

"I'm pretend. You can pretend with me. Stop pretending about other stuff."

Maura slides back into the booth, says, "What's the matter?"

Tony asks what she means.

And then she apologizes. To him. Again.

"What? What for?"

"I forget. I mean, I don't forget. Who could forget? I'm sorry you feel like I'm treating you differently. I don't mean to. I just want to make it easy on you. Easier."

Tony says, "You don't need to apologize to me for anything."

"Come on. I went totally Mean Girls on you back there for nothing."

"Not for nothing."

The food shows up. Maura smiles at the waitress, thanks her. Mikey pokes his head out from under the table, says, "Pretend with me. Not her. Say sorry."

After the waitress goes, Tony says, "Hey. Everything you're doing's helping."

Mikey slaps his forehead.

Maura smiles, thin and less than genuine.

Tony counts all the things he should apologize for.

They eat their burgers without saying much of anything.

***

Karen suggested the place.

They drove there separately.

Tony texted Maura the entire way to the bar. He told her he has things to take care of, that he might need to stay at his parents' for the night. Told her he was holding up okay, that he loves her too and he'll call if he needs anything.

He bit his nails between texts. He didn't turn on any music. He was shaking. Whether it was the cold, or some sort of post-traumatic stress reaction or his nerves from spending more time with Karen in one night than he had in the past three years combined, he couldn't tell.

At the bar, sitting behind golden antique taps, Karen told Tony what he should try, said the brewmaster is a genius. She made stupid small talk, filled the gaps Tony was leaving in the air between them.

He answered questions about teaching. About his reasoning behind continuing to pour money into his shit car. About how he and Chris manage to stay mostly out of trouble.

His head was spinning halfway through the third beer Karen told him he had to try. He read the alcohol content of each one he'd had from a blackboard mounted above the liquor bottles. His first was five percent. Second, Six. Third, Nine.

So he waved over the bartender to order shots.

Karen said, "No thanks, but—"

"I'm having one."

He chose whiskey, picked it up as soon as the glass touched the bar. He said, "Thanks for this," then ripped the shot without making a face.

Karen smiled into her glass, nursing her third drink. She said, "You don't need to thank me."

Tony finished his beer, ordered another of the same, said, "I have a question."

"Okay."

"You've been hanging out with my parents?"

Karen dropped her eyes to the bar, said, "Life's weird, Tony. We kept in touch a little. Once Nate got bad your mom reached out."

"That's it?"

"Yes and no. Your relationship with your parents is...I don't know. It's complicated. They like the company. So do I."

"They ever talk about me?"

"Of course they do, Tony. Come on. Look, it's okay to be friends with people older than us."

"Not when those older people are your ex-boyfriend's parents."

"I think there's a statute of limitations on the term 'ex-boyfriend.'"

"How do you reference them in front of Sam?"

Karen took a pull from her glass, swallowed, said, "Family friends."

Tony nodded, said, "What do you call me?"

"You didn't exist until today."

Neither said anything for a while. Karen ordered another beer. Tony nursed his, a little too uncomfortable to get drunker than he already was.

Then Karen asked where Maura was.

"Home."

"Home, as in?"

"Home. My home. Where we live. Together."

Karen played with her engagement ring, and then her wedding band; spun them around her finger with her thumb. "Why didn't you call her?"

"I did. And don't think my calling you means anything more than—"

"I'm not concerned with what I think this is. What I'm worried about is what you think is happening here."

"You're the one who showed up. I just made the call."

"I would've shown up anyway. Somebody was going to call. You were first. Why were you first?"

Tony finished his beer, ordered another.

Karen said, "Maybe we should be talking about Nate."

"Maybe I don't want to."

Karen sat back in her chair, told Tony she knows that tone. Told him not to think for a second she'd forgotten how to read him. "It's not like it's hard," she said. "You can't still think your sad excuse for subtlety doesn't scream what you're thinking."

Tony took a drink, laughed, said, "You showed up."

"Yeah, I did. And now I'm leaving." Karen called the bartender over, asked for her tab.

Tony said, "I'm pretty sure I hate Nate. Hated."

Karen turned, her face morphing into something Tony had never seen before. From her, anyway. It looked the way his mother's did when she had him found smoking a bowl in the backyard. The way his father had looked at him when he told the old man he'd never really amounted to anything, just a manager of a factory always almost closing.

Karen said, "You can't be serious. You're serious?"

"Wasn't it me who was supposed to end up that way? Isn't that what you told me? That I won't do anything with myself? He got every ounce of attention, made whatever I did look small. And now it's almost like he took the life I was supposed to have. Stole it from me. But he won't be remembered like that. Like the fuck up he was. He'll be the quarterback, the honor's student, the student ambassador. And I'll just be his younger fucking brother."

"So, if you were the one who'd died, you think people would remember you only as the fuck up? The bullshitter? Because, yeah, you are those things. I may have said nasty things to you, but I know what you are beyond all that. Or what you could be, anyway." She signed her receipt, said, "You don't wish you were dead, do you? You don't want to die, right?"

"No, I don't want to fucking die. That's ridiculous."

"I need to smoke." Karen stood up, walked halfway to the door before turning around. She said, "Well?"

Tony laid cash on the bar, followed Karen out the door.

They stood underneath a canvas awning, stared out at the emptying parking lot. They shivered as they smoked one, two, three cigarettes saying nothing, watching people walk out of the building, get into their cars, go home.

Karen asked about the car again, said, "You don't want to let go of that thing, do you?"

"Why should I? It still runs. Gets me where I need to go. It's got history."

The car, red and shedding paint, sat straddling yellow lines across the parking lot from where they stood.

Karen said, "Does it still smell?"

"French fries and cigarettes."

"People call history 'history' for a reason."

"I'm not people. I call history a roadmap. I remember everywhere I went in that car. Everything that happened in it."

"I remember what happened in there too."

"Hey, remember—"

"That was a long time ago." Then she said, "I'm cold."

Tony walked her to her car, thanked her, hugged her, said goodnight.

He walked slowly. Got into his car.

The engine coughed to life. The heater blew cold air onto his feet. He shivered for two, three, four minutes before he figured he could shift into drive without the car stalling out.

Then Karen knocked on the shotgun window.

He reached across, unlocked the door, let her in. They hotboxed the car with cigarette smoke, listened to Operation Ivy and Stiff Little Fingers, other stuff from high school. And college. And the last time they'd sat in the car together—when Nate was forced into rehab the second time. Before Maura. Before Karen's rings.

Karen turned the music down after lighting her third smoke. "Hey, what was that shit in there? You hate Nate? What the fuck was that?"

"What do you want from me?"

"Nothing. I know how shitty he was. I was there for a lot of it. And your parents have told me even more. But I also know what you guys were like when you were kids, posing the same in every photo. Wearing the same outfits. It was almost weird."

Tony smoked, said, "So?"

Karen lowered her window, dropped her cigarette outside, said she was leaving. But she didn't go for the door handle.

Tony reached for her chin, turned her head to face him.

He kissed her.

It was short, cautious. Nostalgic.

He took his hand back, reached into his jacket for his cigarettes.

But Karen climbed, stretched her leg over the center console, planted her knee at his hip. She spilled a can of Coke in a cup holder, knocked the rearview mirror onto the dash, honked the horn with her ass. Through the awkward movements, the groping, their faces never came apart.

Karen pulled away, slapped him across the face.

He said he was sorry.

"No, you're not."

"Yeah, and you're not pissed at me."

She told Tony to shut up, and mashed her lips into his.

***

Tony doesn't tell Maura that Chris is already waiting for them at them bar.

They walk in, see Chris, and Tony says he figured Maura wouldn't mind. Says Chris only texted him a little bit ago, after they'd decided to get a beer after dinner.

Maura makes a face at Tony when she hugs Chris hello. A face not in a mood to spare his feelings.

It's beer, then pool, then darts with Maura talking to Chris. And Tony watching Mikey drink a Shirley Temple at the bar.

The dartboard bleeps when Maura hits the bullseye.

Tony claps, says, "Nice shot."

Maura glances at him looks away.

Chris coughs into his beer, says she got lucky.

Maura laughs, flips Chris off. Tells him to do better.

Tony steps away to use the bathroom thinking of the things he'll say to Maura on the way home. "I figured it'd be a nice surprise."

Or, "Come on, it's Chris. You love Chris."

Or, "He's been lonely lately. Maybe we should set him up with your sister."

All true things. Flimsy true things. Nothing to explain away Chris' involvement in their only night out as a couple since well before Nate.

Tony washes his hands, doesn't flinch when Mikey's reflection appears in the mirror, says, "Pretty sure my getting used to you is scarier than you are."

"You should have told her," Mikey says.

"She didn't need to know. It's fine; she's having fun."

"Not that. Chris is going to say something. You know how he is."

"Shut up. Get the fuck out of here."

Mikey's gone. A drunken regular tells Tony to say what the fuck again.

"Sorry. That wasn't mean for you...I talk to myself sometimes."

The guy hiccups, says, "Better have been talking to yourself. Dickhead."

Back at the table, it's Maura sitting by herself, three darts in front of her. She tells Tony it's his turn while she stares at the television hanging from the wall behind the pool table.

Chris brings over refills. Stumbles over words. Flops into a seat next to Maura.

Then Tony knows what Mikey was talking about.

He throws his darts listening to every word coming from Chris' mouth. Listens for the subject to shift from shitty dart skills to shitty life skills, to shitty untold truths. Moves across the room to pull the darts from the board as Maura says it's a shame the last time they all saw each other was at the memorial.

Tony says, "Chris, your turn."

Chris says, "I feel like don't see anyone anymore outside of funerals and weddings."

"Chris, it's your turn."

Chris says, "Like Tony's parents. You guys together. Shit, I haven't seen Karen since freshman year of college."

Tony takes Chris's hand, digs the plastic darts into his palm, tells him it's his turn. Again.

"Fuck, dude. Shit," Chris says, standing, moving to the white line taped to the floor.

Maura says, "Yeah, Tony was surprised she was there too."

Chris throws his first dart, says, "His parents sure weren't."

Tony, voice loud enough for people at the bar to turn to look, says, "Who needs a refill? Anyone need another beer?"

Maura asks Chris what he means.

Chris pauses for a beat, says, "Nothing."

Maura says, "Tony? Why's your friend lying for you?"

"What?" Tony says. "He's not lying."

"Seriously, Tony?"

"Fuck," Tony says. He sits down, glares at Chris, says, "Look, Karen's apparently been friends with my parents since we broke up."

"Since college?"

"Apparently. I didn't tell you because it's kind of weird. And awkward."

"It is fucking weird and awkward." Maura's jaw clenches, unclenches once, twice. Then, "Have you been talking to her too?"

"Hell no. She was at the memorial service. I found out then."

Maura doesn't say anything. But her face does. It tightens, pulls the muscles into bundles of stiff tissue. Her mouth disappears, becomes thin and flat—her lips turn white.

Tony watches her swallow; her throat struggles to keep down whatever she's keeping trapped in her chest.

Chris curses and says, "I'm going to, uh, go drink. Over there."

When he does, Maura pulls on her coat.

Tony asks her where she's going.

Maura says, "Seriously? You lied to me tonight. Twice. Maybe more than that."

"I'm sorry, I—"

She spits out a string of questions like, "Why didn't you tell me?"

Like, "What does this mean?"

Like, "Have you seen each other since you broke up?"

And Tony tries to answer each in turn. He tells her he didn't tell her because he figured she would wonder what his parents think of her. Tells her it doesn't mean anything other than Karen not having any friends. And, "No, the funeral was the first time I've seen her."

"I'm going home," Maura says.

"Come on, please don't go. I know I lied earlier, but I'm not anymore."

Maura walks to Chris sitting at the bar. She smiles, says goodnight, it was good to see him. She asks, "Can you get him home safe for me?"

Chris says, "Sure. Sorry."

Tony calls her name. Says, "Wait," follows her to the door.

Maura turns and tells him if he follows her outside she'll run him over.

Mikey, sitting a seat away from Chris at the bar says, "She's not going to run you over. But stay here anyways."

Before, Tony and Chris and Maura would come here and close the place on the weekends. Sometimes on weeknights. But those nights never once ended with Maura leaving Tony behind. She'd let him get drunk, whisper nasty things in her ear about what he was going to do to her when they got home. And Chris would pretend not to hear a thing.

Now, sitting between Chris and his imaginary friend, Tony curses, orders another beer, a shot of whiskey. Two shots of whiskey after Chris knocks on the bar.

Chris says he's sorry, says he didn't mean to blow it like that.

"Forget it." Tony doesn't mean that. He wants to grab the back Chris's head, slam his face into the bar over and over until he hears his nose pop, his eye sockets buckle.

But he lets it go, watches Mikey sip from the tiny straw in his red drink, watches him retie the knot of orange cloth behind his head, his eyes concentrating on keeping his lips around the straw, the straw in the drink, while his hands work.

Mikey laughs when he finishes, says, "How cool was that?"

"Pretty cool."

Chris says, "What?"

"Nothing."

"I'm sorry. Really."

Tony gets up from his seat, pulls a pool cue from the wall. He tells Chris to stop worrying about it, says, "Buy the next round and we're even."

Chris orders beers and feeds a dollar into the pool table. Mikey jumps to the sound of the balls rumbling on their tracks, laughs, then hops up onto the bar trying scissor kicks and yelling cowabunga distracting Tony enough to take an entire game of pool to send a text.

And after the second game—after a beer, a shot, another beer—Tony tells Chris he can get going. That Maura's coming to get him.

"Think you're ready for a fight in your state?"

Tony responds to a text from Karen telling him Sam's away for the night, that she'll be right there. Then he says, "Not really."

The boy ties the orange mask around his head, fits the green plastic nose over his own. He breathes deep. He smiles. The smell reminds him of Christmas and Saturday mornings. He velcros his foam shell at his side, buckles a belt he borrowed from his father's closet around the shell at his waist. He stuffs his orange nunchucks between the belt and shell.

He poses in the mirror. Karate stances and semi-sneers.

He says, "Cowabunga, dude," then jumps on his bed, uses its springs to send him into the air. He kicks, yells hiyah, lands on his bedroom floor hard enough to knock over Krang's battle-suit standing on his dresser.

He laughs, says, "Next time, Dimension X, ugly brain-dude," and barrels through his door into the hallway.

His mother calls his name, says something he doesn't listen to.

He says, "Sorry, Mom."

Then he slams into his brother's locked door, crumples to the floor, says, "Whoa."

This time he hears what his mother says. "Stop running around up there. You're going to break your neck."

From inside the bedroom his brother says, "Leave me alone. I'm sleeping."

The boy calls his brother Raph, says, "Shredder took all the pizza."

His mother, now at the bottom of the stairs, calls his name, says, "Leave your brother alone. If he doesn't want to play he doesn't have to play."

The boy crawls across the floor. He lays on his stomach, presses his check down on the hardwood, closes one eye to look under the door. He whispers, "Raph, April's getting mad at me. I think it's because she wants pizza, too. I need your help."

After a minute, two, the boy hears his mother's footsteps move away from the staircase. He says, "Raph?"

There's nothing from inside the bedroom.

He says Raph again.

Still nothing.

He stands, presses his ear to the door. And for a moment, a sound. Another. Then the door's pulled open, and the boy stumbles inside.

His face against a foam turtle shell, held up by arms decorated with elbow pads, he looks up into his brother's eyes—seen through almond-shaped eyeholes cut into a orange mask.

His brother says, "Let's go get our pizza back."

***

On the front lawn, the boy and his brother fight a hoard of Foot Clan.

Plastic sai swinging, stabbing, slashing, the boy's brother maims the robotic soldiers. He punts the severed heads into the air, makes the sound of a metallic crash, the sizzle of ruined circuitry when they hit the blacktop.

The boy somersaults on the lawn. He pulls his nunchucks from his belt, twirls them to distract the Foot Clan, kicks one in the chest, punches another in the face. He screams they need to tell him where Shredder is right now or he'll shred them. He laughs.

"Don't laugh at your own jokes, Mikey," his brother says.

"Shred, though, Raph. That's funny."

"Just keep fighting, there's more coming."

Back to back, the brothers swing their weapons, knock aside their enemies as they come.

The boy tumbles away. On his back, in the grass, he rolls side to side taking imaginary blows from the Foot Clan after they pin him to the ground.

His brother says, "I'm coming, Mikey." But he's knocked to the ground himself.

Two turtles on their backs, rolling, unable to get up, call for help. They yell for Leonardo. They yell for Donatello. They yell for Master Splinter. But no one comes.

The boy, still fending off punches, says, "Master Splinter's in a prison in Dimension X. Krang took him before Shredder took the pizza."

His brother says, "Donnie's in the sewers trying to build a machine to shut down all the Foot all at once."

The boy says, "Leo's dead."

His brother sits up, says, "What? You can't kill Leo."

Still rolling in the grass, the boy says, "I mean he's knocked out."

His brother lays back down, does a backward roll into a crouch, says, "Donnie's machine's working."

Both brothers use their teeth and tongues to make the sound of sparks spraying from the dying Foot Soldiers' necks and eyes.

They stand, brush themselves off, and look at each other. The boy watches his brother's mouth morph, form silent numbers. Once it looks like a smile, it means three. And both brothers jump into the air. They high-five. Yell cowabunga.

But then the brother says, "Shit."

"Swear Jar," the boy says, repeating his mother after his father would say the S-word, or the A-word, or sometimes the F-word. Then he laughs. He doesn't know for certain if he's ever heard his brother say that. And it's hilarious.

His brother says, "Shut up," grabs the boy's arm, and drags him across the lawn. The boy gets shushed every time he asks where they're going, or says his arm hurts, or says stop it.

"Mikey, it's Beebop and Rocksteady, okay?" his brother says, shoving him behind the hedges to the side of the house. "You have to be quiet and hide with me."

The boy says, "Oh, okay," and dives into the mulch, crawls into the bush, ignores the itchiness of the branches.

Behind him, his brother says they have to wait a minute to let the bad-guys pass.

Through the tangles of sharp leaves and brittle sticks, the boy keeps his eyes on the street, waits for invisible walking, talking, mutated animals to walk by. But it's just two boys on bikes, zig-zagging down the street past the house in slow helix-shaped patterns.

He says, "Hey, that's not Beebop and Rocksteady."

His brother says, "No shit."

The boy laughs. But he feels funny. Like he does when his parents yell at him.

The brothers says nothing until the boys on bikes pass.

5

Nate told Tony to go change. He said, "You can't go like that."

Tony's shoulders slumped. He'd spent the last forty minutes deciding what to wear, picking his favorite Bad Religion shirt out of the pile of laundry his mother had laid on his bed. He'd spread pomade into his cobalt blue hair. Spritzed his neck with cologne stolen from Nate's room.

He asked why, his voice whiny, young.

"Because I won't drive you. How's that?"

Tony's mother called them from downstairs, said it was pizza time. "Let's go," she said.

"Button-down shirt. Maybe a sweater. Shave your head, too," Nate said, smiling with his last bit of advice.

Nate left the room, and over the groaning floorboards in the hall he said, "You put on too much Acqua di Gio. Don't think I don't know you steal my shit."

From the bottom of the steps, Tony's mother said, "It'd be really embarrassing for teenagers to have to use the Swear Jar, Nathan. Watch your mouth."

Tony laughed, closed his bedroom door.

The shirt he found in his closet was something he only wore to family parties, baptisms, first holy communions. He hated it. It would hang down too low, bunch up at his hips, make him look fat. And there was a horse on the left breast. Which was a crime punishable by scene-ejection by some of the more hardcore kids he'd met at basement shows.

But he put in on anyway. Buttoned it over his Bad Religion shirt so when he puffed his chest he could still see the crossbuster in a mirror. He'd get the credit he deserved, even if it was given to him by his own self. The blue hair helped.

Downstairs, at the kitchen table, his mother told him he looked nice.

Nate said, "You're welcome."

His father said, "The hair's a little ridiculous."

Tony didn't say much. He ate his pizza.

Tony's father asked Nate about how training for crew was going, asked him if he'd miss turkey season again.

"Only if we make the Stotesbury Cup."

"So, no turkey then?"

They laughed.

"My boats never made it through the Stotesbury qualifiers," Tony's father said. "I never missed turkey." Then he laughed, went on about how smart turkeys are, about throwing the perfect turkey call out into the woods, about decoys, gobblers, hens.

Then it was Nate talking about how well his boat should do this year, talking about being strokeman, about being a leader, setting the tempo, being intense.

Tony got up to get another slice of pizza. He said, "Why do you always get extra cheese?"

His mother said, "Because we like it."

"Who's we? It feels like I'm biting through a flap of skin."

His father said Tony's full name, told him not to be so gross.

The conversation shifted from crew to the college applications Nate had sent away. Nate listed them all. Penn. Drexel. LaSalle.

All the schools in the area Tony hoped his brother would pick from. He ignored the mention of Columbia, Pitt, and BU. Tony knew Nate wasn't going to go to any of them. He wouldn't, couldn't. Even if he got in.

Tony gave up on keeping up with the conversation, let himself sink back into the things he thought he'd said right to Karen on AOL the night before. He limited the smiley faces. Asked her heaps of questions. Wrote "haha" instead of LOL to make himself seem less of a follower.

The dance wasn't something he'd planned on. His friends had all agreed that the music played at those things was bullshit. And Bangarang was playing the VFW. Easy choice. But it wasn't as if he could go anyway.

Then Karen had asked if Tony was going to the dance.

He typed yes without thinking. It took him the rest of the night to convince Chris he was asked by Karen, that he wouldn't be going if she hadn't asked. It took most of the next day to convince Nate to help him convince his parents to let him out of the house.

Gnawing on his crust, Tony heard his name, said, "Huh?"

Three pairs of eyes were on him. Nate's were the only set he took some comfort in.

His father asked him about the algebra test.

"It was good," Tony said.

"What did you get?"

"I don't know."

"You don't know? How'd you feel about it?"

"Good."

"Good?"

"Yeah. Good."

Tony's mother cocked her head to the side. Maybe she felt sorry for how intense Tony's father was being. But she said, "We don't need the attitude. It's not like we're off base here, asking you these questions."

Mrs. Garvin had called the house a few weeks back. Tony had known she was going to, read the letter she told him was for his parents. He'd sat in the kitchen next to the phone that night pretending to do homework. The boredom sunk in sooner than he'd planned. So he'd snuck around the house shutting off all the ringers on all of the phones.

The caller ID. He'd forgotten about the caller ID. The blinking red light, the dozen or so missed calls lead to weeks of algebra drills, monitored homework time, checked notebooks. And blue hair. Because fuck it.

Nate had convinced their parents about the dance on Tony's behalf. He'd said it was a good idea, told them he'd go with Tony. Drive him, too. He'd planned on going anyhow.

And now Tony was ruining it. Sitting, being shitty to his parents, ignoring his brother's glare. Tony said, "It was good. It felt good. Sorry. I'll get it back Monday."

The conversation went back to Nate again after that.

Tony watched his brother, how he handled the attention. The smiles, the jokes, the stories he was sure Nate was making up.

He stayed quiet, waited until Nate asked if he was ready to go.

Tony's mother kissed him on the head, told him to have fun. His father shook his hand, said he should try to bring home some phone numbers.

Tony said, "Thanks."

Said, "I will."

Said goodbye, hoping the hours between leaving and coming home would drag on long enough that he wouldn't have to say hello to them again until the next morning.

A live version of O.A.R.'s "That Was a Crazy Game of Poker" played on the stereo in Nate's car. Nate sang along with the stupid song. Tony stared out the window. It took most of the bloated twelve minute track for Tony to realize they'd been driving too long.

He asked where they were.

"We're going to loosen you up a little."

"By not going to the dance?"

"I didn't think you wanted to go anyway."

"I don't. I mean, I do. I have friends going."

"You meeting a girl there or something?"

Tony said nothing, stared out the window again until Nate said, "Holy shit. You are meeting a girl there, aren't you?"

Tony told him to shut up, leave him alone.

Nate pulled into a neighborhood park's empty lot, said, "Well, all the more reason."

He reached behind Tony, pulled a Teenage Mutant Ninja

Turtles fannypack from underneath the passenger seat. Tony stopped himself from asking if the pack was his, taken without permission. Nate would have told him to shut up, stop whining if he had.

Tony asked what they were doing. Said, "Let's just go. Please?" Nate unzipped the pack, pulled out a glass fish wrapped in neon. And a baggy.

Tony said, "What's that?" But he knew. He'd never done it, but he wasn't stupid.

"It's weed, you idiot."

"I didn't know you—"

"I'm slick like that."

Nate packed the bowl, bent a swivel-necked lighter into a U— he must've swiped it from their father's barbeque supplies—and took a hit.

He handed the bowl, the lighter to Tony, said, "Your turn."

***

The array of colored lights on stage matched the rhythm from the speakers beat for beat, made Tony stare into them. Dazed, mesmerized, whatever, he couldn't look away. The music added a pulse to the air, gave Tony goosebumps despite the auditorium's wet heat.

When they'd shown up, Nate acted as Tony's puppetmaster, pushed him through the doors, steered him onto the dance floor. Tony had felt better with his brother moving his body for him. But then he was gone, he'd left Tony swaying on his feet, fighting gravity. Tony hadn't moved from the spot where he'd been left.

Karen, black hair in a ponytail hanging in front of her shoulder, made her way into the auditorium with a group of girls. Tony stared, uncertain it was her. He waved, because fuck it. His hand had no weight—or any weight he could understand in his fogged up skull. It swung back, forth at his side when he let it drop. It wasn't weightless. And that was hysterical.

Karen hugged him, asked what was funny. She was smiling. Which was weird. It was odd enough she'd been spending some evenings online with him.

He said, "Hi." His voice cracked. Licking his lips didn't work.

His tongue was gummed up to every tooth it touched. There was nothing to swallow, nothing to help him sound like he wasn't still jammed right in the middle of puberty.

Karen said, "Do you want to dance with me?"

"Do you want to get a soda?"

They said yes at the same time. Karen laughed. Tony couldn't catch his breath, his chest shook while he tried to calm himself.

He turned, left the auditorium. Whether Karen was behind him or not wasn't a question until, somewhere out there in the distance, he felt her take his hand. It was numb, but he felt her. Then he felt a tug in the front of his pants, but that was all him. He pulled his shirttail down to cover himself. And kept pulling at it until she asked him what he was doing.

He almost said, "I'm nervous."

Almost said, "Boner."

But he said, "This shirt's too big."

"I like it," Karen said. "You look really nice."

Tony felt blood well up under his skin. He could almost feel every drop fill the network of capillaries in his cheeks as if he were conscious of it. He said, "Thanks."

And they kept walking.

He whipped around to face her, his forehead covered in sweat. "You look really..."

There, in the middle of the hall, Tony was chewing on his words, the inside of his mouth. His eyes went to her lips, her breasts, the freckle cluster on her hand.

She said, "What?"

"Beautiful. You look really beautiful."

He turned around before he saw her reaction. He couldn't turn back. He had to wait, mull over what he thought she thought about what he said.

But Karen's hand was still in his.

In the cafeteria Tony bought two cans of soda from the vending machine, opened Karen's before handing it to her.

They sat together at one of the hundred lunch tables, sipping from their drinks, looking at everything else in the room, everyone else in the room, saying nothing.

The soda tasted off to Tony. It was a more complete experience. Like he could feel the bubbles burst, spill sugar on his tongue.

The fizzing in his mouth was static in his ears. He felt he could do a science experiment based on everything happening, present it in Integrated Science class for the project he'd been putting off for a month.

Karen said, "Are you okay?"

Tony choked on his soda, hacked until his face went red, saying it went down the wrong pipe rasped from his throat in chunks.

Karen waited until his fit ended before she spoke again.

His apology collided with her questions about his sweating.

He let her do the talking after that, nodded when she told him about school, and her parents. He had no idea whether his reactions were appropriate or not. He reacted out of instinct, aware his instincts were smoked stupid.

There was a slap to Tony's back, a familiar voice. But Tony's synapses weren't firing well enough to make the connection.

He saw Karen look past him, smile, say hello.

Nate said, "Nice," punched Tony's arm.

"Hmm?"

"Good work," Nate said taking a seat. "I'm Nate," he said, holding his hand out to Karen.

Karen said her name, shook his hand.

And Tony sat still, attempted to hold back the potential freak-out burning through his brain.

Nate said, "Heard a lot about you."

"Tony's talked about me? You talked about me?"

Tony shrugged, smiled. His lips were tacky, stuck together.

Karen smiled.

Nate said, "You guys in class together? How'd you meet?"

Karen mentioned a football game, Tony's nonchalance bordering on indifference, the band he and Chris were listening to with a Discman and a set of headphones.

"He pretends he's so badass, doesn't he?" Nate said.

Karen smiled, looked at the table.

Nate put his hand to the side of his mouth, whispered, "He doesn't even like football."

"Why did he go?"

"I told him he could meet pretty girls there."

Karen's face went red, she said, "Didn't you play quarter—"

"You're in honors classes, right?"

"How'd you know that?"

Nate stuck out his thumb, pointed to Tony. He slapped Tony's back again, told Karen it was nice to meet her. And he was gone just as fast as he'd shown up.

Tony was sick. His stomach was hanging lower than the seat in was sitting in.

But Karen asked if he wanted to go upstairs to dance, said, "You don't need to be so nervous. I already like you."

***

Tony had kissed girls in parking lots. In basements at parties he'd snuck his father's booze into. In movie theaters.

Never on a crowded, sweaty dance floor.

Never Karen.

At the beginning of the school year he and Chris had sat at lunch, pointed out the girls who'd be lucky enough to be graced by their presence.

Tony had picked Karen. Chris had said, "Bullshit."

But in that crowd, under a manic neon light show, her arms were wrapped around his neck. His hands were on her hips, and he felt her lips touch his. He opened his mouth when she did. Made sure not to be too aggressive with his tongue.

He'd done this enough to know what he was doing. But with Karen, whether he was good, bad, awful, he didn't know.

He didn't care. It was Karen.

He bent his hips, stuck out his ass to hide how much he was enjoying the whole experience. When he pulled his face away he smiled.

So did she.

They kissed again. They kept going, song after song.

Then white light tore through Tony's eyelids.

"Mr. D'Angelo."

Tony shoved himself from Karen.

Mr. Adler stood in front of Tony, a circle of wet people surrounding the three of them, staring, not moving. He said, "I know Miss Kelly here has better sense than this, so I'm assuming you're responsible for the display."

Karen opened her mouth, tried to say something, but Adler

held up a hand. He said, "Goodbye, Miss Kelly."

She backed up, took her place in the circle of bodies, mouthed apologies to Tony.

Adler said, "You're a far cry from Nathan, Mr. D'Angelo."

Tony stared into the flashlight, his eyes never meeting Adler's. Until the only thing in his line of sight was the disciplinarian's face.

"Your eyes are a bit red, Mr. D'Angelo."

"You're holding a flashlight in my face."

"Is that all?"

"Mouthwash would help."

Mr. Adler waved two fingers, told Tony to follow him. The crowd opened up where they passed through. Kids shuffled to the sides, pushed each other out of the way.

The high was gone. Either that or Tony forgot about it.

In the office, Tony said nothing. He stared into Adler's eyes without blinking, without hearing a word that was coming from his mouth. With only a few exceptions.

He heard, "Disciplinary problem."

And, "Familial responsibility."

And, "Black sheep."

Tony said, "Chris Farley was way funnier than I am."

Adler leafed through the rolodex at the corner of his desk. He pulled a card, didn't bother to look at it while dialing the number.

On speaker, Tony's father said, "Hello?"

"Nathan. It's Martin."

Then came his father's follow-up question. It was just a name. Adler said, "Yeah. Anthony."

***

The car ride home was silent. Which was nice. It lulled Tony into a post-high reverie.

The lecture Tony got later on in the kitchen was different, filled with screaming. Cursing. Accusations. People slamming their fists onto tables. Questions about where Tony got the drugs. How long he'd been using drugs. The repetition of "drugs" made the concept hold less weight. It became only a word to say.

"I've never done drugs before."

"I don't have a drug problem."

"The drugs were Nate's."

His father asked Nate if he'd ever smoked pot. Nate said he doesn't even know where he could get pot, or anyone who sells the stuff.

Tony called Nate a fucking liar in front of his red-faced father, his crying mother.

His mother slid a chair around the table, sat down next to Tony. She said, "Was it me? Did I do something wrong?"

Nate said, "Mom. Seriously. He's young. This has nothing to do with anything else than that. He doesn't have a problem. He's fine."

"Enough, Nathan. This is partially your fault. We trusted you to get him to the dance and back without any issues. If you'd watched him a little better—"

"Dad, come on, I—"

"Out."

Once Nate was gone, once the floorboards upstairs creaked and stopped, Tony's father sat across the table from him, said, "Are we doing something wrong? Is it me?"

Tony said nothing, stared.

"I don't mean to be the bad guy, Anth. I don't want you to feel like you need to hate me. But you're so pissed off all the time. You hide in your room. Do nothing but hang out with Chris. Don't you have any other friends?"

Nothing.

"Anthony?"

"Can I go now?"

His father said, "Sure." Then he slammed his hand flat on the table, made Tony flinch. "You can go. First thing tomorrow you can go get your head shaved. Then you can go to bed before nine every night. Then you can only leave the house to go to school. Any other questions?"

Tony said, "Yeah. What would you say if you found out Nate's not what you think he is?"

His father pinched the bridge of his nose.

His mother dabbed her eyes with a paper towel, said, "Anthony, enough. Just go to bed."

Tony said, "I'm serious. I want to know. How bad would Nate

have to fuck up for you to look at him like you're looking at me right now?"

His father said, "Guess we'll wait have to wait and see."

Tony left the kitchen, strained to listen to the whispers from his parents.

Up the stairs, through the hallway, he ignored Nate's voice.

Tony's computer dialed up, connected to AOL. No email from Karen waiting for him. She wasn't signed on.

Nate leaned a shoulder against the door jam, said, "Hey."

"Leave me alone."

"Don't do that. I'll handle it."

"I think you already did."

Nate checked the hall for their parents, lowered his voice, told Tony that he has his own way of dealing with things. He said, "You need to trust me."

"To do what? Get me in more trouble?"

"Dude, you're the one who got caught. You didn't exactly protect me down there."

Tony said nothing, watched the computer screen. A door creaked open over the speakers, Karen's screenname in italics on his Buddy List.

He typed he was sorry, hit enter.

"What," Nate said. "You're not talking to me anymore?"

Karen responded, said Tony had nothing to apologize for, that she hoped everything was okay. "I hope you're not mad at me," she said.

Tony turned to Nate, said, "Leave. Now."

Nate said, "Fine." But he stayed where he was standing.

Tony typed a message. There was no way he could be mad, Karen did nothing wrong. It was Nate. Nate did this, he wrote.

But he deleted that bit.

He took a breath, wrote he really liked kissing her, sent it away before he could regret writing something so stupid.

"Nate," he said.

"Yeah?"

"I don't care what I have to do, but I'm going to make sure Mom and Dad know you're not what they think you are. I won't fight anymore. Never really could defend myself anyway. But you're my new job."

Nate laughed, rubbed the back of his neck. His breaths were heavy, got louder before he said, "Tony, I'm sorry, man. But you know I can't—"

"Don't apologize. I won't. You'll see."

Nate said nothing. His eyes shifted to the floor. His mouth moved, formed words that were never said.

Tony looked away without saying anything else. He kept his eyes fixed to the computer screen so he wouldn't see his brother struggle to find something to say.

Tony knew Nate was gone by the sound of the floorboards in the hallway.

Karen's response popped onto the screen. It said, "I really liked kissing you too."

6

They put off getting rid of Nate's bed until now. Kept it behind a door covered in psychedelic posters, stickers, and Phish lyrics. Since Nate was carried out of the room, his paraphernalia and leftover heroin bagged up and removed, no one's been back inside.

His mother, in the kitchen again, calls to Tony when he falls into the house. Something cheery, forced.

His father stands up from the couch, says, "Ready?" No hello, no handshake.

Tony and his father go upstairs, open Nate's bedroom door, walk inside not looking at anything other than the bed. They strip the covers, stuff them into a garbage bag, slide the mattress from the box spring without speaking.

They lift, flip the bed onto its side, lift again.

Tony's face pressed up against the side of the mattress, he stops himself from asking about the awful hello. From asking if Tony's mother forced the call the other day. From asking if Wyoming's still happening. He concentrates on the mattress smell. Wonders if he's breathing in bits of Nate.

Then Mikey's in the doorway using his nunchucks to direct traffic.

Tony's father says, "Pivot."

"Are you guys going to get another mattress or just let it go?"

"Anthony, pivot."

"I am. Jesus."

They get the mattress out the bedroom door without much trouble. But it scrapes against the hallway wall, knocks photos from their nails. Tony's father curses, drops his corner to the floor, says, "Goddammit."

Tony apologizes. Monotone and dull. It gets muffled beneath his father's foul language.

From downstairs, Tony's mother calls up, asks if everything's alright up there, says, "Do you need help?"

Tony says, "No."

And his mother's only response is footsteps through the dining room, cabinets and drawers opening, closing in the kitchen.

"Don't talk to your mother like that."

"Like what?"

There's talking downstairs now. A joke, a laugh track. The television in the kitchen at a volume that will kill any sound from up here. Unless Tony falls down the steps. Which is possible. His father picks up his end, shoves the bed into Tony.

At the bottom of the stairs, Mikey says, "Don't fall."

Tony says he's not going to fall.

His father says, "What?"

"Slow down. I don't want to fall down the steps. You don't want to kill me, do you?"

They stop moving. Tony below, his father staring down at him, Nate's bed between them.

Tony says, "Sorry. I didn't mean—"

"Shut up."

"Dad, I—"

"Once we finish moving this fucking bed, you can go home. I'm sure you don't want to be here anyway."

Tony says it's nice to see his father too, calls him a fucker under his breath.

His father says, "What was that?"

Tony doesn't say anything.

The stairs are easy. The front door merits a son of a bitch and a shit.

They carry the mattress flat down the driveway. Tony and his father face one another, looking anywhere else but into each other's eyes.

Mikey's hand rests on top of the bed, he looks straight ahead. And for the first time since he began popping into Tony's imagination, he's silent. They cut across the front lawn, and Tony watches Mikey's fingers on the bed.

At the bottom of the driveway, they drop the mattress onto the curb. It bounces, a corner slides off onto the street.

Mikey sits down next to it.

Tony's father asks Tony what he's staring at. He says, "Well?"

"What? Nothing."

"Then go on. Go home."

"What if I don't want to?"

"You don't have a choice here. I'm asking you to leave."

Tony kicks the mattress, says, "That's what you fucking want?"

His father laughs, rubs the back of his neck. His breath is heavy, visible in the cold, thickening before he speaks. He says, "This might be the first time in your entire life you don't want to leave."

"What's your deal? You call, I show up. What else do you want?"

"Forget it." Tony's father walks up the driveway. But he turns, says, "Get in the car I gave you and go home. Soon as you started driving all you did was drive away from here. Now I'm telling you to go and you won't."

"Is this because I didn't call you back after your forced-ass voicemail?"

"What? Jesus. This isn't high school, Anthony."

"What the fuck's this about then?"

"It's about your brother being dead, and you not wanting to do anything but stay away from here. From your mother. From me. We call, you show up. You never just show up."

Tony stuffs his hands in his coat pockets to keep them hidden, to keep his middle fingers in check.

His father says, "What are you still doing here?"

Tony wants to tell him to fuck off. Wants to tell him he's wrong. But he doesn't say anything.

"This time," his father says, "I'm walking away from you." He turns, walks the rest of the way up the driveway.

Tony knows his father's going to slam the door. He still flinches when it happens. Laughs when his father has to open, close, open, close the door before it stops sticking.

He sits on the curb next to Mikey, lights a cigarette. He smokes one, lights another, and ignores his phone. Whether it's Chris, Karen, Maura, it doesn't matter. He'd scream at whoever it is. So he lets it go, picks pebbles off the blacktop, strains his arm throwing them down the road.

When it would snow, the plows used to pile up mountains of the stuff where he's sitting now. He and Nate would dig through it, make forts that were meant to be a base when they were G.I. Joes hiding from Cobra. Or Ghostbusters putting together a plan to trap an abominable snowspectre. Or when Tony would run away from home after breaking something in the house, bored out of his skull on snow days.

Nate would sit with him—Tony remembers that—try to convince him he wasn't going to be in as much trouble as he thought.

Once he said, "It was only a lamp." Another time, a chair. Then, a window.

Now, sitting with Mikey, he flicks a cigarette butt into the street. He says, "You working full time now?"

"Huh?"

"Popping up whenever? Used to be a stress thing I thought."

"Maybe you're stressed all the time."

"Maybe I'm batshit all the time."

Mikey says Swear Jar, then, "You cursed at your dad."

"So? He cursed at me first."

"Curse at Splinter, dude? No pizza for a month."

"Jesus." Tony stands, takes a few swipes at his ass to clear whatever was stuck there from the wet cement. He says, "I'm leaving. Do I need to open the car door for you or will you just be there?"

Mikey looks away from him, trains his eyes on the street. He says, "I'm going to make a list for you."

"Of what? More cartoons to dress up as?"

"First, cut your dad a break."

"What were those rollerblading talking sharks called?"

"Street Sharks?"

"That's it."

"You're distracting me."

"I'm distracting you?" Tony's face contorts, his lip curls, his eyebrow arcs. "What do you want from me?"

"Second, make up with Maura. And you know what I want."

"Really. I don't."

"Ever think people might be trying to help you?"

"Do you count as people?"

Mikey stands, stomps his foot, says, "Let's just go. Can we go? Please?"

Tony unlocks the car, opens the door. He says, "Get in."

Mikey, already buckled into the passenger seat, says, "Getting your own hallucination upset. Good job."

Tony forms his fingers into a gun, puts the barrel to his own temple, and blows his imaginary brains out.

***

The day Nate was released from his last rehab stint, Tony's parents were ready. His father had become obsessed, his mother had supported it. The family counseling sessions were fresh. They had plans set in place. Backup plans for every scenario. They had taken precautions. They had stacks of printed-out research, bookcases full of books full of positive reinforcement tactics, techniques, and personal stories of dealing with addiction. They'd done everything they could based on Tony's father's need to know anything he could.

But Tony had argued, months ago, that putting too much pressure on Nate may make him relapse. It had happened before. He'd told them to be careful.

His mother had said, "Consistency and support is what your brother needs."

Tony had shaken his head, said, "Remember when I was a kid? The more rules you put on me, the more often I tried to find away to do the opposite of what you told me to do. Remember?"

"Well," his father had said, "You weren't addicted to being a jerk. You just were one. This is different."

Then Tony found Nate's body cooling, losing color. And all that planning was broken down into ridiculous catch-all phrases and pop-psychology.

The routine of waking up, going to work, going to bed, and waking up again hadn't taken.

The journal Nate was writing had ended weeks before his death.

And the plan to limit Nate's funds must have backfired.

The morning after Karen, after Nate's body was found, over coffee, Tony's father said, "Maybe he found a way to get into his bank account."

Tony didn't say anything, alcohol bubbling up in the back of his throat.

"Maybe we were too restrictive?"

"Dad, I don't think this was on you," he said, sipping coffee that was burning away the layer of Tums from his stomach lining.

His father said, "We were told to be consistent. Not to let up. Maybe we didn't do enough?"

The conversation broke down into a string of questions with answers Tony didn't want to say out loud. Questions like, "Do you think we did enough?"

Tony held back, didn't say, "No. Of course not. Not when it mattered, anyway."

"Do you regret your relationship with your brother?"

Tony didn't say, "Honestly? Not really."

"Was it us? Were we too hard on him?"

Tony didn't laugh in his father's face. He didn't stand up and scream that his parents weren't hard on him at all. Ever. He didn't bring up Nate's possession charges, or his parents blaming the people he was hanging around with for his arrest. Didn't bring up the stolen television, the stolen stereo, the CDs, the DVDs, the jewelry, the smashed front windows—punched out from the inside—feigning a burglary. Or his parents' refusal to come down on Nate for any of it, their insistence on giving him handfuls of second chances to make things right.

He didn't say, "If every rehab appearance, every other horrible thing he's done wasn't enough to convince you that something needed to be done about Nate a decade ago, his death will."

Instead, with his brain foggy and throbbing, he said, "Really, Dad, this was out of anyone's control for a long time. Even Nate's."

"Then why do I feel like the whole thing is my fault?"

"You shouldn't. It's not."

"But it is. It really is."

"What's that supposed to mean?"

Tony's mother shuffled into the kitchen before his father could answer the question. She kissed Tony on the top of the head, said good morning, started cooking. She made omelets with bacon and cheddar cheese. She fried up slabs of scrapple. She toasted chunks of a sourdough loaf, spread butter—hot from the microwave—onto the pieces. Then she plated four helpings.

Tony let it go, watched the food cool where Nate used to sit.

And for a while they ate in silence.

One plate getting cold at the end of the table.

Tony's father said, "Goddammit," and shoved his plate forward, replaced the empty space with the breakfast meant for Nate and ate the entire cooling breakfast. His silverware clanked on the ceramic, food fell from his open mouth while he shoveled more in. And Tony thought his father choked himself. He coughed splattered food onto the plate, the table. He coughed again, gasped for breath, and covered his eyes with his hand, the fork still wrapped in his fingers.

Then he got up and left the room, took the fork with him.

Tony sat, watched his mother react by taking a sip from her coffee mug and staring, listened to the floorboards upstairs creak and groan specific tune.

He knew where his father was. Standing outside Nate's room. Shifting his weight back and forth, foot to foot.

And then, listening for his father to move from that spot on the hardwood flooring upstairs, his mother asked how Maura is, if she's coming over later.

"Yeah, she'll be here. She says she's sorry for our loss."

He didn't tell his mother that he lied to Maura over the phone. That he'd told Maura Chris came over, had a few beers. That his phone had died after Chris left. That he'd fallen asleep on the couch before he could charge it.

"She's going to stop in on her lunch hour," Tony said.

"I hope she doesn't feel like she has to," his mother said. "It's really nice she wants to come by. Work's okay with you being out a few days?"

"Fuck."

His mother, eating again, said, "Anthony. Language."

Tony apologized, told her he had to make a call.

In the living room, he called the school's main office, told them what had happened. There were condolences from the ladies in the front office. Principal Adler couldn't say much at all. But into the phone, Tony said, "Thank you, I appreciate that," and "We're as shocked as you are," and "He'll certainly be missed."

Over the voices of people who cared more for Nate than for him, Tony was listening for the floorboards upstairs, for his father to move away from Nate's door.

He heard nothing.

∗∗∗

It's a couple days before Maura talks about the Karen situation. The days leading up to it are quiet, cordial. Cold.

But Tony doesn't push anything.

He cooks, he cleans, he stays home nights, doesn't text Karen. He waits for Maura to explode.

But she doesn't. She says, "I know you keep things to yourself. Didn't think you'd lie like that."

Tony talks, sentimental and rehearsed. He says all the things that Mikey made him believe were his ideas. Then he says, "I bought these," hands Maura tickets. "We can go if you want. We don't have to. Just figured we could go, get our minds off things."

"I'm still mad."

"I'm not asking you not to be."

They listen to music on the drive. Don't say much.

Tony follows Maura into the crowd, doesn't bother to ask her if she wants to go upstairs to the balcony.

He watches Maura during the opening band's set. She smiles,

sways to the music.

Once the band finishes up, Tony asks her if she wants beer. She nods, he goes to the opener's merch table first. He spends more on a hoodie and the band's shit album than he did for his ticket to the show.

Then two Miller Lites in sixteen ounce cups at the bar, the last twenty from his wallet.

Maura thanks him for the beer, turns away.

Tony says, "Hey," hands her the CD.

She says, "Thanks, they were good," turns away again.

Tony unzips the new hoodie, spreads it across Maura's shoulders. When she turns around, he smiles.

"You're terrible at this."

"Is it working?"

"This sucks for me, Tony. It sucks that I feel bad for being pissed."

Tony checks the crowd for anyone listening in. He lowers his voice, says, "You don't have to feel bad."

"Why do I, then?"

"Because you can't help but empathize when someone's in pain." The sentence tastes fake. He knows it's true, but saying it feels like lying. "It's hard to be mad at someone when you feel like that."

Maura takes a sip of beer, says, "You can't lie to me. I won't deal with it."

"You won't have to."

It's canned music played from the sound booth for a beat, two.

Then she smiles, sad, shy. She says, "Thank you for my stuff," and leans into him.

Tony hugs her.

"I'm still pissed at you," she says.

"I know."

They talk through most of the second opener's set by leaning in and yelling into each other's ears. About the music. How good it is. Tony lies, says he likes it.

During the second intermission Tony answers all the questions he hasn't heard asked since Chris was stupid enough not to keep his mouth shut. About not knowing Karen was so close to his parents. About why he kept it from her. Whether or not he's still in touch with Karen.

Tony's as honest as he can be.

Then Mumford & Sons gets on stage, starts singing songs Tony knows but hates.

A couple songs in, Maura's singing along, and Tony pulls his phone to take pictures for her to post to Facebook later.

But there's a text from Karen asking what he's doing here.

Tony looks around, sees nothing but the crowd, the light show.

Another text telling him to stop looking around, then one asking him to meet her outside.

Tony taps Maura's shoulder, yells over the music he's going to catch a smoke, get more beer.

She nods, points to her empty cup.

Outside, Karen stands with the shivering smokers talking bullshit in a roped off section.

She says, "Well?"

"Well what?"

"You hate this stuff."

"I'm trying to make up with Maura."

"About what?"

"She found out about your friendship with my parents."

Karen nods, asks for a cigarette.

Tony hands her his pack, his lighter, says, "What's up? I've got to get back."

She lights a cigarette, says, "Haven't heard from you in a couple days."

"I just told you what I've been trying to do."

"Look, we're in the balcony. Stay where you are and everything will be fine."

"Who's we?"

"Don't be dumb."

"I've got to go, I'll text you later."

"Hope so."

Inside, Mikey screams hiyah, flings himself from a merch table, makes Tony jump out of the way of a scissor kick, say holy shit, forcing people to stare.

In line at the bar Mikey says, "Dude, she likes you a lot."

Tony asks for two beers, ignores Mikey, pays with a card.

"Who do you like better? Karen or Maura?"

Tony weaves through the crowd, Mikey, right behind him, talking about lying, the list. Adding Karen to a list of people to stay away from, hers the only name on it.

Tony finds Maura, hands her a beer. They cheers. He kisses her cheek.

Mumford & Sons plays for the better part of an hour. Tony zones out for most of it. Watches Maura shift from having a tentative good time to full on fun. Wonders if Karen is watching them from the railing upstairs, if Sam sees them.

He curses when his phone vibrates, lets it go.

It vibrates again.

And again.

When the fourth call comes through Tony pulls it from his pocket.

Tony's father.

Mikey steps through the crowd, his hand at the side of his head, thumb in his ear, pinky to his lips. He says, "Answer it."

Tony almost gives Mikey the finger. He shows Maura his phone instead.

On the way to the bathrooms Tony swipes his arms behind himself, shoos Mikey away so he can concentrate.

The bathroom door drowns out the music. He leans his back against it, leaves Mikey on the other side.

Tony watches his phone alert him he's got another missed call. He goes to the sweating sink, splashes water on his face, wastes time before returning his father's call.

And then Sam steps into the room.

They stare at each other through the mirror.

Sam says, "Hey."

Tony says, "Hey, man," talking to Sam's reflection.

"Tony, right?"

Tony turns, reaches out his hand, says, "Yeah. Sam?"

They shake, Sam says, "Yeah. Sorry about your brother."

"Ah, yeah, thanks. That's—I appreciate that."

"Yeah."

Sam washes his hands. Tony pretends to, waiting for Sam to leave.

"Hey, listen," Sam says. "Karen told me she's been pretty good friends with your parents since college. But I didn't realize you guys were a thing."

"That was like ten or so years ago. But yeah, no, I just found out about the parent thing, myself."

"Yeah, that's what she said. Look, I don't mean to be a dick or anything, but the whole thing makes me really uncomfortable."

"Oh, yeah. Me too. Sorry about—"

"When things calm down let's sort of let this go. Know what I mean?"

"Trust me. It makes my girlfriend feel just as weird."

"Good."

"Cool."

Sam runs his hands under the electric dryer, says, "Take it easy."

Tony says, "Yeah. You too."

When Sam leaves, the door swings open. The band says thank you to the crowd. People cheer. A rush of guys trying to hit the bathroom keeps the door from staying closed long.

He pictures Maura standing alone, looking around trying to find him.

Pictures her searching the floor unsure if he really went to take his father's call.

Pictures her throwing the CD and the hoodie in the trash and leaving without him.

Then Tony's father calls again.

Tony answers, says hello.

Over the line it's just, "I need you to come home."

"What? No, Dad. I'm out right now."

"Anthony. Please."

"Dad—"

"There's something I need to tell you."

"Tell Mom."

There's a pause, an emptiness on the line. Tony says, "Hello?"

"I can't tell your mother. Just come home. It's about Nathan."

"No shit. Everything's about Nate."

"Anthony. This is my fault. Everything. I need you to come home. Now."

"Dad—"

"If it weren't for me your brother would still be alive, okay?"

Then the call goes dead.

Tony scrapes his foot over the filthy tile floor.

He kicks the trash can across the room, ignores the looks he gets.

He goes to find Maura just as the band starts their encore.

7

Tony's father says, "I killed your brother."

Tony says, "Fucking shit," and texts Maura that he's going to be longer than he expected. He types, Sorry. And, You don't need to wait up.

His father says, "I'm serious."

"That doesn't make any sense."

"Well, I did," Tony's father sips at a coffee mug, winces like he does when he drinks whiskey, like Nate did at loud noises while going through withdrawal.

Tony says, "Got any more?"

"Bottle's empty."

"I meant coffee."

Tony's father tosses a thumbed fist over his shoulder, tells Tony to help himself.

All that's left are the dregs. Greasy and burnt enough to stain ceramic. But Tony pours a mug, sips it anyway. He sets it on the table, sits across from his father. "So," he says, "You killed Nate."

"Everything's a joke to you?"

"Only funny things."

Tony's father doesn't laugh, just rubs the back of his neck. Then he goes off talking about all the books he'd read. All the research he'd done. All the hours spent not sleeping, not eating, not working, absorbing every drop of minutiae, becoming a veritable expert, getting hooked on the shit.

Tony mostly remembers the lectures his father held for him and his mother. The clichéd lines and buzzwords, the counselor-speak. Tony walked out of the house without saying goodbye most nights he was called in for a lesson, fed up, furious.

Now, Tony says, "Can we stop for a second," turning his hands to fists.

His father finishes his mug, swallows twice.

Tony says, "There's nothing you, me, Mom, anybody, could have done. Nate was an—"

Mikey sniffs at Tony's father's mug on the table, makes a face, waves his hand in front of his nose. He says, "Yuck," dragging the end of the word across the back of his throat.

Tony says, "Stop it."

His father says, "Huh?"

"What?"

"You okay?"

Mikey holds two fingers behind Tony's father's head, laughs.

Tony says, "Yeah, I'm good. I was saying that this is all Nate's—"

"Moose ears," Mikey says, his hands forming high-fives, thumbs at Tony's father's temples.

"Nate's what?" Tony's father says. "Anthony?"

"Hmm? Oh. What was I saying?"

Mikey says, "You were saying, 'I'm being a big dummy and want to hear what you have to say, Dad.'"

Tony pinches the bridge of his nose, sighs, says something under his breath, says, "What were you saying, Dad?"

Mikey smiles, gives two thumbs up.

Tony's father stares at Tony, eyebrow cocked, eyes wide.

"I'm good," Tony says.

Tony's father talks about Nate's last release from rehab, how well he'd done there. So much better than the last time. Then, the conditions under which he was allowed to return to work. Twenty to thirty hours a week. Otherwise homebound. "We did everything the counselor suggested."

They did everything the court ordered, too. Nate wasn't allowed to drive, wasn't allowed to leave the state. He wasn't allowed to have a cell phone, wasn't allowed to be within ninety feet of the people he used to spend his free time with—Jason.

Nate didn't argue. He was quiet. He'd watch *Seinfeld* with his father, Major Crimes with his mother.

"He was a good boy again," Tony's father says.

There was the journal he'd write in every night before going to bed. There wasn't much in there, just notes on the day, things at work he couldn't believe he used to do stoned out of his face.

"You could tell he wanted to be better, Anthony."

Tony wants to say, "Yeah, but what the fuck happened, then?" But Mikey circles the table twirling a nunchuck. And Tony stays quiet.

"And he was," his father says.

Tony skipped the family counseling session at which Nate's progress merited a bit of leeway. Not much, but enough. Tony's mother said Nate smiled when he was told of some of the concessions they were all allowed to make. She said he shook his counselor's hand, smiling, saying thank you over and over.

When Tony heard about all of this afterward over the phone, he asked if the counselor reiterated that Nate was still facing a hearing for possession and possible intent to distribute, still facing a stint in jail.

His mother told him that these things take time, that he should give his brother some credit.

Tony remembers apologizing, remembers hanging up, acting as if his nose was just smeared into a stain he'd left on the carpet.

Now, Tony's father says, "Things were getting better. Then I killed him."

Mikey stands in a karate pose, hands molded into half prayers, one held in front of the other.

Tony says, "You didn't kill Nate, Dad."

"Yes. I did."

There was an arrangement made at work. Tony's father had Nate's paychecks deposited into an account Nate was unable to access. Nate would get an allowance. It was called a stipend—to soften it. But it was still lunch money handed over before work. Five for a meal, one for a soda, one for a snack.

"I left my wallet out," Tony's father says. "Once. Then he died."

Tony stares, says nothing, balls his fist.

"He picked the debit card out, guessed the pin."

"He didn't have to guess. Did he?"

"I didn't think he'd ever get a hand on—"

"How fucking stupid can you be?"

Mikey says, "Swear Jar. Watch it, mister."

Tony's father says, "Birth years are easier to remember than random sets of numbers."

"Well no shit, Dad."

"You can't tell your mother."

"Why are you telling me this?"

"Because I have to. And that should be enough for you."

"Just felt the need to dump your shit on me? You and Nate, man. Fuck."

Mikey takes a swipe at Tony's forehead with a nunchuck, screams hi-yah.

Tony flinches hard, hears the bones in his neck crackle. He says, "Shit."

"What's your deal?" Tony's father says.

"No deal. Just—just jumpy. Maybe...maybe Nate saved his allowance or something."

Mikey rolls his eyes, adjusts his shell, says, "You're such a stupid."

Tony's father says, "Don't be stupid, Anthony."

"I'm just trying to help, okay? You call me up, ruin my night, tell me you killed Nate, and now you're giving me shit for trying to take the blame off of your dumbass shoulders."

Tony's father takes a sip from his empty mug, tips his head back, turns the mug upside down. "Goddammit," he says. "That wasn't what I was trying to do. That wasn't my intention."

"What was your intention then, Dad?"

"I wanted to tell you—"

"So you could enjoy your bullshit hunting trip guilt free? So you could relieve yourself, and we could start fresh? So we could be friends now that you decided to start being honest with me?"

Now Tony's standing. And Mikey's punching him in the hip, trying to sweep-kick his feet out from underneath him, saying, "Stop it, stop it, stop it."

Tony says, "You fucking stop it."

Tony's father stares, blinks, swallows, says nothing. The floorboards creak upstairs, and Tony's father says, "You woke your mother up."

"Bye, Dad."

There's an expectation for when Tony storms out of a room. A "Hey, get back here," or a, "Where do you think you're going?" or a, "It'll only get worse if you leave."

But now there's nothing.

Just the creaking, shuffling footsteps from upstairs. The door screaming as Tony rips it open. Mikey saying, "Burr," as the cold sweeps inside. Tony's name being called from upstairs.

Tony says, "Bye, Mom," pulls the door closed behind him once, twice, three times before it shuts.

***

The funeral home had a showroom floor. A white-washed room that stretched for miles. A lane made down the center by caskets, lined up, categorized. The Undertaker—the name Tony assigned the salesman—closed the lid of a casket a third of the way toward an exit sign, said, "This is one of our more higher-end models. This particular model is a rich Mahogany, crafted in one piece, as you can tell by the lack of breakage in the wood grain."

Tony's mother had waited in the lobby. She'd said she couldn't go in; she just couldn't. It was the only true thing Tony had heard her say over the three days since Nate.

Tony's father went to the bathroom after the alloy section. Hadn't come back yet.

Tony was ignoring the Undertaker's sales pitches. He was more focused on the Undertaker's home. Whether it was designed for maximum natural lighting, or if the light sources were human skulls with candles crammed in the eye sockets. If he liked fresh, colorful flowers in potters around the house, or if the walls were painted black.

But then the Undertaker used words like, "Molding."

Like, "Finish."

Like, "Soil."

And Tony had to cover his mouth, wipe the corners of his eyes. He lost it when the Undertaker patted him on the back. Red-faced, trying to breathe. Tony said sorry, said he's good, said he'll be fine. But he couldn't catch his breath. Every time he adjusted his feet, stood up straight, his breath would stick in the back of his throat and choke him.

Tony waved his hand, told the Undertaker to keep going.

So the Undertaker moved on, said, "This model can be hermetically sealed to—"

More hyperventilating, another, "Sorry."

"All of our models come complete with a pre-internment guarantee that—"

"I'm sorry. Again. Sorry."

The Undertaker told Tony he would give him a minute, to find him in his office once he managed to calm himself.

It took two cigarettes leaning against a hearse outside for Tony to compose himself. Another after realizing the hearse was going to be used to transport Nate's body that coming Saturday if they went the traditional route.

Reeking and cursing, Tony went back inside and found his father with the Undertaker mulling over cremation and receptacles.

There was a comment about the smoke smell from Tony's father.

Tony apologized, rolled his eyes.

He followed them across the showroom floor after that. Nodding his head, acting as if every special feature of each urn changed its primary function.

"This one is gold-plated. Adds a beautiful sheen, doesn't it?"

Tony's father said, "Beautiful."

Tony said, "Yeah."

"This piece is exquisite. Platinum, with a built-in glass frame with which you can display a small photo of your loved one."

Tony's father said, "My son."

Tony said, "Yeah." But he was somewhere else. Nude on a steel rack being slid into a cabinet. A cabinet that doubled as a furnace. His skin melting off his bones. His eyeballs bursting in their sockets. He was a skeleton, screaming, sinew falling in strands from the heat.

Then he was outside smoking again.

The texts from Maura were nice, sweet. Everything Tony didn't want to hear at that moment. She asked how he was doing if there was anything special he wanted her to order-in for dinner. She texted clichés about being there for him, doing whatever he needed whenever he needed it done. Tony looked across the parking lot to see if he would be able to toss his phone far enough to make the street.

He put the phone put back into his pocket without responding to a single message.

He tried hiding his cigarette when his mother stepped outside. She said, "Stop it."

He said, "Sorry."

She said, "Do you mind if I have one with you?"

Tony and Nate had pestered her into quitting when they were kids. But now he handed her a smoke, lit it for her, and saw her being cremated in the lighter's flame.

"I haven't had one of these in...I can't even remember," she said. "We used to call them coffin nails."

She burned a hole into Tony's shirt when she fell into him. Then she soaked the front of it, stained it with eye makeup.

Tony said nothing. He stood there waiting for something to say to blurt itself out. But nothing came.

His mother pulled away, stood up straight, wiped her eyes, said, "Think I could have another?"

Tony looked away when lighting the second one for her.

They stood smoking together until Tony's father poked his head outside saying he was wondering where they'd gone.

Both Tony and his mother hid their cigarettes behind their backs.

Tony's father said, "Can't decide between cremation or traditional burial."

Tony's mother dropped her smoke, crushed it under her foot, walked inside. And Tony ignored his phone while finishing off the pack he'd bought that morning.

Then he watched the ashes he left on the blacktop blow away and had to lean on the hearse again.

***

Over the phone, Maura reminds Tony it's a weeknight. Reminds him he's on probation. Reminds him it was late when they left the concert, late when he texted telling her he was at his parents' house, it's later now, and he should just have a beer when he gets home before bed.

"Chris is already there," Tony says. "I just need to process all the shit Dad said."

"I'm not trying to tell you what to do, Tony. And I get it. But—"

"But what, Maura?"

Nothing for a moment.

Then, "Just be careful," she said. "Don't get nuts."

Tony steps out of his car into the parking lot, almost empty, lit by the bar's signage and the street lamp down the way.

Mikey, on top of the car, tying his ratty Nikes, failing, trying again, says, "Know who goes nuts and does dumb things, too? Raph."

Chris pulls up then, and Tony wishes Mikey away with his eyes closed, his fingers crossed.

Walking to the front door, Chris says, "Your dad thinks he killed Nate, huh?"

Tony tells Chris everything his father said over beer and pool.

Chris tells Tony to stop yelling over darts shots of Jim Beam.

Mikey makes fart noises with his hands pressed over his mouth when Tony calls his father That Fucking Guy over Big Buck Hunter and Chris' Irish car bomb refusals.

When Chris asks questions, Tony answers saying, "Maura's fine. Want to play Photohunt?"

And, "No, we're good. We worked things out tonight. Come on, one more beer."

And, "No, there's nothing going on between Karen and me. I thought we were here to talk about Dad."

"He always did have a way with words," Chris says. "Remember in, like, I think it was senior year—"

"I keep asking myself how he'd be acting if I died instead of Nate." Tony finishes his beer, orders another, says, "You didn't have anything important going on, did you?"

"As in, my life?"

"Hey, let's go to a strip club."

Chris asks for his check. Tony asks him what the fuck he's doing.

Chris slides his phone across the bar, the time glowing from its face, says. "It's time to go. I'm drunk, you're hammered, and you're on probation. Come on."

"Come on, what?"

"I'm taking you home is what."

Tony says, "Only if you take me to Karen's." Then he curses.

Mikey, across the bar, gasps so loud he burps, laughs, says, "Did you hear that?"

The bartender slides Chris his check. Despite the country music playing from the TouchTunes, ESPN on the televisions, the Last Call bell, there's no sound. Just Tony's breathing matching Chris'. A pen scratching across the receipt.

Tony tells Chris to say something.

Chris says, "Lied about the Karen thing, then?"

Tony drinks from his glass, tells the bartender to stop serving the kid Shirley Temples, says, "What? No."

"You were the best liar in high school," Chris says. "When did you start sucking at it?"

After another pull of beer, a swallow, Tony says, "Probably when my father killed my brother. Or maybe when my brother decided to start pricking himself up with needles. Or maybe I'm not lying, and you have no idea what you're talking about."

His wallet in his hand, Chris pulls out cash, asks how much Tony thinks he'll need to cover a cab.

Tony says nothing, drinks his beer.

Mikey, at his corner of the bar, sucks down pink soda with his head propped up by his fists.

Chris leaves after Tony calls him a fucker once, twice, three times. And Tony spends Chris' money on a six-pack of beer after the barstools are placed upside down on the bar.

Mikey fights him on the way to the car, swinging punches,

kicking at his ankles. Tony plays the first Kid Dynamite record on his iPod at full volume to drown out the kid in the passenger seat screaming his name, yelling pull over, over and over.

Tony texts Karen, keeps the wheel steady with his knee and free hand.

He slows the car for hidden cops at every intersection, dark parking lot, and driveway. Flicks his spent smokes out the window backward to see the embers arc into nothing in his rearview mirror.

Mikey's gone. Tony turns the music down, says, "Tired of yelling, you little shit? Come on back and talk to me."

Nothing.

"Well? You scared or something? You ditching the only person who can actually see you?"

He grinds over a rumble strip.

He turns without signaling, curses as the tires screech on the street.

He nods off, wakes up, nods off, and wakes up again, and swerves the car around a deer crossing the road.

Most of the texts he writes ask Karen why she's not responding, tell her he's sorry for texting so late, tell her he needs something to do while he's driving so he doesn't wrap his car around a telephone pole.

He asks if she remembers the time they put the seats down and had sex in the school lot. If she remembers how pissed his parents were when they found her earring in their bed. If she kept all the Polaroids they took together in Avalon after his parents told them to behave themselves before leaving for dinner.

A car horn goes off. It's not his. He jerks the wheel, veers off the road.

He rights the car, doesn't stop, drives slow enough to listen for the flopping of a flat, or the rattling of a wrecked engine. Then he pays attention to the road the rest of the way. He parks his car, turns it off, turns the key to keep his favorite song on Kid Dynamite going.

He doesn't remember falling asleep. Just finishing a smoke, tossing it out the window, and leaning back against the headrest.

Then it's Mikey saying, "I think you should wake up."

"Leave me alone."

"I think we're in trouble."

"Seriously?"

"What's that guy's name again? Sam?"

Tony sits up straight, blinks the sunlight away, says, "Where?"

Mikey points out the passenger window.

Even with his hangover vision, Tony says, "Yep. That's him," and waves at Sam staring into the car.

8

Tony smokes the taste of booze away, replaces it with the flavor of a tobacco stained tongue. "Sorry," he says. "I was passing by, thought I'd pop in."

"You were sleeping in your car, man," Sam says.

"My contacts were bothering me."

Sam laughs, but not in a good way. It's a laugh, a sniff, a scratch to the back of the head. "When we talked last night I thought we'd agreed that—"

"We do," Tony ashes his cigarette, says, "One hundred percent. I was just on my way to work, and—"

"Pretty sure you were wearing that last night," Sam says, pointing up and down at Tony's clothes. "And don't ash on my lawn, man."

Mikey drops to the ground, tries to blow the ashes from the grass.

"Sorry," Tony says. "Jesus, what do you do that you start work this early?"

Sam says nothing, stares at Tony, adjusts his tie. He says, "You need to tell me what you're doing at my house."

"Fair enough. I was—"

"Are you trying to fuck my wife?"

"Right now?"

Mikey laughs.

But then it's Sam in Tony's face, jacking him up against the car. It's shaving cream and cologne. It's coffee and breakfast sausage breath. It's whispered fucks and shits. It's questions and crazy-eyes.

Tony almost says Sam does a great Lethal Weapon-era Mel Gibson. He almost asks if he kisses his wife with that mouth. But he says, "Sorry. Really, I'm not. I didn't mean anything by this."

Sam takes a step back, runs his hand through his hair, takes a breath. "Look, I'm trying not to go crazy here, man. But stay away from my house. Stay away from my wife."

"I will."

"It sucks about your brother, okay? But Karen's just a friend trying to help out a friend. She can't be your fucking crutch."

Tony thinks he said crush.

Karen's voice gets Sam to turn around. Gets Tony to wave. She walks across the lawn in a robe, her hair piled up and messy on the top of her head. Tony knows she's holding back when she speaks. She's angry, but keeps her voice quiet, calm. Scared, but keeping a quiver from her voice.

It's Karen's voice that brings back years of texting, promises to grab a drink. Calls about how odd life worked out, questions about what would have happened if one thing or another hadn't. Sex in the backseat of Tony's car. The smell between her legs. The taste of her tongue.

"Sam," Karen says, "It's okay, go to work."

Sam's face turns red. Maybe embarrassment. Maybe anger. He says, "But—"

Karen puts her hand flat on Sam's chest, says, "I can take care of this. Trust me." She kisses his cheek. "Trust me."

Sam purses his lips, nods. Then he stares at Tony, hard.

Karen walks Sam to his car, says things Tony can't hear.

Then Tony says, "Shit."

He opens the car door, picks his phone off the passenger seat. Dead.

Mikey says, "I could have told you that."

He plugs in his charger, connects the phone. No silver apple on the screen. "Shit."

He reaches across the center consol, turns the keys—still in the ignition. Nothing. Just a click. He says, "Fuck."

In the backseat Mikey says, "Swear Jar."

Tony says, "Is it bad that I'm not freaked out by you popping up wherever you want anymore?"

Mikey shrugs, says, "I don't know," and wipes grass from the front of his costume.

Through the windshield, Karen kisses Sam on the mouth, pulls away, pats his cheek light and sweet.

Sam gets in his car, starts it, pulls away.

The car getting smaller, Karen shivers, tightens her robe, waits until Sam turns the corner. Then she contorts her face in a way Tony's never seen.

He turns the keys again, and again, gets nothing but a series of clicks from an old abused car.

Tony's forehead on the steering wheel, Mikey holds a jar to him with Swear Jar scribbled on a piece of paper taped to the side. Tony reaches into the center console for change. He turns, sees Karen through the window, drops a handful of coins onto the empty passenger seat. He smiles.

Outside, Tony tries to speak first, but Karen says, "What are you, stupid?"

"Stupid, no. Crazy's up for debate though."

"What happened, Tony?"

"I was drunk. It was a mistake."

Karen wraps her arms around herself, her lips getting purple in the cold. "Was it? All your texts woke Sam up."

"Sorry."

"Having a hard time believing that."

Tony lights a cigarette. Despite the goosebumps and the chills, the frigid air hasn't registered in his brain until now. He turns to Karen, says, "Look, I don't want to cause any more problems, okay? I just need a jump."

"I think we have cables in the garage."

Neat, organized, the two-door garage is filled with a life Tony doesn't recognize. A pair of kayaks hanging from the ceiling, strapped up with a network of cables and pulleys. Skis, a snowboard on the wall, displayed but accessible. A Triumph motorcycle with two helmets hanging from the handlebars.

Tony says, "Sam likes motorcycles?"

"I like motorcycles."

Tony looks to the floor, says, "I didn't know that."

"I have a life," Karen says, pointing to Tony, herself, back and forth, "Outside of whatever this is."

"I really am sorry. I didn't mean to—"

Karen reaches, wraps her hand around the back of Tony's neck, kisses him with tongue.

He says her name, it comes out muffled with all the lips in play. Pulling away he says, "Karen, stop."

"Why?"

"What if Sam comes back?"

"I'm giving you a jump. Need cables to do that."

"Yeah, well. My breath's awful."

"I like the taste of cigarettes."

This time Tony doesn't stop her. He bites her bottom lip. When he unties her robe, reaches inside, she hisses, says, "Cold." He doesn't stop her groping him through his jeans.

When she kneels down in front of him, Tony turns his head, peaks around the door, down the driveway to the street. Mikey sits on the curb alone picking up small stones and tosses them to the manhole cover in the center of the road.

"Wait," Tony says. "Stop."

Karen doesn't stop, her hand inside his pants now.

"Seriously, stop."

Karen sits back on her calves, curses, looks up at Tony pissed, hurt. Tony zips up, looks down the driveway again. Mikey gets up from the curb smiling.

Tony says, "I'm sorry. I have a weird feeling about this. About Sam."

"You never gave a single fuck before."

"I mean, if you want to get technical..."

Karen stands up, points out the door, says, "Go home, Tony."

Mikey jumps, high-fives the air, yells cowabunga.

Tony walks down the driveway slow. Far enough away that Karen won't hear him, he tells Mikey to shut up.

Then he curses, calls for Karen, says, "Is it still cool that I get a jump?"

***

Tony didn't smoke on the drive home from the funeral parlor. His throat was wrecked, his mouth was dry, his saliva tasted the way the sludge in a cup stuffed with butts smells.

Karen texted, told him she could meet up if he wanted.

He told her his mood was shit, the day was shot, typed then deleted an LOL before hitting send. Then he texted, "I think I need to go home and sleep. Or stare."

The first naked picture of Karen buzzed Tony's phone after he got home. Angled for lighting in the bathroom mirror, she wasn't smiling, but there was a look. Like sympathy.

A text followed the photo, read, "You can stare at this if you want. Hope it makes you feel better."

Maura asked who was texting while they ate burritos on the couch.

Tony said, "Mom."

"I didn't know she texted. So up on technology."

"She's not. That's why I have to respond. Encouragement, I guess."

Maura laughed, reached for the television remote. She turned on a show she would ask Tony to turn to something else under different circumstances.

Everything Maura said while they ate was subtle. Unusual for her. Sometimes brash, others crass, she normally curses while she talks about work, is unafraid to let a burp go loud enough to startle Tony. But at that moment she asked if he wanted anything else. Another beer. More sriracha . If he wanted to watch *Game of Thrones* or something else she hates.

It was nice. And strange.

After dinner, Tony stood to clean the few dishes they'd used.

Like he would any other night. But Maura told him to relax. She made a pot of coffee, handed him a mug, black, went back to work cleaning up.

Tony sat on the couch adjusting himself after each photo Karen sent. After the first there was one with her free hand squeezing her left breast. One with her nipple pinched between her thumb and pointer finger. One with her hand between her legs.

He saved every one to his phone, emailed them to himself, deleted them from his camera roll, and texted nothing in return. Nothing he wrote didn't sound stupid. He Googled How to Password Protect Desktop Files for Windows instead.

Maura sat on the couch after she finished in the kitchen. She folded her legs under herself. The same way Nate sat down before killing himself. Or dying. Or whatever. "Can I do anything for you?" she said.

"No, I think I'm okay."

"Today was rough?"

"Yeah. I guess. Mom and Dad decided on cremation."

Tony kept his eyes on the television. Looking at the way she was sitting would do nothing but make him smoke a second pack of cigarettes.

The phone vibrated on the coffee table. Tony reached, picked it up, said he had to go to the bathroom.

On his way, Maura called his name. "There's nothing I can do? Are you sure? I'm here for you."

Tony smiled, said, "I'm okay. Promise."

He saved another photo while sitting on the closed toilet lid. Karen's ass. Her text said, "I promise to make you feel better if you meet up with me."

He sat for a minute, two.

Then he told her he'd let her know when he was leaving.

He flushed the toilet, ran his hands back and forth under the water in the sink, went back to Maura on the couch.

She hadn't changed the way she was sitting.

If Maura had died, her pink skin—a hue that Tony never believed could exist—would be gone. It would have turned a white-gray, almost translucent. Looking close enough, he'd almost see blue capillaries patterned like tree branches reaching over a road.

Nate's face staring down into his own lap.

Tony liked to think Maura's head would loll backward so she was staring at the sky. She always liked looking up.

Maura said, "What's the matter?"

"Hmm? Nothing."

"Let's watch a movie or something."

Tony sat, told her to pick the movie, that he didn't care what they watched. Through the first act of *10 Things I Hate About You* they sat feet apart. Then it was his arm around her shoulder, the smell of her hair, her breathing out of sync with his, their ribcages fighting each other with every breath.

Maura turned, kissed his neck.

He didn't respond.

After a bit, she turned again, kissed him, climbed into his lap. His phone buzzed in his pocket. Maura told him to let it go.

"It's my mom," Tony said.

Maura nodded, said, "Okay," and climbed off of him. She reached for a blanket draped over the couch's armrest, covered herself with it.

Tony stood, walked into the kitchen with his phone in his hand. He opened the fridge, opened a can of Pepsi, then responded to the text.

Out loud he said, "I have to go."

"Is everything okay?" Maura said.

"I guess? Mom just wants me to come over. Shouldn't be too long. An hour maybe. Maybe a little longer. I'm not sure."

"Want some company?"

"I'm going over there to be her company."

Maura said okay, turned off the movie, put on a DVRed episode of *Grimm*.

Tony stuffed his feet into pre-tied shoes, pulled on a sweatshirt, put on his jacket.

And Maura stared at the television. Her face didn't tell Tony she was pissed off, or even sad. It was just her, staring. If she would have said she was angry, Tony would've told her there was nothing he could do about it. If she'd been upset, Tony would've apologized, told her once everything blows over he'd make it up her. But with her saying nothing, Tony couldn't say anything.

He bent over, kissed her on the cheek, told her he'd be home soon. He promised.

She smiled, weak but sincere, said, "Okay."

"You okay?"

"Yeah. I hope everything's okay with your mom."

On his way out the door Maura said, "I love you."

Tony turned, smiled, said, "I love you, too."

Then he left.

He got in his car and drove to meet Karen.

***

Tony's excuses are shit. So he tells the truth. Most of it.

He tells Principal Adler he hadn't slept, that he can't come in, hangs up before he gets a response.

His mother doesn't say much after he tells her he spent the night at Chris'. The phone call ends faster than he can apologize.

On the phone with Maura he says, "I got too drunk. I pulled over after realizing I couldn't drive. I passed out."

Maura says, "I called your mom. When she said she didn't know where you were it was like...like she assumed you were dead."

Almost home, still shaking with a chill, he says, "I know."

"You let your mom think her second son was dead. I thought you were dead."

"I mean, I feel like death."

Mikey, in the passenger seat, shakes his head, says, "Your jokes are dumb."

Tony hisses, tells him to shut up.

Maura screams what.

"That was to myself," Tony says. "It was a bad joke."

"No shit, Tony."

"I'm almost home, okay? Let me go and we'll talk when I get there."

Maura says nothing, ends the call.

Tony drops the phone into his lap, curses. He cranks the heat, but it blows cold air on his feet. It'll be warm when he parks. Just long enough for the car to prove it's still alive, that Tony's abuse was just a one-off event. Or the last in a series of one-off events. He pets the dashboard, hopes it'll be enough.

Mikey pets the dashboard too, asks why they're doing it.

"You can't talk to me while I'm on the phone," Tony says.

"Why?"

"Because it's rude."

"Why?"

"It just is."

"What just is?"

"Rudeness, just—shut up."

"Can I ask you a question?"

"Will you shut up after I answer?"

"Okay. I'm you, and you're me. So why are you so mean to me all the time?"

Tony pulls onto his street, ignores the question while looking for a place to park.

"Huh?" Mikey says.

"I'm not mean to you."

"Yes you are. And being mean to me is like being mean to yourself, isn't it?"

Tony texts Maura, says he's home, that he'll be there in a minute.

Mikey says, "You must really hate yourself."

"I don't hate myself."

The spot Tony picks is one he's certain he can't fit into. He tries anyway. Arm stretched across the top of the passenger seat, neck turned as far as it will go. He backs up, rolls forward, backs up, bumps the car in front, and continues in this way until he turns the car off.

Walking to the apartment, Mikey follows says, "Can I ask you another question?"

"You haven't stopped asking questions all morning."

"Why do you like that lady you were about to do gross stuff with so much when you have someone at home you can do gross stuff with?"

"It's complicated."

"What is? The gross stuff?"

Tony stops, turns, points a finger into Mikey's face. "Try dealing with death. Not just death, but the death of someone you should have probably liked and didn't. See what happens. You'll do shit that doesn't make much sense, too."

Mikey stares at his sneakers.

"But you've never felt anything like that," Tony says.

Adjusting his mask, Mikey says, "Yuh huh."

Tony doesn't bother to look to see if a neighbor saw him flame out on nothing. Doesn't want to have to apologize for yelling at a rock-salted sidewalk. Doesn't want to have to run from a morning paper-wielding neighborhood watch captain. So he turns, walks the rest of the way to his door concerned with nothing but the icy patches he needs to avoid.

Once inside the apartment, Tony says hello, curls the O to sound like he's asking question. There's no noise. No TV. No shitty music.

Nothing.

Maura, sitting on the couch, stares into a blank television screen, doesn't turn to Tony when he says hi. She says, "I understand what you're going through. I said it before. I haven't dealt with death like this, but I get it. You need to do certain things to get over certain other things. But I'm done."

Tony sits down next to her, says, "Like, with us?"

"Sometimes you can be so fucking stupid."

"I know."

"That's not what I mean, Tony. I mean, it is. But, no, I'm not done with us. But I can't let you do things to yourself like this and kill myself over thinking there's something I could be doing to help. I can't help you anymore."

Tony reaches for her hand, but she pulls it away. She points a finger in his face, says, "You have to get figure your shit out. I'm not going to ask about work—which, by the way, I hope you called out—I'm not going to talk to you like you're a kid—"

Mikey opens the refrigerator, says, "No pizza?"

"—and I'm certainly not going to stick around much longer if you can't figure out some way to stop being such a goddamn idiot."

They sit, stare straight ahead. They stay that way until Maura grabs his face, a hand on each cheek. She says, "People die."

Tony says nothing.

"Your mom and dad are going to die. My parents are going to die. People die in hospitals and leave families without their kids, or siblings, or cousins, or grandparents. People die in car wrecks and plane crashes. People die, Tony."

Tony can't look her in the eye. He looks at the ceiling, the walls, Mikey sitting on the floor watching the show.

"Know what the most common thing about the people left living is? They're alive. And they have to wake up, eat, shit, shower, go to work, go to bed, and wake up and do the same thing again. Every day."

Tony sucks back everything running from his nose. He says, "I know that."

"Yeah? Because if you did, you wouldn't think you're the only one who's ever had something bad happen to you. You'd get drunk. Or cry. Or punch a wall. Whatever. But what you're doing? It's not grief. It's fucking martyrdom."

"I hate Nate, Maura."

"No shit."

"That's bad."

"No it's not. Hate him. Hate him for a year, I don't care. You'll stop. Eventually."

Maura wipes her wet hands on her pants. She wets her hands again after wiping her own eyes. She says, "Go clean yourself up. I called out of work and I've got a half season of *Finding Carter* on the DVR to watch before the finale on Monday."

Mikey follows Tony into the bathroom, stands behind him while Tony washes his face, brushes his teeth, runs water through his hair. Mikey says, "That was mean."

"Harsh," Tony whispers. "Not mean. Maura's not mean."

"It was true though?"

"I guess."

"You going to stay around here more?"

"Think so."

"Can we order pizza?"

"I'll ask...What do you care, you can't...never mind."

Maura already has an episode queued up before Tony gets back. He sits next to her, and they say nothing for a while. They watch another episode together. Then a third.

Tony says, "Can we order pizza for lunch?"

Maura hands him her phone, says the number's saved in her contacts.

When Tony's asked what he wants over the phone, he orders

a Hawaiian pizza even though he hates pineapple, even though Mikey bitches.

It's Maura's favorite.

The boy in the orange mask eats his lunch still dressed up.
His brother took his stuff off, left it on the garage floor before they came inside.
The boy stuffs his face, blows bubbles in his chocolate milk. He says, "Mom, do we have any pizza?"
His mother says, "You love ham and cheese."
"But I'm Michelangelo, and I want pizza, dude," he says, standing, fists on his hips, chin up. "Right, Raph?"
"That's not how Mikey stands," his brother says.
"What?"
"That's Superman, stupid."
Their mother tells the boy's brother to be nice, that if they can't get along they'll have to go to their rooms for the rest of the day.
The boy says, "Mom, I wasn't even doing anything."
"You're being too silly," she says.
The boy crosses his arms, stares across the table at his brother. His brother says nothing. The boy sticks out his tongue. His brother looks past him to their mother, then gives the boy the finger.
"Mom," the boy says, dragging the O out.
His brother mouths, "Rat."
"This is the second time, guys," their mother says. "Stop. It."
The boy crosses his arms over his chest, stares at his brother, out the window, at his half-eaten sandwich.
His brother pays him no mind. He eats his food, sits up straight, wipes his mouth after each bite, after each sip from his glass. He eats slow. Deliberate. After he finishes, in his polite voice, he says, "Mom. Can I ride my bike down to Jason's house?"
The boy says, "Hey," loud and long.
Their mother says, "What about your brother?"
The boy's brother says, "I'll play with him when I get back. He can play my game in Super Mario World."

"But we're playing Ninja Turtles," the boy says.

His brother mouths, "Shut up."

"He just told me to shut up."

At the kitchen sink, their mother says, "I didn't hear anything." Then she says, "Look. Guys. Don't make me tell your father you're being nasty to each other." She says the boy's name, tells him to play video games. She says his brother's name, tells him to back before dinner, and to thank Jason's mother for having him over.

The boy in orange says, "This sucks."

His mother says, "Swear Jar, young man."

He points to his brother, says, "He says sucks all the time. He said shit twice today."

Their mother points, yells, tells the boy to go to his room and wait for his father to get home.

The boy's bottom lip juts out. His eyes burn. He says, "Will you play with me when you come home?"

His brother turns to their mother.

Their mother says, "Not until your father and I decide your punishment."

The boy says, "But you love the Turtles."

His brother says, "Not as much as you do."

The boy runs upstairs. He slams his door. Flings himself onto his bed. He cries loud enough so his mother and brother will hear him downstairs.

But neither of them come for him.

So he stops. Then he goes to the window, waits.

Once his brother rolls down the driveway on his bike, the boy knocks on the window. Not that he could have been heard, but his brother doesn't look back anyway.

***

The boy sneaks into his brother's room. He deletes his brother's game in Super Mario World. He deletes his brother's game in Super Metroid. He hides the Super Mario Land 2 Gameboy cartridge by dropping it behind the headboard.

Then he licks all the buttons on every controller and handheld gaming device in the room.

He has to cover his mouth to stop himself from laughing while he rubs his bare feet on his brother's pillow. But the hand doesn't work. He's laughing so hard he's crying while he drags every writing utensil in the room between his toes.

Back in his own room he cracks up. Face in a pillow, he laughs like he did the first time he and his brother ambushed their father, jumped on his back, called him Shredder.

Then he sits up. A pit in his stomach makes him think of the last time he had a stomach bug. He couldn't make it to the toilet, filled the sink with half-digested Kentucky Fried Chicken.

But it passes.

Then it's the digital clock next to his bed. Then it's trying to subtract dinner time from now. Then it's sneaking back into his brother's room. Then it's dying over and over again as he can't afford to take his time through each level of Super Mario World.

Then it's his mother busting into the room and asking him what exactly he thinks he's doing, young man.

There's screaming, yelling, crying. A hand around a wrist. Resistance. Nikes squeaking as they're dragged along the hardwood floor in the hallway. Threats about what the boy's father will do after he finds out how damn bad the boy's being.

"Swear Jar," the boy says, screaming, jumping on his bed. He says the S-word, the A-word, the F-word. Shrieking at random, he watches his words make his mother blink and take a step back with each one.

She slams his door behind her when she leaves.

Dressed in his shell, his mask, he pulls his nunchucks from his father's belt. He swings them both around, around over his head. He jumps off the bed with a cowabunga, back on to it with a radical. Up and down on the bed, the Turtles theme song sung so loud his voice cracks as he screams the lyrics.

His mother doesn't come back.

He gets bored.

Then he feels sick again. And this time it doesn't go away.

9

Tony's hand was up Karen's plaid skirt. He forgot to keep his lips moving while kissing her. He was listening for her breathing to change. His was face locked onto hers, his fingers were fumbling around trying to figure out what's what. When he worked his tongue around her mouth, his hand would stop moving. When he thought he was getting something going for her, his lips would freeze in an open-mouthed breath exchange.

She said, "Ow."

He said, "Sorry."

It was the way they were sitting that wasn't working. Or that they were in the basement with nothing but a couch. And a television. And concrete floors.

Tony asked if Karen wanted to go to his room. He looked away so he wouldn't see her reaction.

She asked about his parents.

He untangled his fingers from her underwear, stood up, kept

his back to her so she wouldn't see his swollen school khakis. Phone in hand, holding it with his ring finger, pinky, and thumb, he flipped it open, said, "Mom'll be home in forty. Ish."

Karen's face was red, but she smiled, stood.

They held hands up the stairs, Tony's arm bent behind him, his hand sweating in hers.

In the kitchen, Tony told Karen to wait a second. He checked the side door, looked through the curtains at the driveway. He opened the front door, walked to the edge of the flowerbed, looked up and down the street turning his head left, right, left, right. Then he led Karen up to the second floor and told her to wait in his room. He went to his parents' room, then their bathroom. Once he felt he'd checked everywhere parents could possibly be hiding, once he figured he'd at least hear a car door close or the honk of a keyfob lock, he adjusted his pants and went to his room.

Karen was naked, standing next to his bed. She was smiling, shivering a bit.

Tony said, "Should I?"

Karen said, "I don't want to be the only one."

He kicked his shoes off, dropped his pants, almost fell over trying to get his feet from his pant legs. Unbuttoning his shirt, he tried to ignore the sight of his underwear pushed out to a point. But when Karen laughed at his bobbing dick after he ripped down his boxers, Tony wanted to pull them back up.

"I'm not laughing at it," Karen said.

"Yes you are."

"I'm just nervous. And it bounced."

"But it's okay?"

"More than that. I like it." Karen covered her face with her hands, said, "Holy shit. That's not what I meant. I mean, it is, but—holy shit."

Tony stood across from Karen for a minute, two, until she spread her fingers so Tony could see her eyes. She lowered her hands, took a breath. Then she got on the bed, propped herself up with an elbow and told him to lay down with her.

So he did.

Her body was warm, warmer than he thought another naked body would be. They were all knees and hands brushing against parts that made them suck down gulps of air. Tony moved from her mouth to her nipples, then between her legs. The taste was strange, but he liked it.

Karen asked if he had a condom.

He said, "Really?"

She said, "Yeah."

Tony got up, crossed the room. He didn't bend over, but got down on his knees. He kept his spine straight, rifled through the bottom drawer of his dresser. Karen's laugh at his dancing boner was already enough embarrassment. If he'd given her the opportunity to laugh while he was bent at the hip—all spread ass-cheeks and dangling balls—he would've had to get dressed and leave the house. Then run down the road, hope to get hit by a car.

He opened an old tin Ninja Turtles lunch box, lifted an old orange mask with a green rubber nose under the eyeholes, and found the pencil case where he'd stashed a pack of cigarettes and some condoms.

Ripping open the condom wrapper, trying to figure out which end was right, he said, "You're sure about this?"

Karen, under the covers, said, "I've been sure for a while." Then she laughed, slapped a palm to her forehead, said, "I'm sorry. That was the corniest thing I've ever said. I don't know what else to say, you know? Like, the movies make it all seem so romantic. When I say it it sounds so stupid."

Tony, condom on—as best as he could figure—said, "It's not stupid when you say it."

Karen laughed again, said, "Now you sound stupid."

Tony pulled away the covers. Karen held out her arms, spread her legs.

Tony was trying to guide himself in while Karen winced and breathed in through her nose, out through her mouth. Tony wanted to ask questions. But he was concentrating, trying not finish before he started.

Then there was the sound of the front door being shoved open, sticking in the doorjamb.

Tony and Karen cursed.

The comforter was flung about by kicking legs and grasping arms. The bed was bouncing, smashing the headboard into the wall.

Footsteps on the stairs.

Tony and Karen jumped back into their clothes.

The floorboards creaking on the other side of the bedroom door.

Nate flung the door open, walked in, said, "Happy birth—what's going on in here?"

Tony, standing, hands on his hips, breathing heavy, said, "Nothing."

Karen, sitting on the bed, red-faced, said, "Hi, Nate."

Nate looked back and forth at them, his glassy eyes lolling along the curved edges of his eyelids. "Holy fucking shit."

Tony said, "What?"

Nate clapped, said, "Sorry I ruined Tony's present, Karen."

"Nate, that is so fucking gross," Karen said.

Tony turned to Karen, stuck out his hand.

She didn't take it, didn't look up at him. She flattened the front of her skirt, tucked a rope of black hair behind her ear. Her palms went to her face a second, but then she stood, fast. Her hands folded in front of her, then dropped to her sides, then behind her back, at her sides again.

Nate laughed, said, "Come on, relax. It's a beautiful, natural act, you guys." He handed Tony a wrapped, flat square, said happy birthday. Called him bro.

"Who talks like that," Tony said, tossing the gift onto his bed.

Karen pushed the both of them aside, walked out of the room into the hall, said, "Tony, can you take me home?"

Nate said, "You're not going to stay for the birthday boy's dinner?"

From the doorway Karen said, "Please, Tony?"

Tony shoved Nate in the chest, hard. His brother's back crashed into the wall.

"I can still fuck you up," Nate said. "You know that, right?"

Tony said, "I hate you, fucker."

There was a smell to Nate. And while Tony was running through the list of smells of the things he'd smoked himself, or watched other people smoke, he stared at the red whites of Nate's eyes. The mussed hair, the greasy skin. He listened to the wheeze from his brother's nose, a faint and sporadic sniffing. He said, "Might want to shower before Mom and Dad get home. You stink."

"Yeah? Well. You smell like pussy."

Karen said Tony's name again.

Then there was the honk of a car being locked.

Downstairs, Karen said nothing. Her face was red, her hair was a mess, she was biting her nails. Tony took her hand, led her to the front door. He said he was sorry, said he felt like such an idiot. He told her he was going to take care of Nate. Whatever that meant. But he meant it.

The front door was shoved open before Tony could get his hand around the doorknob.

His mother jumped, said, "Oh, jeez. You scared me. Hi, Karen. You're staying for dinner, right?"

Karen looked at the floor, said, "I'm actually not feeling all that well."

"I'm going to take her home," Tony said. "I'll be back in time."

Tony's mother rubbed Karen's arm, said "That's such a shame. We'll miss you, sweetie. Come for dinner Sunday if you're feeling better, okay?"

Karen kept her eyes down, nodded.

Tony's mother kissed Tony on the cheek, wished him a happy birthday.

On the way out the door, he turned, said, "Mom. Nate's upstairs."

His mother turned around, changed her face from shocked to aloof, said, "That's great, right?"

"Yeah," Tony said. "He smells like drugs."

Before his mother could say anything, before she had the opportunity to tell him to stop giving his brother such a hard time all the time, Tony shut the door with the first try and walked Karen to the car.

***

Tony's mother made his favorite. Pan-fried crisps of bacon with olive oil and crushed garlic folded into a couple pounds of linguini. Boneless pork chops, and buttered, boiled cauliflower and broccoli. He was served first. He was the first to get seconds. But after a happy birthday handshake from his father, after everyone was eating, it was all Nate.

"How's school going?" Tony's father said.

"Still like the dorms?" Tony's mother said.

How were the professors, how were the classes, how was the food? Were the girls pretty, were they nice, did they like him the same way the high school girls had? How was crew, how were the coaches, were the practices much different?

Every question Tony's parents asked Nate were answered with Good, or Great, or Of course. He didn't elaborate. He wasn't asked to.

His phone under the table, Tony wrote text messages with the numbered keypad without looking, apologizing to Karen over and over.

His mother said, "No phones at the table, Anthony."

"It's under the table."

His father said, "Doesn't matter."

Then Tony turned to his brother, said, "How did you get here, Nate?"

"Train," Nate said.

"Who picked you up at the train station, Nate?"

"Jason."

"I heard Jason sells drugs now."

Tony's father said Tony's name, then said, "Enough."

"Do you do drugs, Nate?" Tony said.

"What did Karen get you for your birthday, Tony?"

"What'd you get me, Nate?"

"She got you tickets to the Cherry Poppin' Daddies concert, right?"

Tony's mother said, "Guys. That's it. Come on." Then, "Oh, what a great gift. I love that song." She sang a line from "Zoot Suit Riot" and laughed. "Maybe your father and I will get tickets and go with you two."

Nate said, "Not sure that's a show Tony and Karen would want you guys to see."

"Wasn't fall break a month ago or so?" Tony said.

Tony's father said both of their names, alternating his stare between them. He said enough, then, "I don't know what's going on between the two of you, but it ends now. Anthony, your brother wouldn't do drugs. What his friends do is their own business. But, Nathan, Jason's been a problem for a while, you know that. Mind yourself. And, Anthony? I'm not stupid. That cherry popping thing was a sex joke. Are you having sex?"

"What?" Tony said. "Are you serious?"

"Do I look like I'm joking?"

Tony breathed in through his nose, deep. He said, "I can honestly say that I am not having, nor have I ever had sex."

"How about cake and presents?" Tony's mother said.

Nate's face was still stupid from whatever he had done before showing up at the house. But his mouth was curved at the corner, the tiny smirk he used to paste on when they were kids. When Tony could stand him.

Tony ignored his brother, ignored the feeling Nate's dilated pupils gave him as they watched what he would do or say next.

Then Nate's phone rang. He excused himself, got up, stumbled a little, and went into another room.

The sound from Tony then was more laugh than scoff. But still like mucus coughed up during a cold.

His father said, "Problem?"

"No cell phones at the table," Tony said.

"Well—"

Tony finished the sentence he'd heard before, "Technically he's not at the table."

Tony's mother placed the cake in the center of the table. She went back and forth between the kitchen and living room bringing one gift back with each trip. She stacked them all on the kitchen counter, making a show of it. And once Nate returned to the table, she lit the candles on the cake and counted to three.

Nate and Tony's parents sang happy birthday while Tony stared at the flames melting the top of the one, the seven.

Tony smiled after he was served cake. He thanked his parents for the Vans, the t-shirts, the CDs that his mother picked off the list he wrote up for her.

After all the wrapping paper was thrown away, the coffee was served, Nate was staring at his plate until he jumped up, said, "You didn't open mine."

He bumbled his way through the house, up the stairs. Tony

said nothing when he remembered where he'd left Nate's gift. In his room.

When he was back downstairs, Nate stumbled into the kitchen a bit, handed over his gift, said happy birthday. Called Tony bro again.

Tony tore away the wrapping paper. He didn't smile. He held up the Clash record, tattered with white veins of bent cardboard stretching across Joe Strummer. Like the red capillaries in his brother's eyes. The lack of care Nate had taken for the record that Tony had given him four, maybe five years ago made the air stall in his throat. He pulled the record itself from the sleeve. Black and slick, and warped in the center, distorting the light from the fixtures on the kitchen ceiling.

Tony's mother said, "Wow," sounding disappointed underneath her phony tone.

"Yeah," Tony said. "Wow."

Tony's father cleared his throat, said, "Anything to say to your brother, Anthony?"

"Yeah," Tony said. He turned to Nate, said, "This is great, Nate. Thanks for the regift."

"Jesus Christ," Tony's father said. "You can't treat people like this."

Nate sat, said nothing.

"Like what?" Tony said. "I bought this for Nate a couple years ago."

Nate said, "You were always a bigger Clash fan than I was. Figured you'd want it back."

"I do. Thanks." Tony stood up, said, "Really. The bend in the middle will make it sound even better." Then he thanked his mother for dinner, thanked both his parents for the gifts.

He left the kitchen ignoring questions of what he was doing. He put his coat on, grabbed the car keys. He passed back through the kitchen, said, "Karen's family has a gift for me."

He looked at Nate sitting, staring. He wondered if his brother was embarrassed about the gift, or too fucked to give a shit. Either one could've kept him from saying anything. On Tony's way out the door he told himself it didn't matter. Not anymore, so fuck it.

***

Tony and Karen went to a diner. They ate ice cream, shared a piece of pie. Any other night they would be laughing, or foot-wrestling under the table, holding hands on top of it. But they weren't doing those things.

Tony was answering Karen's questions.

No, Nate didn't tell their parents. No, even if they did find out, they wouldn't think she was a slut—they like Tony better when she's around. Yes, they missed her at dinner. No, Tony didn't think she was a whore.

He didn't tell her about the sex questions. He didn't tell her that Nate has one more thing to hold over his head.

She said, "I just wanted to give you something special."

Tony said she did, and he loved it, and he loved her. And once the check was brought to the table, Karen was less nervous. She was asking about the gifts he'd gotten, if he liked them.

Tony told her about the record.

Karen said, "Is he being serious? What's wrong with him?"

"I don't care."

"Come on."

"I'm serious. I don't. At this point he could die—his train could derail, a bus could hit him, a drug dealer could stab him—it wouldn't do anything to me. I'd be fine."

"Tony st—"

"I hate him. Fuck him."

They sat for minute, silent. Tony didn't look at Karen, but could feel her looking at him.

Then she picked up the check.

Tony said he'd get it.

Karen said, "Stop. Tip if you want."

Tony left a couple bucks on the table, followed Karen to the counter.

She paid. They left, held hands through the parking lot.

Tony turned on Dead Kennedy's *Give Me Convenience or Give Me Death* when they got in the car. They talked about school through "Police Truck," and "Too Drunk to Fuck." Karen pulled a wrapped CD-shaped gift from her coat pocket, and Tony opened it through "California Über Alles." It was the only All record he could never get his hands on. He smiled, thanked her, then kissed her cheek. He thanked her again, then kissed her on the mouth.

Then they were making out. And Tony was groping.

Karen said, "Move the car."

Tony did what he was told, drove to the far end of the lot behind the diner near the woods where the lampposts' lights couldn't reach.

They climbed between the front seats one at a time. They fought against the seatbacks, empty soda cans, a book of CDs, the almost vertical back to the backseat bench while they pulled up and unzipped pieces of clothing to expose parts they'd only seen in full light once.

Karen said, "Still want your present?"

"I don't have a condom."

"Girls at school say pulling out is just as good."

"Are you sure?"

"Just—" Karen struggled getting her leg out of her jeans. The fast, jerky motions rocked the car. "Yes I'm sure."

Karen was half sitting, half lying in the corner. The back of her head was propped up by the window, her hair was crushed into the glass. Half of a breast was showing, one bare leg was bent and pressed up against the seatback.

Then Tony remembered how it was earlier in his bedroom.

Karen said, "I love you."

Tony said he did too.

He had to plant a knee one the floor to get into a position where he was in line with her. He asked her about her underwear.

"Just push it to the side," Karen said.

When he did, she hissed, said, "Your hands are cold."

"Sorry."

It took a few tries to get inside Karen. Tony kept stopping, starting every time she clenched her teeth, or shut her eyes too tight, or looked down at her crotch. He apologized once, twice, three times. Karen told him not to worry about it after every sorry, told him it was supposed to be like this.

But it wasn't.

There was no sun coming through the window. Nothing soft

and clean to lie on. Nothing sweet to say. Their foreheads weren't pressed together, they weren't kissing, they never fell into a rhythm.

Instead, the windows fogged up. The car rocked, squeaked on shitty shocks. Neither of them made much noise at all aside from breathing. It was just dark. And cold. And a little smelly.

Tony lasted longer than he thought he would—which still wasn't very long. He made it through "Short Songs," and "Straight A's." But then he pulled out and sprayed down Karen's jeans during "Kinky Sex Makes the World Go 'Round."

"Shit," he said. "Sorry."

"It's okay. I'm sorry."

"What? Why?"

"I got blood on you."

It was too dark to see. Tony thought the stickiness was just part of the whole thing. But she was right.

All they had to clean themselves up with were napkins from an old McDonald's bag. They picked red bits of paper off themselves the best they could. They dressed, scraped at drying stains with their finger nails.

On the drive home, they were silent.

Tony had to keep adjusting himself, his underwear sticking to him.

He caught Karen doing the same, shifting in her seat.

Every so often Karen said she loved Tony. He turned to her every time, smiled, said he loved her too. But most of the ride was All filling the silence.

Tony walked Karen to her door when they got to her house. They kissed, hugged, said goodnight, said they loved each other. Then Tony left.

He changed as soon as he got home.

***

Tony smelled Karen on his pillow. Her shampoo, her perfume, whatever. Something was embedded in the fibers. He tried to sleep on his stomach, but he couldn't. She was there, or he wanted her to be. He rolled around, tried to sleep on his back. But she was in his nostrils.

There were images. He closed his eyes, saw her mouth open and close as she made quiet little gasps with a bit of melody to them. A shadowy scene of pushing himself into her. He concentrated on sleeping, saw her breast bouncing even though it was pinched in half by the underwire of her bra.

It would've been different if they'd done it right. The heat of their bodies pressed into each other. He would have gone slower. He would have kissed her more. He would have had his nose in her hair and smelled what she'd left on his pillow in real life.

He wouldn't have come on her fucking jeans.

Tony threw off his covers, put on pants, Vans, a hoodie. Then he grabbed the pack of cigarettes from the Ninja Turtles lunch box.

He walked a pattern in hall. The one Nate had taught him, the one his father had taught Nate. He tip-toed over the floorboards, worked from muscle memory. The floors didn't make a sound under his feet.

The stairs were more difficult, but even those he had down. He'd learned never to open the front door while trying to be discreet. He went out the side door, crept around the house, sat down on the stoop out front.

He lit up, coughed a bit, then let his head spin. His favorite part of having to space out his cigarette breaks.

Halfway through his smoke a car pulled up front. A minute passed, two. And then Nate was ambling down the driveway toward the street from the side of the house.

Tony watched Nate get in the car. He lit another cigarette, waited. Then another. His head wasn't weightless after his third smoke. But his mouth was dry, his saliva tasted like hot shit.

But he waited through the drymouth and the chill in the air that started taking over. He waited until Nate opened the car door down at the street, stepped outside with a plume of smoke pouring out behind him. Nate leaned down, shook hands with Jason, pocketed whatever was left in his hand.

Instead of the driveway, Nate cut up the lawn right toward Tony.

"Hi Nate," Tony said loud enough for his voice to bounce down the street.

Nate hissed, put a finger to his lips. He stumbled through the flowerbed, turned, sat next to Tony, and said, "Can I bum one?" Tony took a cigarette from his pack, handed it to Nate, took one for himself too. Nate pulled a lighter from his pocket, tried to light Tony's smoke for him. He missed the tip with the flame until Tony said, "I got it."

Tony had to light Nate's cigarette for him.

"Sorry, man," Nate said, his eyes half open. "About the record."

"Don't make it a thing. Seriously."

"I am being serious." Nate sniffed hard, sucked back something wet.

"Jesus."

"Allergies."

"Got it."

They sat quiet for a bit, smoking.

Then Nate started in on a string of apologies. About not calling. About not visiting. About the gift again. He said he was under a ton a pressure. From his father. From himself. From Columbia.

He said, "I don't get high a lot. Just when it feels like the weight of everything turns into a tightness in my neck and chest."

And, "I hyper-focus. I get all into something, crash, and after a little binge I move on to the next thing."

And, "I was way too high when I got home. I didn't mean to be an asshole."

Tony stubbed out his cigarette on the bottom of his shoe, collected the butts and stuffed them into his half empty pack.

Nate said, "I'm really not a bad guy."

Tony said, "Okay," stood up.

"You don't hate me, do you?"

Tony'd heard that before. More than once. From more than one source. He almost laughed at how it almost worked. Again. He said,

"Nope," turned, walked away.

Behind him Nate said, "Hey, I know it's your birthday and all. But do you think you could lend me a couple bucks for the train back tomorrow?"

Tony didn't turn, scream. Didn't run at his brother, try to hit him. He said, "Sell whatever Jason gave you. Or ask Mom and Dad. They'll help you out."

He smiled at the side door, opened it without making a sound. He used his brother's, his father's pattern to get up the stairs, down the hall to his room.

Walking away from Nate made up for everything. It was all he had to do. If it worked on Nate, it'd work on his father, anyone. He'd won. And it was good.

But then he was in his bedroom. Where he'd stood when he saw Karen waiting for him. He took off his clothes, this time alone, in the dark. He went to the dresser, dug through to the lunch box, tucked his near empty pack of cigarettes, the smoked butts next to the condoms he'd saved for nothing.

He got in bed, took a breath.

All he could smell was smoke.

Part 2

10

Seasonal Depression.

That's what Tony's started calling it.

Never mind Nate's death. Death's everywhere. People deal with worse, and as such, so could he.

He did the research, picked his symptoms off lists, wrote down the ways his actions correlated with each one. And then, he self-diagnosed. Seasonal Depression Exacerbated by the Untimely Death of a Family Member.

It wasn't Nate's death that caused him to get put on a second and less lenient level of probation at work. It was the constant gray tint to the sky. It wasn't his parents hollowing themselves out that drove him to cheat on Maura. It was not having seen a living blade of grass in months. It wasn't his meltdown at the funeral that caused the excessive drinking. It was that he'd seen every breath he's blown out of himself since he ignored the last one out of Nate.

But the sun's out. The jackets are stowed for the spring. At night all there's need for is a sweatshirt.

Now he comes right home after work, writes lesson plans, prints handouts, rereads the sections of the books he's assigned. Most of the time he has to cheat, find the materials on the internet, but everybody does that.

Now when Maura gets home, he'll be halfway through making dinner. Most of the time it's bad. He's not a cook. But he's trying. So far he's only had to order takeout a half dozen times.

He contacted Karen once. To tell her he was blocking her number. He said he wasn't mad at her or anything, that it was just something he needed to do. But he waited too long to block her. Her response got through, said something like she'd heard bullshit like that before, that it wasn't a surprise.

Mikey had to tell Tony not to respond, that he didn't need to be the last one to say something.

So he didn't.

Chris asks Tony how he's doing every morning. Every time they hang out. Every time they get a beer or see a show or spin vinyl records in Tony and Maura's apartment. And Tony tells him the truth, which is he's great. That shit's really looking up. He's thinking of picking the guitar up again, maybe getting a band together. Something heavy, but melodic. Like a Drop C Weezer.

He's opening himself up to things. To Maura's music. To advice from other teachers. To everything.

He's making moves. Big ones.

Now, he's reading comics. He bought the first volume in a series of hardcover reprints of the original Teenage Mutant Ninja Turtles comics. The Eastman and Laird stuff.

He and Mikey, sitting on the living room floor, read through the pages, make comments as they go.

Tony says, "This stuff is dark."

"I don't like it," Mikey says. "It's not even funny."

"Sure it is. Just in a different way. It's satire. You know that word?"

"Duh. Still, doesn't mean I like it. It's like they're making fun of me."

"Actually, the stuff I grew up on? The stuff I'm basing you on? That was all kind of a slap in the face to this stuff."

Mikey shoves Tony—which does nothing—and gets up, says, "Let's play or something." Then kicks, punches, does a somersault into the refrigerator, which, again, does nothing.

"Can't," Tony says. "Soon as Maura comes home we're leaving. Big night."

Then the door opens.

Tony gets up, goes to Maura, hugs her, kisses her, grabs her ass.

Maura says she hates doing it before seeing his parents. But Tony presses the issue, and they do it on the couch anyway. It's quick. But loud, and fun. And after, they laugh at each other while they tuck themselves back into their clothes.

Maura goes to the refrigerator, but Tony tells her he just thinks they should get going. "Forget the dip. Let's go," he says.

"I thought you wanted me to make it. You said your mom really likes it."

"I did. And she does. But, I don't know. It's nice out, and I want to drive around a bit with you. Listen to music or something."

Maura cocks an eyebrow, crosses her arms. She says, "You okay?"

"Yeah, why?"

"You're acting kind of—"

"Like my old self?"

Mikey taps the handle of one of his plastic nunchucks on the kitchen counter, holds it to his ear, says, "This doesn't sound right to me."

Ignoring Mikey, Tony asks Maura why she's still looking at him funny. But Mikey's walking toward him, shaking his nunchuck, then listening to it. Again. Again, until he reaches Tony and holds it up to him. He says, "Try it. It sounds funny."

Tony says, "I'm good." He smiles.

Then both Maura and Mikey say okay at the same time, stretching out the tail end of the word.

They leave after that without saying much. Just Tony singing songs to himself, and watching Maura watch him.

Tony doesn't smoke in the car. Even if he wanted to, he'd have to pull over on Redcoat Drive. Crawl down the bank just beyond the sidewalk to the creek that runs under the road. That's where he threw his last pack. His last-last pack.

He drove past Karen's for the last time, the last-last time, tossed the smokes.

It was the only thing left on Mikey's list of things Tony needed to take care of. Everything else was easy. The smokes were hard. It proved addiction comes down to choice. Tony chose to stop seeing Karen. He chose to fix his career. Chose to be better to Maura. Chose to get better.

That's where Nate fucked up.

Nate chose wrong. With everything. He drank too much, smoked too much, partied too much. Then killed himself.

Tony says, "He killed himself."

Maura says, "What?"

"Hmm?'

"What, hmm? You were whispering."

"I was? Sorry." Tony turns on the radio, hits Seek until he hears a song that he's pretty sure he's heard Maura singing once in the shower.

But Maura changes the station, says she hates that song. Then she says, "Hey, so, where are we?"

"Hmm?"

"Is Redcoat a shortcut to your parents?"

Karen's house passes behind Maura through the passenger side window. Tony looks past her.

Mikey tries a backflip in Karen's front yard, and back flops onto the grass.

Tony, quick, looks back at the road, shakes the wheel a bit, and speeds up. "Um," he says. "Not a short cut as much as it is the scenic route."

"I mean, these are nice houses," Maura says. "Maybe we can move into this neighborhood? Like, if we get married or something?"

Tony says yeah. Then, "Fuck."

"What?"

"Forgot something."

He turns right, makes another right, and heads back to their apartment to pick up the ring he left in his Ninja Turtles lunchbox.

***

Maura had to walk Tony down the aisle.

He was taking nips from a flask in the bathroom longer than he'd intended, and she'd caught him.

She was sweet, though. Called him Hun, Babe. But that was before she smelled the booze. Then she said, "Jesus, Tony," and gave him a piece of gum.

They walked past a series of easels displaying Styrofoam poster-board collages of photos of Nate. The first poster was all Polaroids. Nathan's 1st Birthday scrawled in Tony's mother's handwriting. Christmas 1984. Nathan AKA Superman.

Tony was in a few. Screaming, crying, ruining the picture. Nate posing. Nate smiling. Nate playing.

Maura said, "You guys were cute together."

Tony didn't say anything, tried keeping his eyes on the floor in front of him. But the displays lined most of the trip to the altar. There were Nate's first few years in school. His first year in peewee football. Little league. Then it was Nate at banquets. Holding trophies. Smiling.

There was one with Nate and Tony dressed as Ninja Turtles. Hollow plastic pumpkins filled to the brim with candy in their hands. They were smiling-smiling, not posing for a photo. Happy.

He tried concentrating on something else again. The sound of his chewing.

He wasn't sure if chewing gum was allowed in church. He'd gotten demerits for it in middle school, but whether that was a school rule that bled into the First Friday masses or a church rule that bled all over Catholic schools, he didn't know. But he chewed louder when the priest popped into his line of sight, asked him if it was okay to open to the public yet.

Lips smacking, chewing with his mouth open he said, "What'd my parents say?"

"I didn't want to disturb them."

His mother was on the kneeler set up in front of the urn display. His father was staring at the blown-up glam shot of Nate in his high school cap and gown next to the flower arrangements.

Tony's voice bounced off the walls, jumped down the aisle, calling for his father.

The altar servers setting up for the service jumped, startled.

The deacon made a face.

"Is it cool if we let people in?" Tony said.

His father nodded. Looked back at the picture.

"It's cool," Tony said.

The priest's face almost made Tony laugh. But he smiled instead. And when Maura tugged him down the aisle once the priest walked away he said, "Did you see his face?"

Maura shushed him, kissed his cheek.

"You're mad at me?"

She patted his arm, said, "Of course not."

Tony wondered what he would have to do before she'd tell him she was pissed off at him during his brother's memorial service.

Maura put Tony in his place. Right next to Nate's urn. She straightened his tie, told him she loved him, then she went to her seat next to her sister. And Tony watched her watching him.

People showed up fast. Dozens of them. People Tony never met, people Tony never wanted to meet. And people he wished he hadn't.

It was an hour of shaking hands, thanking people for their condolences, saying things like, "Yeah, he was something, wasn't he."

And, "He'll be missed."

And, "We appreciate you being here."

Then he tried crying after seeing how much more of a shit people gave about his brother than he did. They were crying. Really crying. Soap opera crying. All snot and gasps and watery sounds from sucking back whatever poured out of their faces.

He gave up on it fast.

Then Karen showed up. With Sam.

She hugged Tony's mother. Kissed his father on the cheek, hugged him too. Then she looked at Tony and lost it. She hugged him hard. Her breath on his neck. Her lips on his cheek.

She pulled away, moved to the kneeler after touching his face.

Then Sam put his hand out, said, "Really sorry for your loss, man."

Tony hadn't expected him to be so nice. The things he imagined about the guy painted him as a sycophantic suck-up with money, or a big dick-swinging southern oil tycoon, or, sometimes, just a better version of Tony.

The priest whispered into Tony's ear after the stream of people died down a bit. He said they'd better get started, that they'd need time to set up for the five-fifteen mass.

Maura held Tony's hand through the service.

It was nice. But he was sure he didn't need her to do that.

He stared at people. Turned his head to the left, right, watched how people were reacting to the whole thing. All varying degrees of sadness.

Then there was Jason. Strung out. Sobbing.

Tony didn't see him come in.

He was glad he didn't. He would've fucked Jason up before he'd made it to the urn.

He would have to wait until after the ceremony.

"See you in a bit," Tony said.

Maura said, "What?"

"Hmm? Nothing."

Tony waited, figured the parking lot would be the best place.

***

In the living room, standing next to a pile of packed army-green duffel bags, Tony has to pretend to be excited when his father tells him about his new hunting coat. But it's easier now. He's happy his father's happy thinking he's interested. "This thing can withstand below-zero temperatures," his father says, "while still keeping my core-temp up."

Then Tony's father hands him a boot, says, "Feel it. Feel that?"

Tony doesn't roll his eyes, doesn't curse. He takes the boot, says, "What I am feeling for?"

"The weight, Bozo," his father says. "Lighter than a leather dress shoe."

Tony laughs. A real one. "I wouldn't go that far."

"Says so on the box."

He shows Tony the new gun, the laser dot scope. Shows him the bullets, says they're guaranteed to take an elk to the ground from a hundred yards with one shot.

"Isn't that what bullets are supposed to do, Dad?" Tony says.

He doesn't like the way that sounded. Not anymore.

But his father slaps his shoulder, smiles, says, "Do you know how big an elk is?"

They stand for a minute, two, silent. They look at each other, the floor, the television.

Then Tony's father turns his head toward the kitchen, says he's hungry.

Maura peeks into the room, says, "You're going to wait longer if you keep that up. Your wife's making a wonderful dinner and you're acting like—like Tony."

Tony laughs, isn't faking.

His father slaps him on the back, says, "Come here. Look at this."

Tony follows his father upstairs, nods every time he's told he can't tell anyone about this.

In the spare room, Tony's father hands him a backpack, tells him to open the front pocket.

Tony makes a joke about this being some sort of joke, reaches in, pulls out a glass vial full of dust.

"Nathan always wanted to hunt Wyoming," his father says. "So, I'm going to take him with me. At least a little bit of him."

"This," Tony says. "This is really nice, Dad."

"Think so? It's not weird, is it?"

"It's not weird."

Tony holds up the vial, looks close at the big jagged grains of his brother.

Mikey, peeking his head around Tony's father, says, "Weird."

The vial back in the bag, the bag back in his father's hands, Tony smiles.

They stand there for a while, shifting on their feet, looking at each other, looking away, smiling, repeating the whole process once, twice, three times.

"Anthony."

"Yeah?"

"I get so wrapped up in things. Always wanted, or, I don't know, expected more. Could never enjoy what was right in—"

"Dad. It's...You don't need to say any—"

Tony's father wraps himself around Tony, holds him tight with a tinge of Brute. Tony knows what he hears next, but still says,

"What?"

"I love you," his father says.

"Thanks, Dad. I—"

"I'm going to miss you."

"Oh, come on, man. You're going to have a great time."

Tony's father says, "Yeah," pulls away, wipes his eyes. He holds onto the back of Tony's neck, squeezes it a little.

And neither of them look into each other's eyes until Tony's mother calls up the stairs, says dinner's ready.

Tony's father says, "Let's eat," and leaves the room.

Tony doesn't follow far behind.

Dinner's nice. Maura talks about her job. About thinking about going back to school.

Tony answers questions about work. He doesn't hide anything. Talks about everything that's happened. Except Karen.

Tony's father talks about the trip, tells everyone he's going to miss them. He says he's planning on bringing back the biggest elk anyone's ever seen, and won't be back until he gets it.

Tony's mother asks everyone if they like everything. She says she thinks they should all get together like this more often. Says, "Not just on holidays. Or to see your father off on hunting trips. But for little things. Every once in a while."

It's silent for a bit. And Tony can't remember the last time he'd shown up for dinner, or lunch, or anything before Nate had come back from rehab the last time. Easter. No, last Christmas. Maybe.

"Almost forgot," Tony's mother says, too loud to sound like she didn't just figure out a way to kill the quiet. "Karen called earlier asking for you, Anthony. She said she couldn't get through to you on your phone. She thought you might've changed your number or something, but I told her it's still the same. Anyway, note's on the fridge. Her number's on it in case you lost it."

Mikey does a jump-kick out of the kitchen. He holds up a piece of paper. In shaky, horrible handwriting that Tony remembers getting D's for in grade school, it reads, "Tony, don't call me. I hate you. I work for Krang now. Okay bye."

Tony thanks his mother, says he'll take a look later.

Maura cocks an eyebrow.

Tony shrugs his shoulders, makes a face, shakes his head no.

Aside from the Karen note, the rest of the dinner continues like no other dinner with Tony's parents ever has. The odd looks are stifled. The normally off-handed comments are followed up by a chuckle, or a, "Just joking." There's almost an argument about who's taking Tony's father to the airport, but Tony concedes, tells his mother to call him if she has trouble getting back onto 95. There are no curse words. None. Everything is like it never was.

Only took someone dying for Tony to have the nicest meal with his parents since before he could speak. Before he could remember.

Only took fucking Karen until the guilt got too heavy.

Only took Seasonal Depression Exacerbated by the Untimely Death of a Family Member for him to start changing himself into what he needs to be.

Mikey picks from Maura's plate, Tony says, "Stop."

The table goes quiet. Everyone stops eating. Mikey says, "Oooh," like Tony's class did after he cursed at Mrs. Gosnell in second grade. Like they did after he drew a dick on the chalkboard in seventh grade. Like they did when he glued thumbtacks to Sister Diane's chair in eighth.

Tony stands.

Mikey says, "Dude. Don't. Don't do it, dude."

"I have something to say," Tony says.

No one moves. Everyone stares.

"I've been a shit," Tony says. "Not just since Nate. But for pretty much my entire life. And I'm sorry. Really. But I think you've all seen a change in me recently. It's because I figured some stuff out. About me. About what I need to do with myself."

Then everyone's making sounds, but not really saying anything. Tony's on a knee. Ringbox in hand. He asks Maura to marry him. Maura's arms are wrapped around Tony's neck. She's crying, saying yes over and over.

Mikey says gross, loud and long.

Tony's mother is running through the house opening any drawer she finds, saying she needs her camera.

Tony's father stands, shakes Tony's hand, hugs Maura. And after some photos are taken he says, "I hate to cut this short. But I've got to get to the airport."

They clear the table fast once they realize what time it is. Tony helps pack his father's bags in the car. He tells his mother he'll shut the house down and leave a light on before heading home.

Tony's father kisses Maura before getting into the car, says, "Always wanted a daughter. Going to die a happy man."

Tony's mother says she'll call when she gets home. She hugs Maura like Tony's seen her hug Karen.

And once the car backs down the driveway Maura takes Tony's hand, says, "Home?"

Tony nods, says he's ready when she is.

She kisses him, says, "Ready."

He hands his car keys over, tells her to start it up if she can that he'll be right out. Then he heads into the house. Turns off all the lights.

He pulls Karen's note off the fridge, crumples it up, throws it in the trash.

He's halfway to the front door before he turns around.

Mikey stands in the kitchen doorframe, spins a nunchuck.

Tony takes a breath.

Then he walks through Mikey, picks Karen's note out of the trash and pockets it.

11

A dozen phone calls and a Relationship Status update changes things. More Likes than Tony's ever gotten in his life. Enough texts to consider a number change. Smiles from people at work who have only given thin-lipped smirks since the funeral.

Nights in front of the television have shifted to nights in front of the computer screen. Venues. DJs. Photographers. Florists.

Tentative guest lists.

Bridal party candidates.

Theme colors.

And an imaginary friend forcing himself into discussions.

Mikey prefers green table cloths with orange, purple, red, and blue flowers in the center pieces. He thinks pizza is best for the menu, that people could have choices. Meat, fish, and veggie. Pepperoni, anchovy, cheese. He volunteers to be the best man.

Tony gives his opinions but doesn't push too hard for them. Maura gives reasons for her choices while Tony just likes things.

But she bounces her ideas off of him first to be polite. And Tony's good about everything.

When Maura suggests a limo, Mikey says Turtle Van, and Tony says, "I always wanted to ride in a limo."

When Maura says church ceremony, Mikey says Splinter would do it, and Tony says, "I think my parents would appreciate the church thing."

And when Maura volunteers to make all the phone calls, Mikey tells Tony to throw away Karen's note, and Tony says, "I'll make some calls, too. If you want."

Tony doesn't call Karen back, though. Just reads over the words written in his mother's handwriting asking him to call her as soon as he can. Once, twice, three times sometimes.

He almost—a couple of times—opens the password protected file that's embedded in a file, embedded in file, file after file, to look at the nudes Karen sent.

One morning he unblocks her number. He clicks deep into the file series until he stops himself, turns off the computer screen, and blocks her again.

A day or two later he unblocks her, types out a text, but then goes to the computer and reaches the pop-up asking for a password.

And now the only numbers running through his head are those that would unlock the file. The same numbers that get him into everything.

Her number's been unblocked for hours.

Now, with Maura next to him, Chris and Meg on the other side of the table, he pretends to listen. He smiles, laughs. But his attention's on his phone. In his pocket.

Maura says, "You guys both know how important you are to us, right?"

Chris smiles. Meg tears up.

"We want you to be our Best People."

Meg gets up, trots around the table, kisses Tony's cheek and calls him brother. Chris stands and hugs Maura still in her seat. Then they switch.

Maura and Meg hug and cry, and spew sentiment all over the restaurant.

Tony and Chris shake hands, hug. And Chris pulls Tony toward the bar. He doesn't ask if Tony wants a shot or not, but orders two anyway. Tony doesn't say no.

Chris asks the bartender if there's any champagne, asks that it's put on his tab. He hands a shot to Tony, holds his own up, says, "To Best People."

They cheers, down the shots.

Then Tony says, "Did you know about me and Karen before I...alluded to it?"

"I may be dumb. But I'm not stupid."

"Yeah, and Green Day still sucks."

"Come on, man. Insomniac's really good."

Maura and Meg sit on the same side of the table. They're smiling, dabbing their eyes with tissues. Acting like Tony and Chris were never there.

"You mad at me?" Tony says.

"Only because I know what you are. Or what you can be, at least. I don't know what I'd be if what happened to you happened to me. I sort of err on the side of ignorance when it comes to death."

"Thanks, that—"

"That doesn't mean I think it was cool. You using me as an excuse for doing some really heinous shit behind the back of someone who wants to put up with someone like you. Besides me, I mean."

"I thought the whole 'I know what you are' thing meant I'm not that bad of a guy underneath everything."

"You aren't. Doesn't mean you're not a pain in the ass."

Maura whistles from the table, waves Tony and Chris back.

Then Meg yells, tells them not to come back without booze.

Chris says, "You have anything else to say before I start thinking everything's cool for good?"

"Sorry?"

"Anything more current?"

"Karen called my mom, told her she needs me to call her back."

They jump when a cork is popped behind the bar.

Chris says, "Needs or Wants you to call her back?"

"Is there a difference?"

Tony picks up the champagne flutes.

Chris takes the bottle from the bartender, says, "You can't call her back. You know that, right?"

"Yeah. I know that."

"So what's the problem?"

"Nothing. You asked. That's all."

Tony heads back to the table first.

Mikey hops up on the table, pulls his nunchucks. He swings them both in tight circles, glares at Chris.

"Stop it," Tony says.

Maura says, "Stop what?"

"Talking about ways to fix Megatron here up with my best man."

Mikey turns, says, "Ew. She's a girl."

Chris's face goes red. Then he asks if anyone wants champagne.

The champagne gets poured. Chris gets a shade redder every time Maura tells him how great her sister is. Meg fidgets in her seat every time Chris looks to Tony for a hand. And Tony makes faces at Mikey while the kid threatens to hit Chris over the head with a nunchuck telling Tony to tell Chris he can be the Ring Bear.

They all drink, finish off the bottle.

Then Meg says, "Would your brother have been your best man if he hadn't died?"

Maura says, "Meg."

Meg says, "Sorry."

And Tony says, "No. Probably not."

Chris stands, says, "Should I get more beers, maybe?"

Meg says, "How come?"

Chris says, "I'll get beers," and walks off.

"Because," Tony says, "Nate and I—"

Maura puts her hand on Tony's across the table, says, "You don't have to."

"No. I'm good." Tony kisses Maura's cheek, says, "Nate and I weren't like you and Maura. You two, you're friends. You're damn near twins. You talk, laugh, argue, apologize, get over it. It's all really good. Me and Nate? He would fuck around with me, blame shit on me, turn my parents against me, then tell me I was too sensitive. Or too gullible. Or too stupid to realize when I was being fucked with. Then he'd make it a joke."

Chris plunks two pitchers of beer on the table.

Meg says, "Were you ever friends?"

"Sure. When we were kids."

"Do you ever miss him?"

"I miss how he was when we were little."

Chris pours beer in the silence. Meg pulls her phone, answers a text, or pretends to. Maura runs her thumb back and forth across Tony's hand. And Tony thinks he maybe feels his phone vibrate in his pocket.

Then the phone pulses again.

His chest tightens the way it used to.

He pulls his phone from his pocket. A text from Karen saying he needs to call her back, that she has something she needs to talk to him about.

Needs. Twice.

Maura says, "Who's that?"

"Mom," Tony says. "Dad got one. A moose."

"That's great. Wait, wasn't he hunting elk?"

"You know how hunting is, seasons overlap."

"Do you know how hunting is?"

Before Tony says something, says anything, Meg yelps, smiles, says, "Watch your feet, mister."

Chris chugs his beer. Fills it again.

Meg says, "Someone'll take advantage of you if you keep that up."

Mikey makes a face, says, "I don't know what that means, but that sounds gross."

Tony types his response to Karen, asks her when and where she wants to meet up. Just to talk.

Then he deletes the "just to talk" part, taps send.

Maura says Meg and Chris would make a really nice couple. She takes Tony's hand again, says, "It's only fair. He set you and me up. It'll be good if we return the favor, don't you think?"

Meg says, "I think so. I was going to say hello before, but I didn't think it would've been appropriate to introduce myself at a memorial service."

There's the silence again. With Chris bright red, staring at Tony. With Maura rolling her eyes at Meg's comment. And Tony's phone vibrating in his pocket.

***

Jason broke eye-contact first.

Tony whispered bitch, and motherfucker, and cocksucker. No one heard. His teeth were clenched. People were getting up from their pews making all kinds of noise.

Nate's urn was in Tony's hands. He was the first in line, walking down the aisle. He'd passed Chris. Maura. Meg. Some staff from the high school. Then dozens of people he'd never met. Dozens of people with connections to the ashes he was carrying.

But he'd stared Jason in the eye the entire walk.

Jason was in the back. Crying. Fucking bawling.

Tony kept staring. Even turned his head to see if Jason would look up, glance, do anything as Tony passed. But Jason did nothing. And Tony kept cursing to himself.

Outside, Tony's father took Nate's urn, said, "Coming?" before getting in the car.

Tony lit a cigarette, said he'd need a minute.

"Those things'll kill you, Anthony."

Laughing wasn't the response Tony was planning on. He was going to blow smoke in his father's face. Or say fuck you. But instead the smoke caught in the back of his throat, and he laughed. Not hard. Not loud. Just enough for his father to turn away, get in the car, and slam the door so hard the car shook.

The crowd filed out of the church. Slow and somber. Like every movie with a funeral scene Tony had ever watched. Everyone in black, wanting to say anything to cut the tension but saying nothing because it was a goddamn memorial and there's something called decorum.

Maura and Meg stood by the steps. Karen and Sam walked toward their car. And Chris walked over to Tony, slow.

Chris said, "Wish I hadn't quit."

"These things'll kill you."

"That's a joke, right? Can I laugh?"

And they did. Just a bit. Not long.

"Maura wants to set you up with her sister," Tony says.

"Do it. I won't be mad."

"Meg's a little..."

"What?"

"Remember Famke Janssen in GoldenEye?"

"Jesus."

Tony lit another cigarette.

His father stuck his head out from the car window, called his name.

"Dad, let me mourn in my own way, goddammit."

His father disappeared. The window closed.

Tony and Chris were quiet for a moment. Tony didn't regret what he said to his father. More the way he said it. His tone. He regretted embarrassing Chris even more than that.

But then Jason skulked out of the church, used the handicap ramp instead of the stairs.

Tony called his name.

Again, but louder.

Then he screamed it.

He was moving through a crowd of people still lingering at the bottom of the church steps. He heard his name. From Chris. From Maura. From his father. But he ignored all of them.

He said, "Jason, hold up."

And, "I just want to talk."

Then, "Fucking listen to me."

Jason turned around at the bottom of the ramp. He put his hands up, smiled, said, "Hey, Tony. I'm s—sorry for your loss. Awful."

Tony had thought of some things to say in the church. Some witty things. Some angry things. Things laden with words that would make his mother pass out if she heard him saying them in front of a church.

He went with, "Fuck you," and socked Jason in his cheek.

Jason crumpled, collapsed to the ground.

Tony cursed while waving his stinging hand in the air.

The crowd produced an almost collective gasp.

On the ground, Jason crab-walked away from Tony. Half apologizing, half asking what the fuck.

Tony grabbed Jason by the lapels, hoisted him off the concrete.

He threw one, two, three punches into his gut. Then dropped the limp body to the ground again.

Tony told Chris to get the fuck off of him when he was being held back from getting to Jason again. He said he has to do this. Not for Nate. For himself.

Jason said, "I'm calling the cops."

"You're a drug dealer, asshole," Tony said. "Call the cops and I'll turn your ass in."

"I'm clean now, Tony."

"Since when? Since you saw Nate's obituary? Not shooting up for a week doesn't count as clean."

Chris got in front of Tony, told him to calm down. Said stop. And come on, man. And relax.

Then Tony's father was there saying similar things. But instead of calling him Anthony, he was calling him son. "It's okay, son," his father said. "This is useless, son."

Tony's face was tucked between his father's shoulder and neck. All Brute and stubble. His breath warm and rank reflecting off his father's skin back into his face.

His father said, "It's alright, everyone. Head on over to the house. We've got some food and drinks. Hope to see you all there."

Tony heard some of the crowd asking if they could do anything to help, if anyone needed a ride. Or a Kleenex.

Tony laughed at the Kleenex question. But stopped when he realized yeah, he needed a few. He turned, looked for Jason. But he was gone. Like he got up and ran away.

Chris and Tony's father lead Tony to the car. They said, "It's okay," and, "You're okay now," and, "Try not to think about it."

They helped Tony into the car. He buckled himself up. Ignored Nate's urn buckled into the seat next to him. And his mother staring through the windshield at nothing.

Then he tried to remember where Jason used to live, wondered if he still lived there.

***

Tony wakes up with Maura's alarm.

He tells her he needs to get to school earlier than usual.

149

Department meeting.

They shower together. Laugh while washing each other. He pulls her close, squeezes her ass, reaches between her legs. But she says, "Just because you need to be in early doesn't mean you get to make me late."

They dry off. He watches her. Her skin pink, pinker from the hot water. Her curves more pronounced than Karen's. Everything's bigger on Maura. Wider hips. Plumper butt. Bigger breasts. Larger nipples. Puffier stomach.

Then he pays attention to drying himself. Maura and Karen see something in him. But he can't see it.

He's made his choice. He's happy with the decision.

That's what he'll say. What he has to say.

They brush their teeth side by side. Tony bumps Maura with his hip. She bumps him back. They spit, kiss, smile, get back to brushing.

He clips nose hairs while she puts on her makeup.

She straightens her hair while he spreads gel in his.

They dress in the bedroom, talk about dinner.

On the way out the door, Maura says, "Shit."

Tony stops, asks her if everything's okay.

"Yeah. I'm just going to be late. I have to print out a report for my presentation."

"Do it at work."

"I won't have time."

They kiss goodbye. Maura steps back inside, closes the door behind her.

Tony walks to his car, Mikey trailing behind him asking questions about what he's going to say. How he's going to say it.

The ride to the diner is short. But Mikey grills Tony, says, "What if she wants you to be her boyfriend?"

"She's married."

"What if she doesn't care?"

"She does."

"What if she's mean?"

"She won't be. I'll say what I have to say and leave. Simple."

"You're funny."

"Why? Because everything I think should be easy turns out to be anything but? Because I'll be lying when I tell her that I never want to see her again?"

"Now you're getting it."

Tony tells Mikey to shut up, to stay in the car, or in his head. Anywhere where he won't be inclined to make an appearance.

Mikey blows a raspberry, makes faces at Tony through the windshield after the car's shut tight.

Tony points, mouths that he's serious.

Inside, Karen sits at the table they used to sit at in high school. Where they'd spend hours pissing off waitresses by ordering coffee and nothing else, sitting there wasting time.

Tony sits, says hello. He's more formal than he expected he'd be.

Karen doesn't say anything. She stares at him across the table.

The waitress asks for their order. Tony gets a coffee. Karen, orange juice.

"Anything to eat? We've got some breakfast specials."

Tony says, "Coffee's fine, thanks."

Karen asks for orange juice, says thank you without looking.

They stare at each other long enough for Tony to have to look away. Check his phone for the time. Decide he can wait another ten minutes before having to leave. No longer than that. He's made the decision. Ten minutes. That's it.

A minute passes. Two. And Tony opens his mouth to speak, but Karen cuts him off. "Why have you been ignoring me?"

"I told you why."

"That's not good enough."

"Because I was ruining my life with you." Tony made a face, made a note to take the edge out of his voice.

"What about my life, Tony?"

The waitress sets their drinks on the table, slaps down their check, walks off.

"I was a wreck," Tony says. "I didn't mean for any of this to happen. You were there like you always have been, and it felt good. Good. Like it did before...everything. But we both have really good things going on and we've been ignoring them."

Karen sips her orange juice, says, "How can you act like you're up on some moral high-ground now?"

"I'm not."

"You are, Tony. Yes, you are."

"I'm not. Really. I just think I've figured some stuff out." Tony tries not to let his next thought leak out of his mouth. Tries hard. But he says, "Maybe you need to take a look at how good you have it."

"Maybe I just have a soft spot for pricks."

Tony almost says, "Literally?" but stops himself. Too much. Honesty is different than nastiness. That's growth.

He says, "You don't have to be nasty about it. This whole thing was a mistake. I'm trying to do better. Make up for, I don't know, most of my life."

"I've never felt that you had to make up for anything."

"Are you kidding me?"

"No. I'm not. You could be an asshole, yeah, but everybody's got something. You always wanted to be the opposite of Nate and your dad. Most people do whatever they have to so they can stuff themselves into whatever mold they think they're supposed to fit into. But you didn't. You refused. And that made you care harder for the people who never questioned every move you ever made. Now, the person you spent most of your life trying to hate is gone. And you're cramming yourself into his place. You're a liar. You're lying to me. Maura. Your parents. Chris. And yourself."

"No, I was a liar," Tony says, his voice getting low, gravelly. "I'm not doing that anymore. And don't pretend you haven't been lying yourself. At least I'm trying to make up for all of it. I'm trying to do the right thing here."

"And what is the right thing exactly, Tony? To you? Stay with someone you've been cheating on because you don't have the balls to hurt her? Stop using your best friend as an excuse? Stop being horrible to your parents because you think they loved Nate just a little bit more than you?"

"Fuck you." He couldn't help himself with that one.

Karen finishes her juice. She shakes her head. Smirks.

"Something funny?"

"All you had to do was ask."

"Ask what?"

"Let's make a list. If you really wanted what you've got now, you could've asked Maura to go to your parents' house when you found Nate. You could've asked me not to get in your car. You could have asked me to climb out of your lap. Or, and this is the best one, okay? Listening? You could've asked me to pick you."

Tony stares into his coffee.

"I love you. Okay? I do. I can't help it. I would've blown up my life if you'd asked me to. But all I am—actually, was—was some kind of replacement-Nate. Which really brings up some interesting questions about you. And now that you've had some kind of revelation, you don't need me. Or even fucking want me. Maybe I'm wrong about all this, maybe you never did. But you're thirty years old, unfriending people on Facebook. Unfollowing Instagram accounts. Blocking phone numbers."

"What was I supposed to do? I can't help myself whenever I—"

"Tony, for God's sake. You're a real-live grown-up. Grown-ups make choices. You know that, right?"

"What do you want from me, Karen? Seriously."

"Look at you, all pouty and huffy. This isn't going as you'd expected? I'm not going to sit here and tell you'll do great now that you've figured some shit out for yourself. And I'm not going to hold your hand, rub your back, and tell you everything'll be okay when things get bad again. You've tossed me aside too many times for that."

Tony's hands shake, then ball into fists. He slams one down on the table, makes coffee slosh over the top of his mug. "Who are you to say this shit to me? All you're proving is you're just as awful as I am. You made your choice. You got fucking married."

"Only after I got sick of you dumping my ass whenever you thought you didn't need me anymore."

Tony lays napkins down on the spilled coffee. He pulls his wallet from his pocket, puts a five on top of the bill. Then he checks his phone.

He'll be late for work.

He stands, says, "So, what? Are you here to make me feel as bad as you do about all this? You're going to tell me you wasted your life on me? Some shit like that?"

Karen doesn't look at him, stares at his empty seat, says, "Nope. I'm going to tell you I'm pregnant."

Tony flops back into his chair. He pulls at his hair, breaks through the gel he styled it with. His guts tense, relax, tense again, slosh around. His lungs seize up.

Karen says, "But you shouldn't worry. Everything will be okay."

Tony coughs out, "What?"

"Yeah, don't you see? Weren't you listening to anything I said? I said all of that to tell you it doesn't matter if the baby's yours or Sam's. It'll have to be Sam's regardless. And I hope it is. He can play adult really well. I could use a little of that considering you've never tried being one."

Tony says nothing.

"Honestly?" Karen says. "I don't even want to know whose it is. Because I've had a pretty revelatory couple months, myself, and finally knowing what you really are makes me afraid of what I might find out."

Tony sucks back a breath, can feel his face heating up, sweat beading on his forehead, cheeks.

Karen picks up the check, says, "I'm just as horrible as you. If someone like you can learn to live with it, so can I." She pushes Tony's five back across the table to him, says, "I'll take care of this."

She leaves Tony where he sits, pays the bill. She turns away from the counter, says, "So this is what it's like? Feels pretty good."

Karen pushes through the front door, walks out.

Tony watches her cross the parking lot through the plate glass windows. Watches her get into her car, drive away.

Tony's alone, air getting stuck in the back of his throat.

He puts his head to the table, tries to will his lungs into a rhythm.

Mikey rubs his back. Says, "It's okay. It's okay."

12

Tony doesn't go to work.

He leaves the diner, shuts off his phone, and sits in his car smoking for the first hour.

Then he drives in circles. Circles that widen from a circuit around the diner parking lot to 309, 309 to Bethlehem Pike, Sumneytown Pike to North Wales Road, Hancock Road to 202, then back onto 309 again.

Mikey doesn't talk much, but says things like, "We were here already," and, "Where are we going?" and "I think you should go to work."

Tony turns up his music. No Use for a Name's *Hard Rock Bottom*. All speed and melody that does nothing but make him feel old. The lead singer's dead now. Tony bought the album in high school.

But high school ended more than a decade ago.

Before the person who knows him best fell out of his brain.

Before a baby that maybe, could be, possibly his.

Mikey turns off the radio.

"Wait. You can't—" Tony's hand falls from the tuning knob back onto his leg. Which he then uses to open his pack of cigarettes. "Did I?"

"Did you what?"

"I think it's getting worse."

"What's getting worse?"

"You. I think you're getting worse."

"Remember I'm you and you're—"

"Yeah, you're me. I'm you. Whatever. Obviously, you want to say something. Just say it, okay? I'm, like, seconds from crashing this goddamn car into anything hard enough to kill us."

In the passenger seat, Mikey doesn't adjust his costume. Or play with his nunchucks. He sits, staring through the windshield. "Things were getting better."

"Yeah, well."

"You need to go to work."

"Little late for that now."

"Then call. Tell them something bad happened."

"What? Should I say, hey, it's Tony? I won't be in today. Turns out my high school girlfriend—the person I was cheating on my girlfriend, shit, fiancée with—is pregnant and it might be mine, but I'll never know because she doesn't want to know on account of what a shitty person I am?"

"Yeah, tell the truth."

Tony reaches, turns the radio on. Light static through the speakers. The auxiliary cable limp, pulled from his iPod. He doesn't remember doing that. He pretends not to care. Pretends, fuck it, Mikey's gaining purchase through Tony's memory lapses, so what? "The truth," he says. "The truth that I'm a shitty person?"

Mikey says nothing, keeps staring.

"Do you think I'm a shitty person?"

"Do you think you're a sh—bad person?"

"If I do, you do."

"Do you?"

Tony doesn't answer the question. But he turns on his phone, listens to the voicemails.

First, it's Chris. He talks like somebody died, saying dude a lot, asking what could have happened to make Tony do this. "Get here, man. Make something up. Lie. Just get here."

Then it's Principal Adler. No hello. He calls Tony Mr. D'Angelo, not Anthony. He says, "Get to my office as soon as you come in. First thing you do, understand? If you come in."

And then one from Maura. There's nothing. A second of silence.

Tony's missed the first five periods of the school day.

He pulls into the school lot by the end of sixth.

It takes him half a cigarette to get out of the car, walk toward the building. He pinches off the cherry, stuffs the butt in his pocket. He pulls the front door open in time to hear the bell ring, bounce off the tile floors, the painted cinderblock walls.

Students pour into the hall. Tony ducks into the front office before having to answer any questions from teenagers.

In the office, Sandy stays on her phone. Ginny doesn't look up, types at her computer. Sue fills her coffee mug.

Tony says, "Morning."

Nothing.

The clock reads one.

Tony steps into Adler's office, knocks on the open door anyway, smiles, says, "Principal Adler?"

"Close it."

Tony does, shuts Mikey out.

Adler, tearing open pieces of mail with a letter opener, uses his hand, gestures for Tony to sit.

And Tony does.

"Do you know how you got this job, Mr. D'Angelo?" Adler says.

"Yes, sir."

"We post our openings because we have to, not because we're actually searching."

"I understand."

Adler cuts open another envelope, points the letter opener at Tony. "Do you?"

"Yes."

"You were a favor to your father, a friend I grew up with. Nothing else. It wasn't your merits—which are few. It was loyalty. A concept, which now I know, you do not understand." Every word Adler says, every syllable, is accentuated by the letter opener as it dips, points, waves in his hand.

"Sir, I—"

Adler raises a hand. "Mr. D'Angelo. You are indefinitely suspended without pay, pending a hearing with our board. But I assure you, the board hearing is only a formality." He sets the letter opener on his desk. "See that?"

"See what?"

"That's what it looks like when someone does their job properly. If I had your attitude I would have just fired you in a voicemail."

"If I could just—"

"Your father should be ashamed of you. Nathan would be, too, if he were still alive."

Tony's standing.

"Sit down, Mr. D'Angelo."

Whether it's Adler's words, or his stare, or the portrait of the school's founder looking down on him, Tony doesn't stop himself. He snatches the letter opener off Adler's desk. Watches Adler roll his chair into the bookcase behind him. Laughs at the founder as he carves into the portrait.

A diagonal tear from left to right cutting through the face. A cut right to left turning the single scratch into an X. And one, two, three more slashes that leave the painting as an asterisk wearing a fine brown suit.

Tony drops the letter opener to the floor.

Adler tells him to get out.

And Tony gets out. Opens the office door, lets it swing hard enough to slam into the wall.

Mikey stands, says, "What happened?"

Tony doesn't bother to whisper, he says, "You already know. Let's get the fuck out of here."

Sandy, Ginny, and Sue all roll their chairs away from him.

Tony turns to leave, says, "Fucking cowabunga."

***

Tony's father stood in front of Nate's urn on the mantel reading from a sheet of paper.

He didn't mention God. Or heaven. Or better places.

He went off script for the finale. He looked up, eyes blotchy and red, said, "He was a good boy. And my best friend. I wish I could've been a better friend to him."

People cried holding plastic plates of cheese and cups of wine. Tony's father invited anyone who wanted to speak to do so. The room was silent for a bit. Someone cleared their throat. Someone sniffled.

Then people started talking. Telling stories about Nate. Most of which were from when he was a teenager.

All good stories. Funny stories. Stories where Nate did something for someone and won't soon be forgotten for whatever he did when.

Tony stood drinking wine, holding Maura's hand. She squeezed his every so often. He squeezed back, turned, smiled. Or made a face.

Then Karen started to speak. Loud, clear, strong, very Karen. Tony could feel Maura squeeze his hand again.

He didn't squeeze back.

Karen said, "I met Nate, I don't know, fifteen years ago, I guess. Right?"

Tony nodded. As if she were asking him.

"He was a lot of things to a lot of people. He was a wild card around here. Whenever he was involved, something was going to happen. You knew it. In your gut, you know? I think that'll be what people miss most. The endless possibilities."

She told a story. One where she and Tony were watching *The Ring* on the couch in the living room and Nate scared them by stepping out of the shadows of the dark room.

Tony didn't remember the movie. Or the link between Nate's joke and the girl pulling herself from a television set. It had been the smell of Karen's hair. The taste of her lip gloss. And then Nate scaring the shit out of them. Karen cursing. Tony shoving. Nate laughing.

Karen told another story. One where Nate had saved her and Tony by swerving out of the way of a deer standing in the road. She said, "He was always there for us."

Tony remembered the shrooms. That they hadn't worked. Made him gassy and sick to his stomach. Made Karen gropey and foul-mouthed. And made Nate trip balls and drive in zig-zags, dodging the deer he'd been hallucinating.

There were more stories. Short ones. All told to cut the tension. For a smile. Or a laugh.

But Tony knew the true versions. All of which were horrible experiences he and Karen had together with his brother. And they kept getting worse.

Then she said, "I think he was a tether. To a younger time. To really wonderful memories. To old friends. Just by being himself." She was staring at Tony.

Everyone was staring at Tony. Most of them had seen what had happened with Jason.

Tony wondered if they were waiting for him to lose it. Get violent, punch something. Break down, fall to his knees. Weep. Scream. Whatever.

But he did none of that.

He said, "We can all still be friends." He pointed to Nate's urn on the mantel. "He's right there."

Some people awed. Some smiled. Some got teary-eyed and covered their mouths with their hands.

Maura kissed Tony's cheek.

And then, as if Karen's words were too good to follow up, the mingling began.

Tony and Maura talked to Chris for a bit. Then to Adler, some other faculty from school—all faint smiles and sentiment. Then his parents.

His mother hugged Maura. His father did the same, thanked her for coming.

They talked a while. About the weather. About Maura's job. Nothing serious.

Karen and Sam cut in. Tony's parents moved on.

Maura said, "Your speech was so nice."

Karen said, "I'm just glad I'm here. Tony's family was always really sweet to me, so it was really the least I could do."

"I wish I could've got to spend more time with Nate. I barely knew him."

Tony asked Sam what he does for a living.

Sam told him.

Then they watched, listened while Karen answered all of

Maura's questions about what Tony was like in high school.

Karen said, "He was nice. But crotchety. And stubborn. He thought he was this little badass, too, with his multicolored, spiked hair, and his skipping school and everything. But he was a softy. Sweet. Kind. Even when he didn't want to be."

They laughed. Sam did too.

Maura said, "Did he ever get all huffy, stomp out of the room and make noise, like play music, or move stuff around just to make noise loud enough so you'd hear it and come calm him down?"

"He still does that?"

Tony said he was going to smoke. Karen said she and Sam had to get going. Maura found her sister.

Outside on the stoop, Tony smoked, shivered. He flinched and ashed on himself when his father sat next down to him.

"Didn't hear you come out," Tony said.

"Cold out here."

"Yeah."

"I hope you got that out of your system."

Tony stubbed out his cigarette. Lit another. Didn't look at his father, said, "Got what out of my system?"

"That outburst at the church. With Jason."

"You know, I got the distinct feeling you were proud of me for a second back there."

"Didn't say I wasn't."

"What's this about then?"

"This is just some advice from a father to his son, understand?"

"Not sure I like where this is going."

"Don't go with your gut too much, Anthony. Most things take a bit more forethought. If you're all impulse and no brains you can get yourself into trouble. We've all done it from time to time. You. Me."

"Nate."

"Stop it."

Tony dragged from his smoke, hard. Coughed a little.

"Point is, you're a man. Use your head. Don't get yourself into trouble. You have responsibilities. Take your time, but move on."

"Anything else?"

Tony's father stood, patted Tony's shoulder, said, "That's it."

He got through another cigarette before Maura came outside and said, "Finished out here yet, smokey?"

Tony stood, said he was.

"Karen, by the way? No clue why you ever would've broken up with her."

Tony put his arm around Maura's shoulders, said, "Aren't you glad I did, though?"

Maura said, "Very," and kissed him.

***

They eat pizza for lunch. Ice cream for dessert. And Tony buys a new pack of cigarettes to carry him through the rest of the afternoon.

Mikey asks questions. Questions about Tony's next move. About the baby. About how he's feeling about everything that happened.

Tony says he doesn't know what he's going to do next.

He says the baby's probably not his anyway.

He says he thinks he feels a bit liberated. "I can concentrate on the wedding now. On Maura. I'll get another job. Maybe not soon, but I'll get one."

He hides his shaking hands from Mikey. Smokes when pressure builds in his chest enough that it feels like he needs to burp, but can't. Tells Mikey to shut it whenever a question's asked he doesn't want to answer.

They drive around wasting time. Whenever Tony would skip school he'd make sure he was never home earlier than he'd get there on the days he'd stayed until the last bell. Just in case his mother came home early. Or his father had to supervise third shift and didn't have to go into work until after dinner. Or so he could prove otherwise when Nate wanted to fuck with him by telling their parents Tony skipped.

But now, after burning through most of the gas tank, Tony says, "Fuck it."

It's easy to find parking near the apartment when everyone's at work.

Mikey's questions continue on the walk from the car.

Tony shuts his eyes up tight, wills Mikey away.

But Mikey's still there, arms crossed over the front of his shell. He says, "Really?"

Tony unlocks the front door, steps inside. All the lights are on. Maura must've forgotten to turn them off.

But then it's the sound of feet stomping back and forth in the bedroom.

Tony creeps around corners. Most robberies happen during the day.

In the kitchen, he pulls a knife from the silverware drawer. Mikey pulls his nunchucks. Together they tiptoe through the living room.

Past cardboard boxes. Past trash bags full of clothes. Past Tony's record crates. Past his computer wrapped in its own cables.

But it's not a man in a balaclava or a group of teenagers with a gun. It's Maura carrying a box. She says, "Holy shit," and drops it.

Tony says, "I thought you were a burglar."

Mikey says, "Or the Shredder."

Maura kicks the box, curses, says, "Put the fucking knife down."

Tony does, where his turntable was. "What's going on?"

She leans against a wall, says, "Nothing ever works out as good as the movies."

"Not sure what you're talking about. What are you doing?"

"It was supposed to be a grand gesture. I wanted to throw your shit out the window. But I'm not crazy. And my neighbors wouldn't appreciate a hysterical woman flinging shit out windows onto the street."

"Your neighbors? Why aren't you at work?"

"Called out, Tony. I called out. Had someone else do my presentation for me." She slides her back down the wall, sits on the floor, her arms on her knees.

"Why did you—" Tony leans against a wall. Feels his skin go cold. Sweat on his scalp. Oozing down his back. His throat whines when he breathes.

Maura cocks an eyebrow, looks up, says, "Figure it out?"

"Figure what out?"

She laughs, hard. For a while. Then she wipes her eyes, stands. She says, "You use the same password for everything, don't you? I could probably clear out your bank account, pay all my bills. Read all your Facebook messages, see who else you've been fucking."

Tony has nothing to say. There are no apologies that wouldn't sound soap opera. No amount of pleading that wouldn't make him look more pathetic than he does now. Standing next to his imaginary friend, surrounded by all of his stuff boxed up and ready to go. So he says, "You were snooping through my shit?"

Maura gets in his face, says, "You were sexting your high school girlfriend?"

"I thought you said you liked her."

Maura punches Tony in the gut, drops him to the floor.

Mikey crawls on the floor to him, asks if he's alright. He tries to help him stand, but Tony says, "Let go."

Maura says, "Let go of what?"

"I wasn't talking to you."

"Then who the fuck were you talking to?"

Tony stands, points at Mikey, says, "Him."

Her face contorts, severe and angry, soft and sad, then into a teary-eyed smile that Tony sees in his students who get picked on too much. Just before they lose it, turn into squealing, crying monsters and get made fun of even more for it. She says, "You're making fun of me? That's your strategy?"

Tony tries catching his breath, rubs his gut where she punched him. "No," he says. "I'm telling you the truth. For the first time in a while. Okay? Just listen for a second. Please."

Maura turns, goes back into the bedroom, starts throwing clothes at Tony's feet.

Tony says he's serious. That's he's sick. Not sex addict sick. But sick enough to be hanging around with hallucinations—one hallucination. "I'm not making this up. Who could make this up?" he says. "It's a 'Sometimes truth is stranger than fiction' thing. Like the Bad Religion song."

Maura stops, says, "Know what? This is your stuff. You pack it."

"Do you believe me?"

"The only thing I can believe is that you are the only person who makes music references while your fucking fiancée is packing up your shit."

"I got fired today."

"Are you trying to make me feel bad for being pissed that you've been actively ruining my life?"

"I've been ruining my life, too."

"Holy shit." Maura pushes past Tony, walks through Mikey, slings her purse over her shoulder. "How long do you need?"

"With what?"

"To get your shit out of my apartment?"

"Maura, if you would just please—"

"Please what?" Her voice lowers. Her face softens. "Seriously? Please, what? You've turned me into an idiot. I'm smarter than this. Maybe you were a project for me. Maybe you were something I thought I could turn into something you're not. But what's worse is that I let you do this to me. I let you do whatever you wanted because I felt horrible for asking you otherwise. I said it before and didn't take my own advice. Everyone has dead people. What you were doing to yourself was awful, what you did to me was worse. But now I have to live with being a fucking idiot. And I did that to myself."

"Maura—"

"I'll be back in a couple hours. Get your shit out of my apartment. Get your imaginary friend to help."

Tony and Mikey don't move.

The front door slams shut.

After a while, Tony picks up a box. He says, "You going to help or what?"

They pack everything up within an hour.

Load Tony's car for a half hour after that.

Then Tony calls his mother to tell her he's coming for a visit.

The boy's father holds the orange mask in his hands. He uses his hands when he speaks. The green plastic nosepiece flaps while his father talks about how to behave, how to talk to his mother. The wrinkled tips of orange fabric where the boy ties the mask around his head whip around while his father discusses

curse words.

The boy listens. But he doesn't pretend to like it. He sits with his back against the headboard, his Ninja Turtles pillow hugged to his chest, his chin resting on the top.

His father says, "Am I making sense?"

The boys say yes, draws out the E sound.

"It's a wonderful thing you and your brother are so close. But he's growing up. And you will, too. You can't give him such a hard time about it. Then you'll grow up and not be friends at all."

The boy wants nothing to do with his brother. Or growing up. Or cutting his brother a break. But he nods, says that he didn't mean anything by what he did. He says, "I was mad."

"Well, now he's mad. And your mother's mad."

"Are you mad?"

"Far as I'm concerned, no one's killed anybody else. No one's screaming. You guys are clean and clothed. I just need everyone to get along. Think you can do that for me?"

The boy nods again.

"Say 'yes' for me, pal."

"Yes for me, pal."

"Good one." The boy's father waves his hand, tells him to come down to dinner. Tells him he can suit up again for a little before bed if he wants.

The boy is introduced at the dinner table as someone who has something to say. And the boy makes his apologies. He kisses his mother's cheek. He holds out his hand for his brother to shake. Then he sits down and eats. He doesn't look up from his plate. Last time he got in trouble and got involved with dinner conversation he felt that people were nodding but not listening. So he concentrates on his food.

When he's full, he asks to leave.

When he leaves, he goes upstairs.

From upstairs he hears the voices pick up their volume. Laughter. His brother using the voice he uses in front of teachers at school, and, now, his parents.

The boy doesn't bother to get dressed up again. He leaves his gear on the floor—where he threw it at the tail-end of his tantrum.

He puts on PJs, lays on top of the covers on his bed. He turns the Phillies game on the radio like his brother does before bed. But he gets bored.

So he stares at the ceiling and listens to his family downstairs speaking. And laughing.

He drifts off to sleep trying to tell the difference between his brother's voice and his father's.

13

Tony's sophomore year dorm room was a concrete box coated in posters of punk bands. The posters featuring band members throwing up middle fingers were positioned in such a way that every time he opened the door, anyone passing by would know what he thought about them.

It was Milwaukee's Best Ice from the mini fridge and Desaparecidos on the boom box. Karen lying on the bed sipping from her can while Tony blew smoke into a fan that faced the open window.

He had planned on picking her up from school, taking her to the diner, talking to her there. Unlike the last time, he couldn't do it. He asked her what she wanted to do instead. And all she'd wanted to do was go to his dorm.

"Is this a new Bright Eyes?" she said.

"Bright Eyes sucks."

"I'm serious, that sounds like Conor."

"It is Conor. But this isn't Bright Eyes."

Tony finished his cigarette, flicked it out the window, lit another.

"Can you close the window? It's cold," she said.

"After I'm done."

Karen sat up, folded her legs underneath herself, cocked an eyebrow, and stared straight ahead at Tony's desk. All CDs and DVDs, way too many novels for one English course.

Tony said, "What?"

"You're being a dick."

Tony stood, pinched his smoke's cherry out the window and put the short in back in his pack. He said, "Sorry." He closed the window, said, "I don't mean to be."

"What's wrong?"

"Nothing. Why?"

Earlier in the week, Tony had gotten a call from his father. He'd picked it up by mistake. When he was piss drunk. He'd expected it had something to do with school, the dorm violations, the RA catching him puking in the hall.

But it was about Nate. The only other thing his father talks about.

How he'd be coming home from school early—a month before break.

Tony asked questions. Normal ones. Like why. And when. And what happened. But his father said, "We have a plan, and we're working it out. You'll know what's next when we figure it out ourselves."

And Tony had been left with his imagination.

Drugs. Nate had knocked a girl up. He'd killed a guy over drugs. Or a girl. He'd flunked out—Tony had laughed at that one. It was ridiculous.

Karen said, "What's on your mind, Tony? You're staring."

"Seriously. Nothing."

Tony finished his beer. Opened another.

Karen said, "I don't mean to dredge up history or anything, but your mood feels a little familiar to me."

"Stop. It's not that."

Karen put her empty can on the floor. Then she laid down

again, stretched her arms over her head, which pulled her shirt up a bit.

Tony kept looking at the bare skin between her shirt and beltline. Her belly button. The red blotch an inch below it.

Karen watched him. She said, "Then what's the matter? Seeing as you're not thinking about anything."

Tony had practiced everything he was going to say, just like last time. Worded it all in a way that would make sense. He'd talked into every mirror he could find, said, "Karen, I think Nate's issues are giving us both an opportunity to find stuff out about ourselves...separate from each other. He's sick. I need to concentrate on my family. I hope you understand."

But with Karen lying on his bed, all he could say, "I guess I'm just worried about Nate."

He sat on the bed next to her, leaned his back against the wall, kept quiet.

A minute passed, he thought he could say what he needed to say then. Then, then. Then it was silence that lasted until Karen shuffled over making space for him to lie down.

And he laid down.

They were there a while. The album ended, started over again. There was nothing else but the sound of shit beer slurped from cans warming in their hands.

Karen said, "Don't you want to make out with me or something?"

He did. But he didn't. Something always meant more than making out. And he couldn't break up with her after having sex with her.

But, then, maybe he could. One last time. Like a bookend.

He rolled on top of her. They kissed a while. He regretted the taste of his beer-soaked tongue. And the sound she made when he pressed his hips into her. And his fumbling with her front-opening bra.

But then his phone rang, danced over a pile of change on his desk.

He got up, said, "Shit," but didn't mean it.

Karen said, "Can't it wait?"

"What if it's about Nate?"

Karen didn't say anything. She adjusted herself, got up, went to the fridge for another beer.

Tony said, "Hi, Dad," made sure Karen knew who it was.

His father asked him where he was. Asked him if he was busy.

Tony said, "School," and, "No."

"I need you to get Nathan."

"What? No. I'm—"

"Now you're busy?"

"I mean, no, but—"

"Get Nathan. We had to move things up. We need your help."

Tony asked where Nate was, why his father couldn't do it himself, why Nate was back even earlier than Tony had been told he'd be.

Tony's father skirted the questions. Except for the one about where Nate needed to be picked up. He said, "I'll see you later, call me when you have him in the car," and hung up.

Karen was leaning against the wall. Her face had softened. "What's going on?"

"Nate's back."

"What does that mean?"

Tony emptied his backpack, went to the fridge. He put more beers inside than he knew they'd be able to drink.

Karen said his name, said, "What are the beers for?"

"Roadies."

"Can you tell me what's going on? Please?"

Tony didn't say he wanted to break up and drop her off at school on the way to get Nate. He didn't say that he'd take her home and they'd talk the next day. He didn't say he could use Nate as an excuse to dump her now.

He said, "Feel like taking a ride?"

***

30th Street Station wasn't far. It took four cigarettes and three-quarters of the Mighty Mighty Bosstones' *More Noise and Other Disturbances*.

Tony and Karen didn't talk much, drank beer in the dark. When they did talk, it was questions and answers about what could have maybe happened that made this trip necessary. All ridiculous speculation and Karen asking Tony to lower his voice.

Parked out front of the station, Tony texted Nate, told him he was waiting outside.

There was no response.

Tony almost called his father to tell him Nate was a no-show. Almost called to curse at him.

Almost threw the car in drive and left.

But then Karen said, "Tony," shook his arm, pointed out the window.

Nate, on the other side of the pedestrian walkway, was loading suitcases into the trunk of a cab.

Both Tony and Karen were out of the car yelling Nate's name.

Karen was yelling loud enough to be heard. Tony couldn't control himself, was screaming, cursing, then running across the sidewalk, the taxi lane.

Nate jumped, hard. Then he fixed his face—all forehead wrinkles, wide eyes, and a hanging jaw—and smiled, said, "Hey, guys."

Tony said, "What the fuck are you doing?"

"Going home, man. Why?"

"I texted you." Tony shoved Nate.

Karen grabbed Tony's arm before he could go after his brother again. She said, "Nate, we're picking you up."

Nate said, "You didn't have to come all the way out here." Tony's shove hadn't done much else but back Nate into a taillight. "I got a cab. It's cool."

Tony said, "Get your shit out of the trunk. Put it in mine."

"Tony, come on. I don't want to burden you guys."

Karen said, "It's no problem. Really. Just come with us, okay?"

"Yeah," Tony said. "Get in the fucking car, Nate."

Nate ran his hand through his hair, blinked his sagging eyelids too many times.   He shrugged, said, "Alright," then walked to Tony's car, opened the back door, got in.

His luggage was still in the cab.

Karen apologized to the cab driver while Tony dragged Nate's gear, piece by piece to his car, throwing it all into the trunk not giving a shit about what was inside.

Karen said Tony's name.

Face to face she whispered to him. "Calm down. You're freaking out."

Tony didn't give any thought to how loud his voice was. He said, "He was trying to run. You know that right? He knew we were here. He's not stupid."

"No, Tony. But he's stoned. Out of his face, actually."

Through the window, Nate sat in the back seat, his chin on his chest, asleep.

Tony said, "So what?"

"Let's just take him home, okay? Let's just relax. I know this sucks. It's awful. But he's not the bad guy here."

"He's always been the bad guy, Karen. He's like—he's like the fucking Shredder."

Karen laughed.

Tony said, "What?"

"Your brother's passed out in your backseat, and you think of cartoons."

"So?"

"Can I be April?"

Tony lit a cigarette, didn't say anything.

"Come on. Let me be April."

Tony smiled a bit, said, "You'd have to dye your hair."

"You've had plenty of experience with that, but I think my hair's a little too dark for even your level of expertise."

Tony said, "Shut up," and kissed her. Then he remembered everything he was supposed to do, turned away from her, walked to the driver's side door staring at the ground.

The car ride to Tony's parents' house was slow. And quiet. Just whispers between Tony and Karen. Or Nate wheezing in the backseat. The rattle of the car engine that Tony should have gotten fixed the last time he should've gotten an oil change.

Nate woke up halfway home like he was coming out of a nightmare. He sucked back a breath, grabbed for the door handle. Then he asked where he was. Then he said, "Oh, right."

He was asleep again after that.

There were too many cars in the driveway. Tony said what the fuck, parked on the street.

Karen stood behind him while he shook Nate over and over

trying to wake him up.

Tony thought maybe his brother had died during the drive. That he would have to go inside and tell his parents Nate was dead in the car, getting cold and going stiff.

But Nate woke up, cursed.

Tony was almost pissed that he wouldn't get to know what it felt like to be an only child.

Karen might have even gotten mad at him if he'd told her that one.

He pushed the thought away, said, "You're home."

Nate said he needed his stuff. But Tony turned him toward the house and gave him a little shove. There was no protest.

Up the driveway, and walking the path to the front door was slow. Nate was asking why there were so many cars in the driveway. Why Tony was sent to pick him up. How Karen was doing, that she filled out since the last time he saw her.

Tony said nothing, pushed Nate into the front door. Hard. Harder than he'd wanted to.

But the sound Nate's body made against the wood was enough for Tony's mother to open the door, say hello, invite them all inside. It was the way she'd invited guests into the reception after his grandmother's funeral. Formal and sad. Like she'd never met the people she was speaking to before.

The house was filled with people. Some were Nate's high school friends. Some were family from Tony's father's side, his mother's side. Some people Tony had never seen.

There was a pot of coffee. A table of finger foods, cheeses, and crackers.

Nate didn't say anything.

But Tony said, "What the fuck is this shit? This was the fucking plan?"

Karen smacked his arm.

His father called him Anthony, said, "I called you a half dozen times, got your voicemail every time. I had to arrange things sooner than I thought."

His mother said nothing. She scratched her eyebrow, turned away.

Everyone else in the room was either horrified or constipated.

Staring, mouths open, food in hands floating in front of their faces.

Tony said, "Could have told me, Dad. What? No one tells me anything around here, so I figured I had to find out the old crass way."

Even Nate turned, made a face.

"Oh, shut up."

Tony's father weaved around the people in the room. He grabbed Tony by the arm, said hello to Karen, and dragged Tony outside.

Out front, Tony's father said, "You're not a stupid-ass. You had to have some clue what we were planning."

"Well, yeah," Tony got as close to his father's face as he could without the tips of their noses touching. "But no one told me about it."

"I guess I assumed too much of you then."

"The surprise is for the person the intervention is intervening for, Dad."

"You barely come home any more, Tony. You call when you need something. You wait until we leave message after message on your phone to return our calls. You don't react well to anything having to do with your brother."

"Maybe I don't come home or pick up your calls because you don't react well to anything having to do with me."

"I can't deal with this right now." Tony's father opened the door. "You coming?"

Tony lit a cigarette, blew smoke in his father's face, into the house. "I can't deal with this right now."

Tony's father stepped inside. Left the door open.

Tony only had enough time for half a smoke before Karen came outside and told him to get his ass in the house.

He thought about saying, "I can't. Because we're breaking up and I have to take you back to school."

He thought about saying, "You can stay. But I'm leaving."

He thought about saying, "I wish Nate died in the car. Then I'd have a real reason for being here."

Instead, he said, "Fuck. Fine." He dropped his cigarette, smeared a streak of black on the patio under his foot, and went in the house ignoring the looks from Karen.

***

There were tears. Bouts of pleading for Nate to think of his potential. Tony's father spoke. Tony's mother tried to speak, but got choked up and stopped. Aunts and uncles chimed in. Old friends asked Nate to please check himself into a program.

Karen said, "Your life doesn't have to end. It can be put on pause for a little. You can find a local school just as good as Columbia. They don't know what they're missing by tossing you out."

Tony said nothing.

But he listened to everything that was said. About Nate being kicked out of school. About Nate selling drugs to pay for pot, then coke, then pills. About how lucky he was that the police were never involved. About how much Nate could do with himself once he got clean.

Tony hadn't known about any of it. He knew, but never in any official capacity. He had never gotten an update from his parents. He just saw how Nate would act when he visited on the rare occasions they were in the house at the same time. Took note of how he was smelling. Noticed the weight he'd lost, the lack of giving a shit about his appearance.

The group looked to Tony.

Nate, on the couch, bleary-eyed and embarrassed, stared.
Tony said, "What?"
His father said, "Why don't you say a few words."
"Sure." Tony let the silence in the room become uncomfortable, even more so than it already was. Then he said, "Well, Nate, nobody told me about any of this."
Karen said, "Tony. Stop it. That's not true and you know it."
"Look, I don't want to make this about me or anything, but I'm part of this family too. And no one took the time to tell me about any of this. I had to guess. Like I couldn't handle it or something. Like I'm a second cousin who only visits on holidays and doesn't need to know our personal business...no offense. Like I'm some moron who wasn't paying attention while his brother

was morphing into, well, you." He pointed at Nate.

Nate sat back in his chair.

"For a long time I was the loser," Tony said. "I was the one people assumed was doing shit he shouldn't be doing. I was the one with the shitty temper, the one who sucked at school."

Tony's father said, "That's enough."

"I'm the college boy now. Doing pretty okay, too. Aside from calculus, but whatever."

Tony's mother said, "Anthony."

"What, Mom? You should be happy. I'm turning out alright."

Karen said, "Tony, stop."

"I'm turning out alright, Nate. Without having to be a clone of you. Or Dad. Aren't you proud of me?"

Nate said nothing.

The family was pissed.

Nate's friends were angry.

Tony was pulled away by his arm, but he didn't take his eyes off his brother. And Nate didn't stop staring him in eye. Tony wrenched his arm away, said, "Get off me."

Tony heard his father say, "Karen, get him out of here."

There was some shoving after that. Nothing too violent. Just Tony's father's hand on his chest. Karen's hand on his shoulder. Tony slapping his father's hand away, still staring at Nate.

Then footsteps. A slammed door. And Karen asking Tony what was wrong with him.

Tony didn't say anything. He walked to the car, got in, and waited for Karen.

They drove in silence the half hour back to Karen's dorm.

Tony didn't put his blinkers on, which was meant for Karen to just get out and say nothing.

But she said, "You've got some issues, man."

"Guess so."

"Oh, fuck you."

"Fuck me? Fuck you. Since when are you the fifth member of my family? 'Get him out of here?' Like I'm the shitty boyfriend of a daughter they never had."

Tony turned on his blinkers.

Karen said, "That was bad, Tony. That was so bad."

The next few sentences Tony went from anger to more or less

agreeing with her. But he was losing his breath, and his nose ran, and his eyes welled up.

Then he figured he could use it, say what he'd wanted to say all night.

He said, "I'm messed up."

Said, "I don't know what happened to me."

Said, "I used to be different, right? I was different."

Karen's tone changed. It softened, sounded sympathetic. She said all the nice things someone says to someone about to burst, splash a room with brain matter.

"Don't be so hard on yourself," she said. "This is a horrible situation. You handled tonight badly. Everyone has a bad night, you know? You can apologize."

Tony figured putting his forehead to the steering wheel and going for major tears might have been too much. But Karen rubbed his back, said it's okay, it's okay.

Then he said. "I don't think I can do this right now."

"Do what?" Karen's hand was still smoothing circles into the back of his hoodie.

"This."

Karen pulled her hand away.

"I don't know if this is the best time for me to be in a relationship."

Karen stared through the windshield, said nothing.

"My family's falling apart. Nate's—"

"Stop."

There was nothing for a while. Almost two cigarettes.

Tony said, "Karen."

Karen said, "I was right, wasn't I?"

"About what?"

"You. How you were acting earlier."

"No. Seriously? Did you see what just happened?"

"Don't pretend that—"

Tony punched the steering wheel, screamed, said, "We need to break up, okay?

"Fuck." Karen opened the door, got out of the car.

"Maybe when I figure things out with Nate we can get back together. This can be just a break. Like a temporary thing."

"I'm assuming I'll hear from you soon. It happened once already. We'll start this whole thing up again because...I don't even fucking know anymore." Karen slammed the car door, walked to the dorm, went inside, didn't look back.

Tony turned off the blinkers, shifted into drive, and drove away.

When he hit 76, he slid Strike Anywhere's "Change is a Sound" into the CD player.

When he got back to his dorm, he tossed the backpack filled with warm beers onto the bed, flopped himself down onto the mattress.

Turned off his phone.

Breathed in what Karen had left behind in the fibers of his pillowcase and covers.

Then he drank until he fell asleep.

Part 3

14

Pennsylvania is a big barren nothing. Two cities. Nothing but road aside from burned-out towns, yellow grass, and deer smeared down the highway.

When Tony and Chris left there was music, conversation, cigarettes, pit stops with a beer from the cooler in the back.

Now it's silence and sore throats. Too much smoking. Not enough to drink. Tony can't remember how many miles it's been since the last time they spoke. Fifty, seventy-five, maybe a hundred.

Tony says, "Remember the one time we played strip padiddle with Karen and Amanda?"

Chris says, "What?"

"Remember that?"

"Sorry, I zoned out for a while there."

"Strip padiddle."

Chris sits up straight, lights a cigarette, says, "Oh yeah. What was that, twelve years ago?"

"Twelve-ish, I guess."

"To be honest, I don't really want to think about the time we were once naked in this car together, losing strip padiddle."

"We lost?"

"Dude, revisionist history much?"

"Dude, talk like a college freshman much?"

Four cigarettes and Pinkerton later they pull into a rest stop, get out, stretch, and open the back of the car. Tony opens the cooler, pulls a beer, shakes his wet hand off and sprinkles their duffel bags with water.

He holds the can to Chris.

Chris twists open a 5 Hour Energy, says, "My shift."

"Didn't stop me."

Chris laughs, says, "Yeah, well, I'm not you." He stuffs the empty bottle in the plastic bag where they've been keeping the crumpled beers cans, says he'll be back.

Tony lights a smoke, pulls his phone from his pocket, logs into his father's bank account.

Two more charges on his debit card since they left. One at a McDonald's for a little over ten bucks. Number four with a large fry and a ten piece nugget. Standard fare for his father. Tony used to sit in the backseat of his father's Chevy station wagon next to Nate. His father would rattle off their order in a voice loud enough to make the drive-thru attendant mock him with the volume of his own, tinny and electric through the speaker.

The second at a Motel 6 in Salt Lake City.

Tony Googles the motel chain, the city, waits. He holds his thumb on the address once the results load. He taps on the navigation notification asking him if he would like directions.

They've been on 80 for most of the trip. The new set of directions tell Tony to make his way to 70 and take that the most of rest of the way.

Tony curses loud enough for his voice to echo across the empty lot into the woods.

Mikey stands at the edge of the tree line, his back to Tony, looking back and forth all nervous and kid-skittish.

Then Tony feels the pressure of his bloated bladder, walks to

the woods ignoring the restroom doors Chris disappeared into.
Tony says, "Hey."
Mikey shushes him, says, "I can't go when people talk."
"Sorry."
"Shh."
Tony unzips, says, "He's moving again."
"Duh."

Their streams finish in tandem. They both shake, put themselves back together, turn and walk back to the car.

A car pulls into the lot, Tony drinks his beer and smokes, leaning against his car. He says "how's it going" to the people. They say nothing, walk toward the bathroom doors Chris exits.

Chris holds the door for them, says, "Yeah," when they thank him. From across the lot, he says, "Any update?"

"Bank records say Salt Lake."

"Change the route at all?"

"Little bit. Lost some time with the last set of directions."

"How many hours out are we?"

"About thirty. Give or take."

"A lot can happen in thirty hours."

"Good thing he'll be sleeping for the next eight or so. Hopefully."

Tony's father used to rely on eight hours when he was a shift manager. When he did third shift, he'd be in bed by the time Tony and Nate would get off the school bus. Working second he'd be just falling asleep while they were getting ready for school. The first shift was the only one that would allow him to be home for dinner. Even then he'd be in bed before ten.

But he's older now. Maybe he needs ten hours at his age.

No telling what he'll do now, though. He's running.

Tony knows a bit about duplicity. Anything goes.

Chris says, "Ready?"

"One second."

Tony goes to the back, opens the trunk, pulls a beer from the cooler, and trots over to the other car.

Chris says, "What are you doing?"

Tony wedges the unopened can under the front tire, says, "Remember this?"

"What? Being a dick?"

"Stop. This is funny. It's what people do on road trips."

"How would you know?"

Tony tells Chris to shut up, hands the keys over, jogs around to the passenger side door.

In the car, Tony gives Chris a set of instructions about how to drive the thing. If it doesn't start, pull the key a minute and try again. If the car bucks while shifting it into drive, it'll sound like it's shaking itself to pieces, but don't worry about it. If it stalls, pull the key, reinsert, and start it up again quick. If that doesn't work, wait thirty seconds to a minute to try again. If that doesn't work, it'll be about a half hour before Chris can try again.

"We should've flown," Chris says.

"And miss an opportunity to drive across the country?"

"This isn't a fun thing, Tony."

"No. But who says we can't have some fun on the way? You were all about this."

"Agreeing to come along is different than—"

"Shh, start the car."

Chris turns the key, starts the car on the first try.

Tony watches the people from the other car cross the lot, get into their car. He says, "Be cool."

The other car crushes explodes the beer can. Beer foam splashes the wheel well and the passenger door.

Tony says, "Punch it."

Chris throws the car into reverse, backs up, shifts into drive—and the car stalls. He says, "Fuck."

"Start it again. Start it again."

The car starts again, and Chris peels out of the parking lot cursing.

Tony laughs, says, "Take it easy on the car, man."

Chris says, "Fucking piece of shit."

Back on the highway, Chris ramps up the speed until the car shakes.

Tony says, "Slow it down. This thing can't go much past eighty."

"Can you not do that again, please? What if they decide to chase us down and slit our throats?"

Tony laughs through saying, "They won't."

"Promise me you won't be doing any more of that. I'll turn this thing around and save my personal days."

"Sorry, Dad."

Neither of them speaks for a bit.

Mikey, in the backseat says, "Do you think they'll really come slit our throats?"

Then Tony's phone speaks up in the silence, says, "Recalculating."

Tony looks at his phone, says, "Chris?"

"What?"

"We missed our exit."

***

Tony's mother had questions. Dozens of them. Questions about what happened between him and Maura. About how a couple can just decide to call off an engagement only days after agreeing to marry each other. About what Tony had done to ruin his relationship. About the apartment. About the ring. About what he was going to tell his father.

Tony dodged most of the questions. Made up some things. Omitted others. Until he just decided to break the truth to his mother by telling her it turned out Maura had been seeing another guy for a while.

Tony said, "It's not totally her fault. I was dragging my feet about the whole marriage thing. But I found a bunch of emails."

Tony's mother said, "Bitch."

"Mom."

"Who does that to someone they're supposed to love?"

Tony said, for the record, that the last email he had read was Maura breaking it off with the guy. He said she had been worried she would never get married and she'd just be that girl living with a guy who never wanted to commit.

Tony's mother said, "It's inexcusable. And pathetic. Only a pathetic, sad person does something like that."

"Mom, I'm fine. I'm hurt, but, like I said, I'm partially to blame. It wasn't all her."

"Disgusting."

"Can we talk about something else?"

His mother said she had half a mind to call Maura up, tell her how horrible of a person she is. Said she always knew Maura wasn't right for Tony. Said she had an edge. Said she's glad he had the sense to leave her instead of becoming one of those pathetic boys you see on trashy talk shows.

Then she said, "I was looking forward to having grandkids running around. I miss babies. You and Nathan were wonderful little boys."

"Can we not talk about babies, please?"

Over coffee and *Seinfeld* his mother said, "You can stay as long as you need to, Anthony."

"Thanks."

"Think Karen would want to get back together with you?"

"She's married, Mom."

"So? That sort of thing doesn't seem to matter much anymore."

They watched television together until Tony's mother got up, kissed his forehead, told him she'd make his bed before she goes to sleep herself.

Tony waited for the floorboards upstairs to stop creaking before he went to his father's liquor cabinet.

He drank, turned off his phone. Drank some more, turned his phone back on to text Karen. He put the phone down after typing out a long text about the baby and drank some more.

Then he woke up to his mother saying it was seven and asking if he'd make it to work on time.

After a self-induced vomit and a shower, he dressed in wrinkled clothes. Drank a cup of coffee a bit too fast. Then picked the note off the fridge. His father's flight information.

His mother shuffled around the kitchen, staring, confused.

"Want me to get Dad?" Tony said.

"Hmm? Oh, you don't have to. I'm sure you're busy."

Tony laughed, said, "Busy with what?"

His mother kissed his cheek, thanked him, said, "Get to work, you're going to be late."

Tony said he'd see her tonight and left.

He went to the diner, ate breakfast. Talked to Mikey in head-nods and arched eyebrows.

Mikey said, "What do you want to do today?"

Tony shrugged his shoulders.

"Why did you lie to your mom?"

Tony cocked an eyebrow.

"Are you going to tell your dad the truth?"

Tony asked the waitress for the check. He left Mikey at the table when the waitress handed him his bill.

But Mikey was already in the car.

He followed Tony into the mall. Into Best Buy. Into Barnes and Noble. Into Target, and McDonald's, and the movie theater. He talked through *Captain America: The Winter Soldier*, asking questions about why Nick Fury died, and why Bucky is a bad guy now, and why the computer was talking.

Tony shushed Mikey enough times to have to hope a theater attendant hadn't seen him, hadn't called the cops on account of a nut telling an empty seat to just watch the fucking movie.

Mikey was gone for a while after that.

Tony talked to himself, fought traffic to the airport. Practiced what he would say to his father.

"Dad, before you hear it from anyone else, I need to tell you what really happened with work."

And, "Dad, I think we need to have a nice long conversation about my future."

And, "Dad, I blame you for turning me into a motherfucker."

From the backseat, Mikey said, "Why are you talking to yourself?"

Tony talked to the rearview mirror, said he was, they were—no, he was hilarious.

Once Mikey stopped laughing he blew a raspberry, said, "Don't be a dummy. Tell your dad the truth. You can start over after that."

"Start over?"

"Yeah, like when someone blows up a Lego castle you built with a football on accident."

"Like the time when Nate—"

"What do you do with a pile of Legos?"

"Build something?"

"Yeah, the blocks don't break. You can use them again."

"That was shockingly wise."

"See? You're not a big dummy all the time."

They talked about other things the rest of the way to the airport.

Things that didn't make Tony's chest swell with pressure.

Even at the airport, Tony wasn't bothered by the kid. Tony leaned against the car, smoking. Mikey showed off his new karate moves that were just his old karate moves done a little bit better.

Then the arrival time for Tony's father's flight came and went. He wasn't in the stream of people pouring out the doors. Wasn't standing down the sidewalk a ways looking confused or pissed. He didn't text. Didn't call.

Tony said, "Think he missed the flight?"

Mikey shrugged, tried a roundhouse kick and fell to the concrete.

Tony called his father's phone. It went straight to voicemail. He said, "Hey, it's me. I'm outside. Where are you?"

Three cigarettes and two phone calls later Mikey said he'd go inside and look.

Tony watched Mikey through the glass, weaving in and out of crowds, diving over luggage into ugly somersaults. He laughed as he watched even though he knew his father wasn't there. Even though he knew his father probably had never intended to get on the plane in the first place. Even though Tony wasn't surprised, not even a little bit.

Tony knew.

All he wanted to do was run, too.

***

Tony wakes up halfway through Ohio. A sunny morning rush hour—as rush hour as Middle Jabip, Ohio can get.

It's a rest stop bathroom break, a smoke, and coffee before Tony's back behind the wheel. Before Chris is snoring, sprawled across the backseat. Before Mikey's sitting shotgun playing with Tony's iPod.

Tony drops a butt-smoked cigarette into the dregs in his paper coffee cup, switches lanes. And after considering lighting another, ignoring his wrecked throat, it's the right turn signal arrow in the dash. Solid green.

Tony's seen something like this before. A while ago. But it blinked off after a bit, then.

Now Tony can't make it go away.

He taps the plastic panel behind the steering wheel. Flicks the turn signal switch left, right, left, right. He turns on the high-beams, turns them off.

But the arrow stays green.

Then smoke wisps out of the steering column.

And Tony says holy shit.

He jerks the wheel right, sends the car careening through three lanes of traffic.

Car horns blare. Chris wakes up screaming. Mikey yells cowabunga dude.

Tony steers the car over the rumble strip and into the shoulder and cranks the gearshift into park.

Chris says, "What's going on? What's happening?"

Tony says, "Think the car's on fire, dude."

Tony's outside, running around the front of the car. He opens the passenger side door, says, "Get out," to Mikey.

Chris says, "I'm fucking trying, man. Goddamn two-door piece of shit."

Tony tells Chris not to talk about his car like that, rolls the seat forward and moves out of the way.

All three of them back up toward the trees bordering the road, watch the smoke start to pour out of the steering column.

Then Tony runs at the car, jumps inside from the open passenger door, and turns the car off. He pulls the keys, trips falls, and lands on the street outside covering his head before the car explodes.

But nothing happens.

Chris asks what the fuck.

Mikey laughs.

And Tony pulls himself up, peeks inside the car.

No smoke. No fire. No impending explosion. He says, "We're good."

Chris says, "We're good? What does that mean?"

"It means we're cool."

"Jesus, man."

Tony laughs says, "She's got quirks like that. Now we know what to do if it happens again."

"All seventeen-year-old cars have quirks, Tony. That wasn't a quirk. That was an oh my god, oh my god, we're all going to die situation."

Tony walks to the back of the car, says, "Relax. We're fine. If it happens again we should be worried, but this was just a freak thing." He opens the trunk, opens the cooler, pulls two beers and tosses one to Chris.

Chris says, "It's like eight in the morning."

Between cracking the can open, slurping through his first sip, Tony says, "And this is a road trip."

"A road trip only by definition. We didn't plot out hotels or cities to visit; we're tracking down your runaway dad." Chris opens his beer, sits in the grass.

Tony sits next to him.

They sit and sip their beers, light cigarettes. They don't say anything.

Mikey sits like Nate, his shell up against the car.

"I think we can get in a ton of trouble doing this," Chris says after a drink from his can. "This is probably DUIable."

"Probably. It'd be one more thing to add to the list."

"Not for me."

"Yeah. Not for you."

Tony finishes his beer, drops his cigarette into the can, tosses it over his shoulder, stands.

Chris pours what's left of his beer onto the grass, coughs through the last drag of his smoke.

Tony says, "Ready?"

"Why are we doing this, Tony?"

"To get my dad back."

Chris cocks an eyebrow, says, "What else?"

Behind him, Tony hears Mikey say, "Psst. Tell him. You can't get in trouble. Not with him."

Tony leans against the car, takes a breath. Then tells Chris everything. About Maura finding the photos. About Karen being pregnant. About the possibility that it could be his.

Chris lights a cigarette opens another beer through all of it. He doesn't say anything. But Tony watches his face react. Like it did when Tony broke up with Karen the first, second, third time. Like it did when Nate died and Tony told him how he found the body. Every heinous thing Tony's ever done has affected Chris this way. Convincing reaction faces. A beer, a smoke. Some stupid, canned, clichéd catch phrase afterward. But this time Chris says, "Holy shit."

"Yeah."

"Do you want a hug or something?"

"What? No."

"I wasn't serious."

Mikey wraps his arms around Tony's waste, hugs his hip. Tony rolls his eyes, says, "Well, what if I was just deflecting the question by my reaction right there?"

Chris drinks, smokes, looks at the car.

"What? Nothing else? That's all?" Tony says.

"Can I just say that I think it would've been best if we'd taken my car?"

"You can say it. But I'll ignore it. See that? Ignored it."

"Next time then," Chris says handing his beer to Tony.

Tony drinks, says, "Next time? You're not going to get all pissy and demand we turn my shitty car around? Most people would be appalled at me if I told them what I just told you."

"I'm not most people."

"You're more like me than you think."

Chris laughs, says, "I'm nothing like you."

"Yeah, you are."

"No. I'm not."

Tony says yuh-huh, takes a drink.

Chris says he's not like Tony again, takes the can, drinks, hands it back.

They go back and forth until the can's empty and Tony crushes it under his foot.

Chris says, "Ready?"

Tony tosses Chris the keys, says it's his shift.

15

Tony's father moves southwesterly. From Salt Lake City to Fillmore, Utah, hitting gas stations and fast food joints in between. He hasn't made a full stop since the Motel 6. And he wasn't there as long as Tony had predicted.

Tony leaves voicemails on his father's phone every couple hours. He hasn't said a word about tracking him down, but once they hit Iowa, the next time Tony checks his father's bank records, there's an ATM withdraw for three-hundred dollars. That means either there's nothing in Fillmore that takes plastic, or he'll be working on cash and driving until he can't. Tony wonders if the voicemails made his father figure out he's being followed. That maybe he's cut off the trail he's been leaving behind. But Tony doesn't mention the possibility to Chris, keeps driving.

Tony and Chris take shorter shifts. Between the leg cramps and drowsiness, the cigarette sore throats and dehydration headaches, neither of them can stand driving for more than a few hours at a time.

Even Mikey in the backseat has trouble sticking around. Tony figures his brain is too exhausted to manifest the kid. But when Tony's eyes shut while he's driving, Mikey's back asking questions.

"Are we there yet?" he says.

"Not sure where there is yet."

"Do you want to sing the *Turtles* theme song with me?"

After everything Tony told Chris after Chris took everything as well as any concerned friend could, Tony continued to leave Mikey out of the story.

He's gotten better at concealing his imaginary, stress-induced whatever, but when he tells Mikey he will not pull over to watch him try a back flip, his voice raised, angry, Chris stirs. Then it's a good morning, a yawn, a question about how his real, live, actual friend slept.

Chris sits up in his seat, shrugs, clears his throat, spits out the window.

A few hours ago, if Chris had made the suggestion of getting a motel room, Tony would have told him no. That they needed to keep moving. But now, seventeen hours on the road after the smoke incident with nothing but car-sleep, Tony says, "We should stop. Want to stop?"

Chris says nothing, pulls his phone, taps at the screen for a bit, and sets the phone down in an empty cup holder, a new set of directions displayed.

When they pull into the Quality Inn parking lot after a couple dozen miles, Tony doesn't have to use the key to turn the car off. It shuts itself down.

Chris says, "I'd be worried if I could give a shit right now."

They rent a room, close the blinds, get in bed.

Chris is out in seconds.

And Tony stares at the ceiling.

For an hour.

Two.

Then he gets up. Walks with Mikey out the door, down the halls, through the lobby.

He pours coffee, meanders past the gym doors, the business center with high-speed internet access. The pool.

Before Tony can say stop, Mikey's through the door yelling cowabunga and flinging himself into the water.

Then Tony says fuck it, strips to his underwear and cannonballs into the pool.

He floats on his back, imagines drifting in Mikey's wake every time the kid jumps in. Which is often.

Then there's a voice. Someone saying, "You're not dead are you?"

Tony thinks, no, dead people have a color to them. Gray, ashen. He's seen it. But he stands up in the water, turns.

A woman—the voice—stands at the edge of the pool. Short hair graying in streaks, tired eyes looking this way, that, younger than the sockets they sit in. A towel and a novel tucked under one arm. The other arm bent at the elbow, the rest hidden behind her back. A bikini top and boyshorts.

"No," Tony says. "Not dead. Dead tired, maybe." He laughs, phony, forced.

She does too, says, "They've got beds here, you know."

If Karen had said that it would've meant sex.

If Maura had said that it would've meant sleep.

This woman saying it leaves Tony with nothing to say.

Mikey swims up to Tony from behind, says something about how his shell makes him float like the Turtles did after fighting Super Shredder at the end of the second film.

Tony says, "I figured I'd take a swim instead of sleeping. Sleep doesn't come too easy most of the time."

She says, "Yeah? Why's that?"

"I'm Tony." He bobs through the water to the edge of the pool, puts out his hand.

The woman pulls the towel and book from under her arm, stuffs them into the pit of the other, puts out her left hand. "Marie."

Tony switches hands, gives her an awkward, left-handed, dead fish handshake. He says, "Sorry."

"For what?"

"Bad handshake."

Marie backs away, drops her stuff onto a white plastic table, drops herself into a white plastic chair. She crosses her legs, tucks her hands under her thighs. She says, "I'm used to it."

"I'll get better at it after a while."

Mikey laughs, swims away, says, "That was dumb."

Tony says, "Sorry. That wasn't meant to—"

Marie says, "Where are you from, Tony?"

"Philadelphia."

"Road trip?"

"How'd you know?"

"You're in a Quality Inn in Iowa. No real reason to be in a Quality Inn in Iowa otherwise."

Tony pulls himself out of the pool, sits in a chair far enough from Marie to make himself feel that distance may make her judgments about his fattening body less severe. Close up he's gooseflesh and glass-cutting nipples, bloated no matter how much he sucks in the gut he's been working on. He crosses his legs to keep Marie from judging other parts through a thin sheet on cotton. He says, "Yeah, road trip."

"To where?"

He tells her about his father. It sounds stupid. It tastes desperate. Stinks of Too Much Information.

But Marie sits, listens, nods the way Tony thinks a person should when hearing about a runaway father.

Tony says, "Sorry for unloading there."

"Hey, I asked. You don't have anything to apologize for."

"You don't know that." Tony laughs. The same bullshit chuckle from before.

"No. I don't," Marie says. "But since we're sharing." She pulls her right hand from under her leg, holds it up for Tony to see.

A claw, four fingers, and a thumb melded into a hooked set of pincers tipped in two painted fingernails.

Tony holds back a flinch, concentrates on Marie's eyes. He says things like, "You didn't need to hide that—not that your hand's a that," and "Nothing I haven't seen before—not that it's weird or anything," and, "Shit. I'm sorry."

Marie laughs, loud, genuine this time. She tells Tony he has nothing to apologize for again. She tells him that everyone has ugly parts. She says, "Some people are better at hiding them than others."

***

Tony's mother said his father was always good at hiding things. "Not that he's done anything to make me question my trust in him," she said.

But he'd never talk about the things that were bothering him.

He'd collected every bad thing—work, money, Tony's problems, and Nate's issues—kept it all in his chest.

It was too much sometimes. He'd explode every so often. But he'd directed those explosions at something else. Or someone else. Like Tony.

He was impulsive. He would just do things. Buy things. Get wrapped up in things.

"Like the aquarium," Tony's mother said. "Remember that? He loved taking care of those fish when he'd come home from work."

There were the volumes of How To books about buying, flipping, and selling houses.

There was the research into getting involved with starting up a small business.

"He would get so wrapped up in something that whatever he was doing became the only thing that was important. Until it helped him work out what was actually bothering him."

Tony remembered every obsession his father had, all the things he let slide. Eventually, the fish had died in their cloudy water. The books had collected dust on the bathroom counter. The office space that was going to be his very own air conditioning business was sold off. He'd just go back to what he'd been ignoring. Every time.

Tony's mother talked for an hour, two. Spoke like Tony's father's not coming home was unexpected, but not a complete surprise.

She said, "We'll see him again."

She kept going. All past tense and funeral phrases.

After his mother had gone to bed, Tony and Mikey stayed up. Nick at Nite. Beer. Cereal. Whiskey. Leftovers from the fridge. More beer.

Tony asked questions, "Do you think he wants someone to chase him? Is that why he's doing this?"

Mikey answered in shrugs and follow-up questions. "Would you want someone to chase you?"

"Do you think he needed to clear his head or just totally quit his life?" Tony said.

"Would you have quit your life if everyone hadn't quit you first?"

"What was he thinking?"

Mikey stood, then paced around the room. He made a list of all the things Tony didn't want help with when he needed it. Kept asking whether or not he would accept help if someone were willing to go further than anyone else to do so.

Tony said, "What are you saying?"

"No one except me was able to bring you back from what you were doing. And because I'm you, that means I wasn't enough, right?"

"I think we've done a pretty nice job together."

Mikey laughed, rolled his eyes, said he was serious. He said, "What if we go get him?"

There was no job to go to everyday. No fiancée to plan a wedding with. No mistress to fuck. But there was a baby. The baby.

Mikey said, "Karen doesn't even want to see you again. Like ever."

Tony talked about Karen changing her mind. He talked about how having a baby would give him a set of rules. That if he had rules, he would be able to follow them. That it's easy to follow a series of parameters. That structure may be the only thing he'd been missing.

Mikey said, "You had rules. You broke all of them."

"I'm talking about real rules. A baby's different."

"Than what?"

"Than everything. It's a living, breathing thing that needs to be taken care of."

"Didn't you need to take care of Maura? Or let her take care of you?"

Tony told Mikey to shut up. He sat on the couch. Stood up. Went outside and smoked.

The cigarette went straight to his face. All the beer and booze seeped into his brain. It was the spins, then heavy eyelids, then stumbling into the house and sitting on the couch.

He fell asleep sitting up.

He woke up with a stiff neck to reruns of *The Fresh Prince of Bel-Air*. Will was screaming, high-pitched and shrill. Jazz was thrown out of the house. Then Carlton helped Will fix whatever had happened earlier in the episode, the parts Tony had snored through.

Tony stood up, leaned against the wall to keep from falling over.

Then Mikey strolled into the room with a bowl of Trix, stuffing his face, saying good morning.

Tony coughed, swallowed back the stomach acid that bubbled up his throat. Then he said, "Should we go get him?"

With a mouthful of cereal, Mikey said, "Duh," dribbling ropes of rainbow colored milk down his chin.

"Okay. Let's get him."

The floorboards creaked upstairs. A door closed, a toilet flushed. And Tony's mother came downstairs asking Tony why he wasn't ready for work yet, saying he'll be late again.

Tony said, "Called out."

"But—"

"Do you have an online user ID? For your bank accounts?"

"What? Why?"

"Do you have it?"

"I can probably look it up. Why?"

"Let's look it up." Tony kissed his mother, said good morning and shooed her upstairs.

They dug through lockboxes stuffed with bills, banking statements, student loan letters, college acceptances—most were Nate's, Tony had only gotten a couple. It was almost an hour before Tony's mother handed him a stack of ripped up envelopes. Papers asking his parents to go paperless, a Post-It note with nine digits scrawled in his father's handwriting.

Tony pulled his phone, opened the same banking app he used for himself, typed in the numbers. He answered a security question about his grandmother's maiden name, another about the name of his father's high school. Then he guessed at the password—Nate's birth date.

The app told him it was wrong in red letters, gave him a warning about failing at more than three log-in attempts.

Tony said, "Fuck."

His mother said, "Anthony."

He said, "Sorry."

He keyed in the user ID number again, made sure he got all the digits right. Then he tried his own birth date for the password.

The app opened up the bank account's virtual wallet. It gave Tony a list of transactions. Dates. The amount of money spent where and when.

Tony said, "Huh."

His mother said, "What?"

"I found Dad."

Tony handed his phone to his mother.

She stared at the screen.

Then she started to cry.

***

Over coffee in the hotel lobby, Tony tells Marie about Nate. He tells her about Maura and Karen. His job. The baby. He leaves Mikey out of it. Dumping everything on a stranger is fine until craziness enters the conversation. Then it's fake smiles and excuses about having just remembered that something urgent is going on anywhere else.

He tries to stop himself from staring at her claw hand the best he can. But it's strange. And grotesque. Something from a David Cronenberg film.

Marie isn't hiding it. Her coffee cup is gripped between the pincers.

She says, "So you're running, then?"

"I'm sort of thinking about it as playing hide and seek."

"Usually the hiders aren't seeking at the same time."

"I'm playing both sides."

Tony adjusts himself, his soggy underwear soaking his jeans. He says, "What are you running from?"

Marie stands, holds out her hand, asks if he needs a refill.

Tony hands her his cup, says yeah. "Come on. My guts are all over the floor here."

Marie fills both cups from the pot, says, "I'm not running. I'm looking around. Ever feel homesick when you're still at home?"

"Didn't know that could happen."

"It can. Happened to me. Is happening to me. I don't know. It's that feeling you get when there's no one to talk to at a party." She hands Tony his coffee. "All these people around talking about mortgages, baby names—no offense, by the way—and you think, holy shit, I don't belong here at all."

"Aren't you talking about loneliness?"

"No, I wasn't lonely. That's way too melodramatic a thing to say, hanging around a bunch of people I grew up with. It was just a feeling I got. Like I had nothing to say or do there that was going to help me make up for whatever I was missing."

"What do you think you're missing?"

"Don't know. Just figure I'll drive around until I find it. And maybe I won't find anything. That's fine. If that's the case I'll just go home."

"Just like that?"

"Just like that."

"So, are you always sage-like and mystifying?"

"Not always. I figure tonight I'll find a bar a couple hours from here, and get drunk and perform party tricks." She holds up her claw, flexes it, snaps it shut, clicks the fingernails together over and over until Tony realizes he's staring and laughs.

Tony says, "Mind if I ask what happened there?"

"Played with matches and gasoline when I was little."

"Seriously?"

Marie laughs, says, "No. I came out like this."

"Do you have any other, uh...special features?"

"Two vaginas."

"What?"

"God, you're easy."

Tony flips her off, laughs.

They sit a while longer. Mikey asks Tony to ask Marie if she wants to order a pizza.

He does. She does. So they do.

They eat, talk about movies, music, books, all the things that would drive a conversation for Tony before he collapsed everything onto himself before Nate died. And for a minute—a short one—Tony doesn't think about what he's going to say next. He doesn't wait to talk while Marie speaks. He sits, listens, comments adds to the conversation. Like people who don't have imaginary friends do. Like people who have more than one live-in-the-flesh friend do. Like he used to.

But nothing is familiar. The content's the same, but all Tony wants to do is keep going. And they do. They keep talking until Chris walks, sleepy and bleary-eyed, through the lobby.

Tony introduces Chris to Marie.

Marie, hiding her right hand, uses her left, reaches out and confuses Chris.

Chris smiles, shakes her hand, says it's nice to meet her.

Tony says, "How'd you sleep?"

"The best anyone can sleep in the middle of the day. Did you sleep?"

Tony tells him that he and Marie have been sitting around talking, drinking coffee. That he's fine to drive if Chris wants to catch a few more hours in the car.

Chris cocks an eyebrow, smirks, puts his hand out, says, "I'll start the car up. Ready when you are."

Tony hands over the keys. "Remember to start—"

"I remember. You learn fast driving that thing."

Tony and Marie don't say anything until the lobby's automatic doors cut them off from Chris.

"Seems like a good friend," Marie says.

"He's alright." Tony laughs, stands, holds out his left hand. "It was nice meeting you, Marie. Maybe I'll see you around."

"Probably not." Marie holds out her right hand, the claw hand.

Tony takes it, shakes it, and gets a shiver by the feeling of taught skin over fused bone.

They don't say anything.

Tony nods, turns and leaves the hotel.

In the parking lot, Tony remembers his wet pants, figures going back in would be stupid, tells himself he'll change in the back while Chris drives.

He turns around, looks through the glass doors, looks around the parking lot.

No laughing, no karate in his periphery.

He says, "Hello?"

Nothing.

Then it's Mikey through the backseat window, waving.

Tony cocks an eyebrow, shakes his head, figures it'll take more than one positive conversation. But it was a start.

He goes around the side of the car, gets in.

Chris says, "Didn't sleep at all?"

"Nope. But I'm good."

"What were you up to, then?"

"Nothing, why?"

Chris makes the same face he did back in the hotel, says, "I don't need to remind you of your track record with women as of late, do I?"

"It wasn't like that. All we did was talk."

"Just talk?"

"What are you, my dad?"

Chris shifts the car into reverse, stalls it, puts it back in park, starts it again, shifts, backs out of the spot.

Tony climbs into the backseat, says he has to change his pants.

Chris says, "I knew it."

"I was in the pool."

The car stalls again when Chris shifts into drive. He says, "It's getting worse, you know."

"You just haven't gotten the hang of it yet." Tony watches Chris shake his head in the rearview mirror. "Just give it some love, man."

Chris's phone, from the cup holder, directs them to make a series of turns that'll take them back to the highway. Tony is rocked back and forth while changing, asks if Chris is driving like an asshole on purpose.

Once he's changed, Tony climbs back into the front. He reads the ETA to Fillmore from Chris's phone and hopes his old man's ugliness is put back in check by they time they get there.

16

Tony's father posts a charge on his credit card in Carson City, Nevada just as Tony starts seeing signs for Fort Collins, Colorado.

Twelve hours, almost seven hundred miles, and four rest stops through three states, and Tony's more pissed off than tired. A day and a half of just driving, a break he didn't sleep through, and no one to talk to on his shifts besides Chris' sleeping body makes Mikey a constant presence.

When Mikey isn't sitting in the backseat babbling all kid-tired and delirious, he's on the side of the road waving the car on with his nunchucks, an air traffic controller on the tarmac. When he's not talking through plotlines for the next time he plays Ninja Turtles he's standing on the hood, surfing the car, screaming cowabunga.

Sometimes he talks about Marie, about how nice she was, about her weird hand.

Sometimes he talks about Chris, asks about how many days he

took off for the trip, if Tony thinks he's having fun.

Tony wants to scream for Mikey to be quiet, please for just ten minutes. He punches the ceiling until his first hurts instead.

Chris sits up straight, startled, says, "What's the matter?"

"Nothing."

"What was that noise?"

"Must've run over some shit." Tony shakes his aching hand, says it's cramping up from holding the wheel too tight for too long.

Chris rubs his eyes, says whatever, pulls a cigarette from the pack on the dash, lights it, smokes for a bit. Then he asks where they are.

Tony tells him, asks him to light a cigarette for him.

Chris says, "Any update on your dad?"

"Just one. He moved again."

"Shit. How far?"

"However far Fillmore is from Carson City, Nevada."

Chris pulls his phone from his pocket, types for a bit, says, "Shit, man."

"What?"

"That's more than five hundred miles."

This time, Tony screams. He punches the steering wheel, honks the horn once, twice, three times. He calls his father a motherfucker. A cocksucker. A rotten sonofabitch piece of shit.

Mikey says Swear Jar from the backseat after each curse, laughs harder and louder at each one.

Every time Chris starts to speak, Tony cuts him off with, "Fucker," or "Asshole," or "Dickhead."

And after a while, it's just the sound of the car fighting the road.

The wind through the open windows.

Mikey trying to stop himself from giggling.

Until Chris says, "Tony, maybe we should head home."

"Oh, no," Tony says. "That's what the jackoff wants—don't say it." Tony stares into the rearview mirror.

Mikey slaps his hands over his mouth in the reflection, his shoulders shaking, cheeks red.

Chris says, "Sorry."

"Not you. No, we're going to find him. And I'm going to kick his stupid ass all the way home."

This time Tony points at the rearview mirror.

Chris says, "There's no way we can catch up to him, man. He only stops to sleep. We're always going to be five hundred miles behind him. He doesn't want to be found. I doubt he even knows what the hell he's doing, or where he's going. He's just going."

"You told me you'd help me."

"I told you that when you knew exactly where he was."

"I do know exactly where he is."

"But there's no way to know where's he's going to be. Right now he's moving in a straight line, yeah. But what if he heads north for a day, then east for a couple of hours, then turns around again?"

"I need you with me."

"Why?"

Tony says nothing. Even Mikey keeps quiet.

Chris says, "Why, Tony?"

Tony says, "Fuck it." He drives until signs for the next rest stop start peppering the road.

They're thirty miles away.

Then twelve miles away.

Then one.

Then Tony veers off the highway into the rest area. Parks under the flickering bulb from the lone lamppost.

Outside the circle of light is all black. Even the white lines of the handful of parking spaces get swallowed up in it. Then it's just the glorified port-o-potty, a soda machine, a snack machine across the way.

Tony and Chris sit a minute, don't move, stare into the non-color between them and the toilets.

Then Tony says fuck it, gets out, heads for the bathroom.

He listens for Chris following him, but there's nothing. Just his own feet clapping against the blacktop.

In the black, it's Marie's horseshit about ugliness, self-awareness. Useless words that soaked into Tony's exhausted brain. The same exhausted brain that spits out imaginary friends. The exhausted brain that thought up every shitty decision. That hates Nate for living and dying. Hates Tony's father more now than when Nate was still alive.

Tony kicks in a bathroom stall door. He pulls the lid off the toilet tank, throws it into the mirror above the sink. He punches the metal wall between stalls. He punches it again. And again. Leaves a fist-sized blotch of red in the dent. He uses the toilet. Pulls the roll of toilet paper out of its plastic case, drops it in the bowl. Flushes.

Before he leaves the bathroom, Mikey says his name.

Tony turns, grabs Mikey by the yellow front-shell, shakes him, then laughs. He says, "If someone walks in right now they'd see me jacking up nothing but air. How fucked up is that?"

Mikey says, "I think you'll feel better if you sleep a little."

"That's what you think? I'll feel better in the morning?"

"Yes?"

"What are we doing out here?"

"Looking for your dad."

"Why?"

"Because he's your dad."

"Fuck that guy."

"He might not be the best at it. But he's yours."

"So?"

"Besides your mom and me, who else do you have?"

Tony stares, his hands tearing Mikey's shell. He breathes fast. Feels his pulse in his neck. Grinds his teeth hot. Then lets go.

Mikey brushes himself off, says, "I didn't know that could happen."

"What's that?"

"I go through stuff. Why didn't you go through me?"

Tony washes his bloody hand in the sink, works around the glass, the chunks of ceramic. He says, "I'm getting worse."

Mikey says, "Or maybe you need to sleep a little."

"Yeah, let's hope that's the case."

Tony wraps his hand in paper towels. He ignores the water pooling on the floor from the toilet he stuffed with paper and opens the bathroom door to find Chris leaning against the soda machine outside.

Chris' eyebrows are up, high arches wrinkling his forehead. His jaw clenches, unclenches.

Tony says, "Mind if I sleep a bit?"

"Nope. Could use a little myself."

Tony turns, walks to the car. Chris doesn't make much noise walking, but Tony knows he's a few steps back. He says, "What'd you hear?"

"Glass."

"Want to go home?"

"Leaning that way."

"Will you change your mind after some sleep?" Tony unlocks the car, opens the door.

Chris says, "Depends on who you were talking to in there."

"What's the right answer?"

Chris gets in the car, closes the door. Tony does the same.

Chris says, "I think you just answered my question right there."

Tony says nothing. He puts down his seatback, sets a couple of alarms on his phone. He turns onto his side, his back to Chris. He closes his eyes telling himself he'll sleep a half an hour, hour tops. No sleep, he gets back on the road. Whether Chris wants to continue on or not.

***

Tony stood in the staff lot smoking in full view of the students. He stared at the front of the building, the glass doors swinging open, closed as the kids left for the day. He hadn't thought he'd miss the place. He'd figured he'd been there for the last time the day he was fired.

But he missed it, smoking, remembering the things he'd done there as a student, staff. Most of the good memories from when he was a student.

He'd waited for his bus back then, leaning against the wall down a ways from the main doors.

He'd hidden in the bushes, skipping class with Chris near the side entrance.

He'd made out with Karen where he was standing.

Students walked through the student lot staring. Some teachers waved, looked around like they were doing something wrong. Others saw him, dropped their eyes to the ground, looked at their phones, pretended they were late for something.

Most everyone was gone by the time Chris came outside. He walked across the lot heading for Tony, smiled, made a face, said, "Can't you get arrested for having no business on a school campus?"

Tony lit a cigarette, said, "I'm still waiting on the bill for the painting I carved up."

Chris' face changed fast. He said, "What did you do?"

"Never mind."

"So, what? Are you here to take me to an early dinner or something?"

"Maybe after."

"After what?"

Tony talked about his father. About the hunting trip. About the disappearance, the radio silence. About the stupidity of old people

who know nothing about modern technology.

Chris asked for a cigarette when Tony finished.

Tony said, "Thought you wanted to quit."

"You're a bad influence."

"Shut up. You're just like me."

Chris coughed through the smoke, laughed, said, "I'm nothing like you."

"So?"

"So, what?"

"You in?"

Chris laughed again. Coughed again. Started talking, but was cut off by Principal Adler yelling across the parking lot.

Tony said, "Shit."

"Mr. D'Angelo you have thirty seconds to get off campus before I call the police and have escorted you off. And Mr. Hogan, I need to see you a minute. Now."

Tony asked Chris to meet him at the bar after Adler puts the final touches on his new asshole. But before he could get in his car he heard Adler say that he should be expecting a hefty bill for the painting he destroyed.

Tony called across the lot, said, "Good thing I moved then," and got in his car, drove to the bar.

It didn't take long for Chris to show up. A beer, a smoke outside. But when he walked in he called Tony a jackass, said, "You'll be paying my tab."

Tony laughed, said, "I'm unemployed. I was about to tell you the same thing."

It was a beer, a smoke, another beer and a shot of Goldschläger before Chris talked about anything other than the shit that was left in Tony's wake.

He talked about the rumors that had been snuffed out—something about Tony punching Adler.

He talked about the student campaign to bring Tony back—he was popular in the slacker circles.

He talked about Adler turning over a new leaf in his dictatorship—started making daily rounds, popping into classrooms of the teachers thirty and under, giving them notes afterward. Pages of notes.

"You caused some major shit to come down on all of us," Chris said.

"Whatever. Sorry, I guess."

Chris laughed, said, "See? Nothing like you."

Tony gave Chris the finger. "Listen," he said. "I'm going to go get my dad back. I want you to come with me."

"When?"

"Soon as possible."

"When's that, in your mind?"

"I'm ready to go tonight if you can swing it."

Chris ordered another round of shots. "Your mom's cool with you just driving off and leaving her alone?"

"Still working on that one."

After more beer, more cigarettes, Chris stopped asking questions, listened to Tony's plan without saying much.

Tony said it was simple. They get on the road, head in the direction of his father's last whereabouts. They would track his father's movements using the mobile wallet app that gives the names of the places where he pays using his bank card or the credit card linked to that account. From that information, they can Google search the addresses and alter their course when they need to.

"Couple days," Tony said. "Five, max."

"I think you may be underestimating the human need for sleep."

"We'll drive in shifts."

"If you fly and rent a car you'll get him quicker."

"If we fly we'll lose an entire day sitting on a plane while he keeps driving. By the time we land he could be twelve hours ahead of us in any direction. Plus, road trip. We never got to do that. We always said we'd do that someday."

"I think 'someday' has passed, man."

"Come on."

"We were eighteen when we talked about that," Chris said, sipping his beer, looking at Tony funny. The kind of funny that made Tony think, pity. Or worry. Or fucking nuts.

Mikey, at the other side of the bar, waving, Shirley Temple in hand, made Tony think fucking nuts may not be inaccurate. But he didn't want Chris doing anything out of pity, and he told him so.

Chris said, "Tony, man, look. If we go, emphasis on if, you need to promise me that when things get too...bleak out there, that we'll turn back around."

"Deal."

"Don't say it like that. That was too fast."

Tony waited a bit, said deal again.

"Say you promise."

"I promise."

"Again. Too fast. I feel like you're way too excited about this."

Tony stood, went outside for a smoke. Hoped Chris would follow him. Which he did.

They smoked together. They didn't say much until Tony said, "You should have seen, Mom, man. When I told her I found him?"

Chris didn't say anything.

Tony waited, didn't look at Chris, slowed his smoking pace.

Chris said, "What's Maura saying about all this?"

"She's cool with it."

Chris cocked an eyebrow.

"I'm serious."

"What was all that shit about moving?"

"I lied."

"You've been doing a lot of that lately." Chris scraped his cigarette on the wall, tossed the butt in a bucket filled with butts and sludgy black water. He said, "I'm in. Give me a day."

"Yes," Tony said. "Thank you. I need you with me."

"Just as long as we don't take your piece of shit car."

Tony tossed his cigarette in the bucket, laughed, slapped Chris' back, said, "You're the boss."

"Liar."

"At least I'm consistent."

***

It's a tap on the window.

Then it's someone saying wake up.

Then it's Tony sitting upright in the driver's seat staring through the window at a gun barrel.

Tony says Chris' name.

Then he smacks Chris' chest.

Chris says, "What?" Then, "Oh, shit."

Mikey, in the backseat, says, "Let me get him."

Tony shushes Mikey.

The guy outside, all scraggly hair and bug eyes, taps the gun on the window again, says, "Out."

Tony opens his door. Chris opens his.

The guy says, "Give me all your shit—what's taking you so long? Get over here."

Chris apologizes, says, "Just take it easy. We'll do whatever you want." He rounds the front of the car.

Tony roots through his pockets, hands over his wallet, phone, car keys, lighter, pack of Dentyne Ice.

"I don't want your fucking gum," the guy says.

Tony says he can have it if he wants it. He says, "I always carry—"

"Shut the fuck up."

Chris says, "Tony, shut the fuck up."

The guy says, "Both of you shut the fuck up." Then he points the gun at Chris, tells him to hand over everything he has.

While Chris pulls his wallet, keys, and coins out of his pocket, Tony watches Mikey point to places on the guy that Tony could punch, kick, break, stab, and pull. Tony could kick the side of the guy's knee, bust the kneecap, make the leg bend in, send bone through skin. He could karate chop the gun arm, knock the gun to the ground, pick it up and put six bullets in the guy's craggy face. He could grab the guy's balls, squeeze until they pop like grapes in his fist.

But Tony does nothing.

The guy says, "Your phone, too."

Chris says, "I don't have a phone."

"Yeah," Tony says. "He's a Luddite."

The guy says, "The fuck's a Luddite?"

"Like the Amish without religion."

The guy puts the gun to Chris' forehead, tells Tony he talks too much. He turns back to Chris, tells him to give up the phone or he'll kill them both.

Chris says, "Really. I don't have a phone."

The guy looks back and forth between Chris and Tony. Both have their hands up, their legs spread.

Tony wonders if a bullet hurts.

The guy pats Chris down, runs through his pockets, digs down the front of his pants, down the back. He says, "Whatever. Move." Then slides himself behind Chris, tells them both to walk away.

Tony and Chris back away slow.

Tony watches the guy get in the car, put the key in the ignition, turn it. The car chokes sputters, chokes, shakes and coughs itself silent.

Tony almost laughs.

The guy tries again. Same thing. He says, "What the fuck?"

Tony says, "What's the matter?"

"Your car's a piece of shit."

"It's old. Give it another shot."

The guy points the gun at Tony, says, "Keep walking."

The car comes through again. The guy yells, punches the steering wheel, honks the horn. He says, "Get back here. Start this fucking thing."

Tony walks slow, his hands up. He tells the guy he's not doing anything stupid. Tells him he's just walking toward the car. That he's keeping his hands up and away from his pockets even though they're empty.

"Will you hurry the fuck up," the guys says.

The guy gets out, makes way for Tony to get in.

He points the gun at Tony's temple, tells him if he tries to drive away he'll kill him, then Chris. Says, "I'll kill your whole family."

Tony laughs.

"What's funny, motherfucker?"

"Nothing."

Tony tries starting the car, ignores the steps it takes to start the thing after too many failed attempts. It does nothing but shake, buck, and die. Tony says he has no idea what's wrong. "Maybe you can try again in a couple of minutes?"

The guys says, "Fuck this." He walks around the car, puts a bullet in every tire.

Tony jumps at each shot, gets rocked side to side after each tire blows.

The guy stops walking after firing the last shot into the front passenger-side tire. He says, "What the fuck is this?" He bends down out of view, pops up holding Chris' phone.

Mikey, in the backseat, says, "Uh oh."

Tony gets out of the car, runs to the back, turns, runs the other way when he sees the guy moving to cut him off. They go back and forth, running, turning around once, twice before the guy starts unloading into the windows.

Tony's sprayed with glass. A window explodes into his face, trips him up, makes him check his eyes, his ears for blood, bullet holes. Another shot dumps glass onto his back, down his shirt. A third peppers his hair. Shards bite into his skin, fall away, leave microtears in his arms, neck, and face that itch more than hurt.

That's when the cops show up. All red and blue lights and shouting for people to freeze.

Tony lies on the ground, face down, covered in glass and bloody little nicks.

He turns his head, sees Chris in the grass checking himself for bullet holes.

Mikey helps the cops tackle the guy, rough him up, cuff him and drag him to the cruiser.

Once the ambulance shows, the cops interview Tony and Chris while EMTs swab Tony's minor wounds, pull bits of glass from his skin, clean up his bloodied punching-hand. The cops talk about the dispatcher thinking the call was a prank until Chris told the guy he'd do whatever was he was asked. They say it was a smart move hiding the phone in the wheel well. They tell Tony he was lucky to have Chris there all clear-headed and collected. They shake Chris' hand, call him a hero.

Cars pull in every so often while the sun comes up. People gawk at the mess, walk to the bathroom. Tony hears talk about some nut who wrecked the place. He must've caused the mess in the parking lot, too. He must've been one serious psycho to cause such damage.

Tony doesn't say it, but he knows they're right.

The cops write reports.

Tony and Chris are told that refusing the trip to the hospital washes the EMTs of all liability. Tony makes a joke about bedside manner. But no one laughs. Not even Mikey.

When the tow truck pulls into the lot, Chris tells Tony that the second the last new tire is bolted onto the car, the first place they're going is the closest airport.

Then he says, "It won't matter if you get on the plane with me or not."

17

Tony and Chris don't talk much after they check in to the hotel down the road from the autobody shop.

Over breakfast and morning smokes it's how nice Fort Collins is. Then it's morning talk shows on the bolted down hotel television talking for them. A nap that only lasts as long as the sun takes to burn through the closed drapes.

Over lunch and beers Tony picked up at the convenience store next door it's Chris on the phone with work telling them he'll be back sooner than expected. Then it's Tony checking up on his father's whereabouts, closing, and reopening the app for up-to-the-minute updates while Chris sleeps through the afternoon after finishing his food.

And at the Applebee's down the road, it's Tony eating dinner alone while Chris books his flight back at the room.

Tony gets a little drunk. Talks to people who come and go at the bar, makes up some bullshit about how he bloodied up his hand, tells the truth about why he's got hundreds of red lines etched all over his skin. Then he starts talking to Mikey and is asked to leave for weirding out the customers.

Chris is already asleep when Tony spills into the room. Chris' bags are packed, tomorrow's clothes laid out.

Tony flops onto the empty bed, gets a friend request from Marie. He doesn't remember giving her his last name. He drifts off to sleep, his thumb hovering over the Ignore icon next to a picture of her graying hair blowing across her face.

At the shop in the morning, Tony asks for an expected timeframe on the car.

"Couple hours," the shop manager says.

"My friend's trying to catch a flight. Do you have a time in mind?"

"Couple hours."

"If I provide the duct tape and the trash bag for one of the windows will it reduce the price and the time?"

"Maybe."

He calls his mother in a CVS, waiting in line to pay for a box of trash bags and an extra large roll of duct tape.

He says, "Trip's going well."

And, "Shouldn't be much longer. Dad hasn't moved in a couple of days."

And, "How are you?"

His mother tells him she's fine. She's working. Watching her shows at night. She says, "I started a new book, too. *11/22/63* by Stephen King? Read that one? It's about a guy who goes back in time to stop Kennedy from being assassinated."

The shop beeps through on the other line.

Tony tells her he's got to get going. He'll check in soon. He tells his mother he loves her, ends the call.

Four tires, a new windshield, and three windows all on Tony's credit card.

The trash bag in the back thumps in the wind on the ride back to the hotel, doesn't matter how fast he goes. He still doesn't want to think about the sound it'll make on highways.

Mikey says, "That's annoying."

Tony says, "So are you."

He texts Chris, tells him the car's ready.

Chris is waiting outside when Tony pulls up.

Nothing's said. Neither of them looks the other in the face. They load gear into the trunk, nothing but the sound of feet on blacktop.

In the car, Chris says, "Ready?"

Tony says, "Yeah," doesn't ask Chris to change his mind.

The drive to Denver is silent. Aside from the bag. Between sixty and eighty miles an hour it takes on the pitch of a small prop plane.

Tony gets used to it.

Chris doesn't talk about it, his elbow on the armrest, two fingers at the corner of his eyebrow keeping his head up.

Denver International reminds Tony of Nate's outdoor high school sports banquets. Giant white tents folded over one another, forming patterns with the center poles poking up into the sky. Just on a scale that shifts it from a gaudy prep school ego-stroke to a city from a science fiction movie.

Tony pulls over at the American Airlines terminal.

Chris gets out, goes around back, opens the trunk, closes it, steps up onto the sidewalk and starts walking toward the glass doors.

Mikey stays silent in the backseat.

Tony shuts the car off, gets out, tells Chris to stop, wait.

Chris turns, says, "Yeah?"

"I'm sorry."

Chris smiles, laughs a little, says, "This doesn't have to be a thing."

"I'm serious."

"I know you are."

Tony lights a cigarette, leans against the car, runs his finger around a sanded down exit wound in the metal from one of the bullets.

Chris says, "Why don't you come home? Leave that thing here, buy a ticket and come home."

"I can't."

"We're going to need to talk about some things."

"Yeah, I know."

"Things that make me a little more than worried, man."

"Yeah, I know."

Chris points to Tony's cigarette. Tony hands it over. Chris smokes it, says, "I'm quitting. For real this time."

"Just wait until I get home. Me being a bad influence and all." Tony sparks up a new smoke.

"I'll look forward to it. When do you think that'll be?"

"Who knows. Maybe I'll hit California and decide to stay."

"You hate the sun."

"Northern California."

"You're afraid of earthquakes."

"Maybe I'll head up to Seattle."

"You'd rather kill yourself than deal with dreary weather three hundred and thirty days a year."

"I'll get medicine."

"You self-medicate enough."

They laugh, smoke. But things get quiet again.

Tony looks at Chris, waits for him to say something, then looks at his shoes. He does it again. A third time. And every time he does it he knows Chris is staring right at him.

Tony drops his cigarette, crushes it under his foot.

Chris says, "Jesus, man." He smacks Tony's shoulder.

Tony says, "What?" He stands up straight.

Then Chris hugs Tony. Not long enough for Tony to feel like he could laugh. But long enough to keep him quiet.

Chris slaps his back, pulls away, says, "I'll see you when you get home." He slings his duffel bag over his shoulder, turns, walks into the airport. He doesn't look back once.

Tony leans against the car. Watches Mikey walk toward the airport turnstile doors and wave to Chris as he fades into the crowd. Takes a breath, holds it, lets it out slow.

The next breath takes a couple tries to get down.

Mikey turns, says, "What?"

Tony says, "Nothing. I'm good."

Mikey sticks out his thumb, throws it behind his back, says, "I like him."

Tony says, "Me too."

People stare, but Tony ignores them. He says, "Ready?"

"Cowabunga, dude."

In the car, Mikey riding shotgun, Tony turns the engine over on the first try.

The solid directional arrow pops on in the dash.

Tony curses, turns on his hazards, turns them off, and the turn signal stops glowing.

Tony says, "That was easy."

Mikey says, "Where are we going?"

Tony pulls his phone from his pocket, logs into the mobile banking app. He Googles the location of his father's last charge, plugs it into

his GPS, shifts into drive, and pulls away from the curb.

***

Tony's mother stared at his phone while he explained his plan. His plan to drive in shifts with Chris to wherever his father may be.

He said, "If he moves, we'll know."

And, "We'll adjust our route along the way with the GPS."

And, "Shouldn't take more than five, six days. Seven tops."

His mother stood up from the table after he finished talking. She made a pot of coffee, filled a mug for herself, said, "I don't think so."

Tony made a face, looked at Mikey sitting at the end of the table, said, "Why?"

"I don't think this is a good idea."

"Mom, it's the best idea. Actually, it's the only idea. For whatever reason, Dad is freaked out and driving in any direction but the one that leads back here."

"His son is dead."

"Yeah. But you're not. I'm not."

Tony's mother smacked her hand down on the table. She said she didn't care. That everyone copes with loss in their way. That Tony's father not coming home isn't about his wanting to be with his family or not, it's about not having the family he once had. She said, "He'll come home when he's ready."

"What about work, Mom? What happens when they fire him for not showing up, or even calling in to take a leave of absence?"

His mother stood, said, "How do you know he hasn't already done that?"

"Because he didn't bother to call us."

Tony had to run through every excuse he could've made for his father. Over and over. Nate getting his hands on the debit card because his father had gotten careless—or had begun trusting Nate too much. Again. The whole I Killed Your Brother talk that did little else but dump his guilt onto someone else to make himself feel better.

Tony said, "Look." He sat down, said, "Dad feels guilty. I get it. But he can't run out on us like this and not expect one of us to do something about it."

His mother hit the table again, used her fist this time. She said, "So now you're going to run out on me?"

"You wanted me to go with him, Mom. How is this different?"

"Because it is, Anthony."

Tony wanted to say something profound then. Something about putting the family back together. Or trying to make up for the things he's done. Or needing to do this for himself too. But it was all soapy and disingenuous. There was nothing else in his head aside from going and getting his father. Maybe it was spite. Maybe it was an actual need for his father to be where he should be.

Tony said, "Maybe I just need to show him I can do something right."

His mother, said, "You've never needed to prove anything."

"That's bullshit, Mom."

They didn't say anything for a while. Tony watched his mother blow on her coffee, watched her pick at her her fingernails. Watched her look around the room for the first time since Nate died without staring through the walls.

She finished her coffee, said, "You can't leave me."

"I'm not leaving you, Mom. That's not what this is."

"I wanted you to go with him because it would've been good for you both. And you'd both be back on schedule. But if you go out chasing him, I could be here alone for...for however long it takes for one of you to turn around."

Nothing got dramatic. No one started screaming or crying. Tony's mother poured herself another cup of coffee, went into the living room, turned on the television.

Tony followed her. He sat next to her on the couch.

They watched a Supernatural rerun, the news at noon.

Tony responded to Chris' texts about getting time off by telling him he'd call him later.

It was past one when his mother said, "Why aren't you working?"

Without thinking up some story, without backpedaling, without leaving the room and telling her he had something to take care of, he said, "I got fired."

She nodded. She sipped from her mug. She said, "I'm not stupid, you know."

"I know that."

"Was it Karen?"

"What?"

"Karen. Was she the one who broke you and Maura up?"

Tony breathed deep, said, "No. It was just me."

She took Tony's hand, said, "You're a good boy. You want to be anyway. But trying to bring your father back won't fix things. And I can't let another piece of my life go if I can stop it. I couldn't stop Nathan. I couldn't stop your father even if I knew he wasn't going to come home. But I can stop you. Or at least ask you to stop yourself."

Tony's mother stood, walked to the bathroom. After a while, Tony knocked on the bathroom door.

His mother opened the door, tissues in hand, and sat back in the divot she'd left in the couch.

And Tony had nothing to say. Just words floating around his brain about family. What was left of his family. Over and over.

Family.

He stood, picked up his car keys.

Mikey, trying back flips ending in back flops in the dining room, sat up said, "Where are we going?"

Tony walked to the front door.

His mother said, "Where are you going?"

He turned said, "I won't be long."

"You didn't answer my question."

"I'll be back." Tony smiled, opened the door, waited for Mikey to follow him.

In the car, Mikey kept telling Tony how stupid his idea was.

He said, "You're going to get beat up," and, "You can't fight like I can," and, "You're going to make your mom cry again when you come home all gross and bloody."

Tony knew all that.

He didn't say anything. He made the turns he'd memorized. Took the shortcuts he'd figured out by not wanting someone to recognize his car.

And when he pulled up to the curb in front of Karen's house he had to tell Mikey to shut up before he changed his mind.

***

Tony's father drives like he knows he's being chased.

For every rest stop, restaurant, and gas station Tony stops in off I-80 toward Carson City, his father moves south.

Tony takes short breaks. Naps in crowded parking lots. Eats on the run. Takes enough 5 Hour Energy to make him sweat. Mikey's manic rambling is enough to keep Tony's chin from dipping to his chest more than once or twice. But he can't think of a time when he was more exhausted.

His father hits drive-thrus in Mammoth Lakes, California. Fills his rental's tank in Big Pine. Probably orders more coffee than food. Maybe uses empty bottles to empty his bladder. Might be running on so little sleep that his body is operating on some need to keep moving.

It may be the first thing in recent memory Tony can identify that they have in common. Running on empty. Chasing whatever. Despite what they're chasing down they're both defying everything their bodies tell them.

Just outside Carson City, Mikey sounds like he's talking from inside a fish tank. Muffled, distant. But right in front of Tony's face.

Then Tony falls asleep.

The car drifts to the right. Passes over the rumble strip, grinds into the guardrail. And Tony wakes up and screams.

He jerks the wheel to the right just missing the sign welcoming him to Nevada's capital in old-timey letters straight from a Tex Avery cartoon.

Tony looks at Mikey.

Mikey looks at Tony.

Tony says, "I think I need to stop for a while."

"Duh."

Tony keeps himself awake by looking up all of his father's account activity in Carson City, finding the hotel he stayed in. He sets his course, drives on, then notices the mountain range backdrop. Lumpy and massive, imposing themselves over the city. They're everywhere. Straight ahead, left, right. Tony had always heard the western ranges were something to see at least once. But Pennsylvania has mountains, he'd thought. Pennsylvania doesn't have shit.

Mikey says, "Wow."

"Right?"

"Can we climb them?"

"Nope."

"Why?"

"Already feel small enough."

Tony forgets to follow the GPS directions to the Days Inn. He drives down the empty three-lane streets. Reads banners tied to buildings, hanging over intersections telling everyone to conserve water or else. Casinos that look more like corner stores than Atlantic City's glitzy monoliths. A strip of buildings from a spaghetti western all dolled up in flashing lightbulbs. The Bug Spider from *Wayne's World*.

Tony pulls over in front of the VW Bug suspended in the air by eight segmented iron legs. He gets out of the car, walks toward it taking pictures with his phone along the way. He waves for Mikey. He kneels down, switches the camera to face him, takes a photo of himself, Mikey next to him making a face, and the sculpture in the background.

Mikey says, "Can we go now?"

"Yeah. Just felt like I had to stop. Wayne's World was one of Nate's favorites."

Mikey smiles a bit, yawns, says, "Can we go now?" draws out Now like kids do.

Tony pulls up the photo. A picture of his face, the spider car mostly blocked by his head, and the empty space where Mikey would be if he were real.

They get in the car, and Tony follows the directions to the hotel.

He hauls his duffel into the lobby, lays his credit card on the desk, asks for a room.

The girl behind the counter runs his card, says, "You're the second D'Angelo we've had stay with us in the past couple days."

Tony says, "Nathan?"

"Shit—Sorry, I wasn't even supposed to say that."

"If I show you a picture, could you nod if it's a Yes?"

The girl—her name tag says Stephanie—looks around, waves her hand in a way that makes Tony assume she's okay with just looking at a picture.

Tony puts his phone on the desk, his father's picture taking up the whole screen.

Stephanie nods.

"How'd he look?"

"Tired."

"Could you tell me what room he stayed in?"

"That would get me fired." She hands over a keycard, Tony's credit card, and thanks him for staying with them today.

On the walk to the room, Tony turns the keycard over and over in his fingers, says, "Think this was his room?"

Mikey says, "She said she would get fired if she did that."

"But she said that while she was handing me the key. Like, she was saying it without saying it."

"I think you're making stuff up."

"Clearly. I'm talking to you."

Tony unlocks the door, peeks his head inside expecting to find something out of order, some sign his father left for him.

But the room's perfect. Two double beds done up like they've never been used. An end table with a phone, a pad of paper, a Bible, a television remote.

Mikey falls onto one of the beds, falls asleep before Tony can say anything else.

Tony doesn't check pillowcases for a note. He doesn't drop to the floor searching for something his father left behind under the beds. He doesn't tear the room apart thinking his father stayed here when it's clear he didn't.

He turns on the television, tries to sleep. But can't.

He turns off the television, tries again. But can't.

Then he pulls his phone from his pocket, checks his father's bank account. He Googles the hotel from the most recent purchase. A two and a half star Extended Stay America in Temecula, California.

He calls his father. The call goes to voicemail. He says, "Hey, Dad. It's me. Again. Just wanted to let you know that I'm sitting in a room at the Days Inn in Carson City. Thought it was yours for a minute. But it can't be, can it. Even if it were, you wouldn't have left anything for me to find. A note explaining what the hell you're doing and why you're doing it. Just want to let you that I saw something from a movie out here that Nate would have probably loved to see. Maybe that's what you're doing, carrying that vile of dust around to places Nate never got to go? Seeing all the shit he died before he could see. I don't know. Seems to me you're just running. Anyway. I'm tracking you down. Have been for days. I figure I'll eventually catch up with you, or you'll just run out of money and hitchhike home. Whatever. I know where you are. And I'm on my way."

He ends the call.

He fights to get to sleep. When he does drift away the last thought he has is what he'll do when he finally finds his father. He's surprised by what he imagines.

No screaming. No violence.

Just a tired old man asleep in the backseat, his son driving him home.

18

Tony wakes up. Then panics.

He's slept through an entire day, through the night.

But he looks out, the window at the sun just dipping below the desert horizon. A dark navy, hazy sky striped with some pink. He lays back down, figures he couldn't have been asleep for more than an hour or two.

But then he remembers the sun should be setting behind the mountains.

He curses, jumps out of bed, tells Mikey to wake up.

Mikey, in the other bed, says, "What's going on?"

Tony tells him they've been sleeping for the better part of fifteen hours, that his father could be anywhere by now. Mexico. Hawaii. Wherever.

Mikey says, "You can't drive to Hawaii."

"But you can fly. What's stopping him?"

Tony checks his phone. Opens the app.

Still just the Temecula Extended Stay charge.

Tony changes, stuffs his dirties into his duffel bag. The bag's insides smell worse than he does, filled with sweaty, spent clothes. Dressed in his last pair of clean underwear, a shirt he's already worn before, socks on their third day of use and jeans that smell like smoke and fast food, he says, "Ready?"

Mikey tightens the knot of his mask behind his said, says, "Cowabunga."

They're out the door. They jog through the hall. Run through the front doors and into the parking lot.

For sunrise, the humidity makes Tony's armpits sweat, beads up his forehead.

The inside of the car's even worse. Mucky and thick, Tony wipes his forehead on his shoulder. He turns the key. The car doesn't turn over. He tries again.

Nothing.

He waits. Counts to five. Then ten. Then tries again.

The car starts, but the right turn signal flicks on green.

Tony turns on the hazards. Turns them off.

The arrow still glows.

He turns the hazards on again. Leaves them on for a minute, two. He tells Mikey to shut up after a question about catching fire.

He takes a breath, turns the hazards off.

Gray gauges. No lights.

Tony says, "Jesus."

Mikey says, "Really, though. Are we going to catch on fire?"

"Maybe."

Carson City is four hundred sixty-six miles, and eight and a half hours of driving to Temecula according to Tony's GPS. Driving straight through without stopping for anything but gas, food, and toilets would put them in the front of his father's last known whereabouts before sunset. The real sunset.

They pull away from the hotel, stop in the closest convenience store. Tony buys bags of chips, premade breakfast sandwiches, a twelve pack of Coke, two packs of smokes, and a bottle of water the size and shape of a torpedo.

Mikey wants Bagel Bites from the freezer section but Tony tells him to put them back.

The car doesn't start again at first. But the turn signal doesn't come on when Tony's able to get it to turn over.

The car shakes through Carson City. Putts stopped at red lights. Struggles to pick up speed, lets Tony know by screaming through rising RPMs until he gets it rolling up above twenty-five hundred. But once Tony merges onto 395 South the struggle sounds taper off pushing the thing into a consistent groove. But going over sixty-five makes it shudder, so Tony keeps it at sixty. He doesn't bother passing anyone.

Mikey stares out the window.

Tony's father could be sleeping. Wasting time in a hotel room ready to get picked up and go home. He could be replaying Tony's message over and over, swelling with guilt.

Tony turns the radio on full blast to drown out the sound of the trash bag flapping in the back, his father doing whatever the hell. Concentrates, mountains to the right, dead grass and desert to the left.

But the music turns to Tony and his father reuniting to songs Tony grew up on and never let go of. They could talk about music all the way home. They could play songs Nate liked. O.A.R., and Dave Matthews Band, and Phish.

The scenery turns to making a stop at the Grand Canyon together to toss the vial of Nate off the edge. They could stop in Nashville and swim in a guitar shaped pool because Nate never had the chance to. They could stop at Lake Erie because Nate watched Eerie, Indiana as a kid and thought the show took place closer to home than it actually did.

They wouldn't need to talk about why his father ran. It would just be something that happened. And when they got home his father could get Tony a job at the shop. They'd work swing-shifts together. Blue coveralls and lunch pails. Greasy hands and overtime. They could watch the Eagles on Sundays. The Phils during the summer and fall. They could go hunting.

When splitting open a deer with his father fills Tony's head, Mikey taps his shoulder, says, "Pretending is just pretend sometimes."

Tony lights a cigarette, opens a soda can, says, "You're not wrong."

It's a hundred miles before the green arrow pops on again. This time Tony keeps his hazards on for the better part of ten miles.

It's another fifty before Tony checks if his father made any more moves.

Then it's Tony pulling the car to the side of the road, turning it off, getting out and chucking soda cans into the dead grass.

He sits down, leans his back against one of the new tires and smokes.

His father hadn't moved. Not according to his bank records. But he cleared out what was left in his checking account at the ATM in the Extended Stay.

Tony pulls his phone from his pocket, tucks it away.

Repeats that twice.

Then he calls Karen to ask her what the fuck he's supposed to do now.

***

Karen didn't open the door.

She asked him what the fuck he thought he was doing, her voice muffled and distant through the wood. She asked him if he'd heard anything she fucking said to him the last time they were together.

Tony said, "Please just open the door. This has nothing to do with you and me."

"You're talking to me right now, Tony. That literally means there's something to do with you and me."

"You know what I mean. Come on, please?"

"Sam's on his way home. Ever think about what he'll do if he sees you creeping around the house again?"

"It's about Mom and Dad, Karen."

Karen said nothing.

For a while.

Long enough for Tony to knock again, ask hello. Consider stomping his feet with tapering force, saying goodbye, fading his voice to a lesser volume, making her think he was leaving.

But she opened the door, poked her head outside, said, "What about them?"

"Can I come in?"

"No. What about them?"

Tony heard a car, turned his head to look down the lawn at

the street.

Mikey, standing at the curb, said, "Not him."

He turned back to Karen. She raised her eyebrows, shook her head, mouthed what.

"Did you tell—"

"Jesus." She pulls her head back inside, starts closing the door, but

takes her time.

"Wait."

"No, Tony. I didn't tell my husband about our illicit affair, okay?"

"Oh, good."

"That still doesn't mean he won't kick your ass for hanging around our house. And it also doesn't mean that I won't ever decide to tell him even if that means wrecking my life even more than I already have. Or my daughter's life."

"It's a girl?"

"I don't know, I'm just trying out the vocabulary because I wasn't ready for this shit and I hope it'll eventually stop sounding weird."

Another car, another time Tony whipped his head around, another negative from Mikey.

While Tony's head was turned Karen had opened the door a bit wider.

He stared at her stomach. Looked for some swelling. Thought about the birthmark under her bellybutton. Wondered if it would migrate south the bigger she got, or increase in circumference.

When his eyes went to her chest, when he thought that maybe her breasts had plumped a little, Karen said, "Tony. Eyes up."

"Sorry."

"That stuff won't happen for a little while yet. Really looking forward to, it."

Tony made a face, shrugged his shoulders, said he didn't know a whole lot about that sort of thing.

"Your mom and dad?"

"Right. Sorry." He dug his hands into his pockets, rounded his shoulders, said, "Dad never came home from his hunting trip."

"What?" Karen's body shifted. Morphed from rigid and

defensive to something softer, less rehearsed. "What happened? Was there an accident?"

"No. No accident. He's fine. Far as I know."

"What's that mean?"

"He's running. Heading west." He told her how he'd been tracking him. He told her how his father hadn't returned any of his calls, any of his mother's calls. Told her how his mother was handling it, exaggerated some—tears, depression, not bathing.

While Tony explained, Karen's eyes widened, got glassy. She pushed the door all the way open. Let it go. Her arms and hands moved with her questions in the breaks between Tony's sentences.

He said, "I have no one else to go to."

"What about—"

Tony shook his head, said, "She's gone too." He paused a minute, took a breath. "I need to go get him back."

"Good. Yeah, that's good."

"But I can't leave Mom alone."

Karen stiffened. Her shoulders angled. Her jaw clenched.

"Do you know what I'm here for now?" Tony said.

"I'm not sure if you're brave or just fucking stupid."

"I'm leaning toward the latter."

Karen stepped outside, forced Tony to shuffle his feet backward to make room for her on the porch.

Then she slapped him.

"You're a manipulative prick," she said. "You know that, right?"

Tony stared, said nothing. Let the side of his face hum, fill with blood, heat up.

Then he heard another car.

He tried to keep his eyes locked on Karen's, but he turned, saw Mikey running up the lawn, waving. Sam's car screeching to a stop, leaving inches between Tony's bumper and his own.

Tony cursed, turned, watched Sam get out of the car and ask what the fuck.

Hands at his hips, smile on his face—all angles, sinister—Sam walked and talked, calling Tony You, saying he was wondering when Tony would show up again, asking why he showed up again, how he could be so stupid.

Tony took small steps, his hands out in front of him, saying, "Hey, Sam, listen, I'm here for a reason, so if you'll—"

"You trying to fuck my wife?"

"What? No, I—"

"Is he trying to fuck you, Karen?"

Before Karen could say anything, Tony could feel the heat from Sam's face, the tip of his nose grazing his own. He said, "You have three seconds to tell me what you're doing here."

"Sam, I—"

"One."

"You're really counting?"

"Two."

"Sam, just hold on a—"

Sam didn't say three, he backed up, threw his fist at Tony, clobbered him in the side of the head, mashed his ear to his skull, knocked him into the lawn.

It was pain and light. Tinnitus and more pain.

Tony couldn't hear himself say, "Sam, come on. I'm not here to fuck your wife."

He couldn't hear Sam say, "Get up." But he saw his mouth move, form the words.

He couldn't hear anything from Karen. He hoped she was saying something, running down the lawn to stop her husband.

Tony got up. Karen hadn't moved. Sam was squaring up.

They circled each other on the lawn. Sam's hands were in fists, clenched white and held in front of his face. Tony put his hands up, ready to push Sam away, kept telling him he doesn't want to have to hurt him.

They grappled, circled, fell over.

They got up. Tony took another punch to the head, a kick in the ass, and was in the grass again.

Then Sam was sitting on Tony's chest. His hands were in Tony's hair, pulling his head up, driving it back into the dirt, once, twice, three times. Tony was saying he was there to talk about his mother.

Sam said, "Your mother's not going to be able to identify your dead fucking body."

Mikey jumped on to Sam's back. And for a second Tony saw

the kid's hands yanking Sam off him by the ears.

But it was Karen, the back of Sam's collar in her fist.

Sam spat in Tony's face. He said, "Fuck you. If Karen weren't here you'd be dead."

It took Tony a minute to get up, to shake off the lights exploding in his eyes, to wipe the loogie from his cheek. To wave Mikey off, tell him he's good without Karen and Sam seeing.

Tony spit blood into the lawn, said, "I think I bit my tongue."

"You got off light, fucker."

"Do you exclusively talk in clichés? Jesus."

Sam yanked his arm away from Karen, sent a fist into Tony's gut, and Tony back into the grass.

While Tony tried to suck down any air he could, he heard Karen yelling. Heard her telling Sam everything Tony had said. About his mother. His father. How Sam needed to go inside so she could sort this all out for herself. Then she said, "I grew up with him. He's nothing to you. But I'm connected to that family. And not the way you're thinking right now. I swear to God."

Tony was on all fours. He watched Sam stomp inside, slam the door. He let Karen grab his arm, help pull him upright. She said, "You deserved that."

"I know."

Then she grabbed his face, squeezed his cheeks, puckered his lips. She said, "But I do, too. What can I do?"

"You changed your mind?" It came out hoarse, in bursts, belabored and airy.

Her hands fell to her sides. "About me and you? No. But I could use a little redemption."

Mikey, from behind Karen, said, "He could too."

Karen said, "The sooner you get on the road to find your dad the sooner you might be able to get a little yourself."

She walked toward the house, said she'd be back in a minute.

Tony said, "Thanks, Karen. Can't tell you how much—"

"Don't thank me. This isn't for you."

"Okay."

"Go home. I'll meet you there."

Tony got in his car, started driving. He didn't turn on any music, told Mikey to shut up. He listened to the clicking in the

back of his throat. Hoped it was mucus stuck back there, not
something that had come loose from Sam's punch.

***

Tony does what Karen suggests. He drives. As fast as he can
for as long as he and his car can stand it.

He doesn't check for any more charges. Doesn't talk much.

He speeds when he can. Pays attention to the GPS app Karen
suggested that gives the locations of cops on the road. He does
between seventy and eighty, sometimes ramps it up to ninety
when the roads empty.

But the car struggles. Shakes, labors up the dials in the dash.
Turns itself off when he parks to use a bathroom. Refuses to turn
over enough for Tony to attempt to forget how many times he
tries. Burns

through a tank of gas every hundred miles.

He loses an hour trying to start the car in Bishop, California
after filling up.

Just past Lone Pine it's the turn signal arrow popping on
whenever. Then the hazards stop fixing the problem. And Tony
has to pull the car onto the shoulder, shut it off, start it up to get
rid of the green in the dash.

But just south of Owens Lake the arrow glows green every time
Tony taps the brake pedal.

So he doesn't use the brakes.

He tries not to.

He watches the GPS's traffic patterns for the red, orange lines.
He watches the break lights ten, twenty car lengths ahead. And
when he's forced to, he drifts onto the rumble strip to slow the
car down.

When he can't avoid the brakes, Mikey lets him know when
his foot's been on the pedal too long, says, "What's that smell?"

Tony smells it too. Acrid and noxious. The car telling him he's
running out of time.

He drives on anyway.

San Bernardino offers traffic he can't avoid.

He pulls off 215, finds a parking lot, smokes and finishes off
his last sodas.

An hour passes, Mikey says, "Now?"

Tony turns on the car, the arrow follows.

Another hour, Mikey says, "Can we go now?"

Tony turns the car on. No arrow.

He punches the ceiling, screams fuck yes.

The arrow is on in the dash when he checks again.

Tony finishes off his pack of smokes. He buys another in the gas station across the street. Smokes two more cigarettes. Tries again. No arrow.

Forty-eight miles from Temecula, Tony and Mikey talk about anything, everything, trying to ignore all the new sounds coming from underneath the hood. And under their feet. Deep in the dash.

Tony turns on an old Blink-182 album. "Dude Ranch", the one he liked despite calling himself a punk in high school. He assigned songs to specific moments with Karen back then. The nasty words she called him when he was a dick. Watching her dress. Seeing her talking to other guys in the halls at school.

Now, Tony and Mikey sing every word. They don't miss, flub, or mix up a single one. And by the time the last track repeats its title over and over again, Tony can't stop repeating I'm Sorry as the car coughs into the Extended Stay America parking lot, as it shuts down before he can pull into a parking spot.

He lets the car roll into a parking block, buck with the impact, stop dead.

Over the metal clinks from parts that haven't stopped spinning yet, Tony says, "Ready?"

Mikey says nothing, takes a breath, nods.

Tony walks through the lot, pulls up his father's picture on his phone.

He walks through the automatic doors, shivers with the filtered air crawling over his sweaty skin.

But his heart's fast, his pits wet, his breathing's heavy.

He steps up to the counter, smiles, says hello, and lays his phone down for the attendant to see. Tony says, "Has this man stayed here?"

"Sir, I'm sorry—"

"Look, I know you're not allowed to divulge information about your customers, okay? But this is my father. This hotel is the last place I can confirm he's been. I need you to tell me if you've seen him."

The attendant doesn't look at the picture, says, "I haven't seen him."

Tony laughs, looks at Mikey, says, "He didn't even look."

"Excuse me?"

"You didn't look at the picture."

"Even if I did, sir, there's no way I could answer one way or the other. You are not the police. You are not the FBI."

"But I'm a person."

The attendant stands, says, "Yes. With a fairly convincing story. But I'm sorry, unless you want a room our conversation is over."

"I want a room."

"Great."

"Have you seen this man?"

"How long do you expect to say with us?"

Tony takes the phone off the desk without pulling his eyes way from the attendant's. He opens the banking app, checks for recent purchases, says, "Hopefully just a night or two."

"Which?"

"Two."

Tony hands over his credit card, his ID, and waits for his keycard.

Once the attendant slides the key across the counter, Tony says, "More than likely I'll be sitting in the lobby quite a bit, though, waiting to see if my father walks through because you're being so helpful."

"You're welcome to use any and all of the facilities available to you, sir. Enjoy your stay."

On the elevator, Mikey waits until Tony finishes off a breakdown, counts six dollars and seventy-five cents in quarters that Tony needs to add to the Swear Jar.

"Fuck you."

"Seven bucks."

Off the elevator, through the hall, Tony fights the urge to knock on every door, see if his father's there, ask if they've seen him. He'd say, "Hi, Dad. Let's go home." Or, "Hi, have you seen my father," and hold up the picture.

But he doesn't do that.

He unlocks the door to room 408, let's Mikey inside, drops his duffel to the floor.

Tony turns, sticks his foot between the door and the door jam, says, "Huh."

Mikey says, "What?"

Tony laughs, points across the hall at 407. The Do Not Disturb sign crammed in the keycard slot. "What if that's Dad's room?"

Mikey says, "I don't think it is."

"What if it is?"

"You're sleepy. Go to sleep."

"I'll bet it's his room."

Mikey says nothing.

The silence forces Tony to turn around, see the kid standing, fists on hips, saying, "See if you think that when you wake up."

Tony gets in bed.

He stares at the ceiling.

Refuses to think about the possibility of his father sleeping across the hall.

But anything's possible. Anything.

Mikey, from the next bed says, "Not that."

Tony falls asleep with an image of his father opening the door to 407 imprinted on the insides of his eyelids.

19

Tony knocks on 407.

Nothing.

He knocks again.

Nothing.

Mikey says people put Do Not Disturb signs on their doors for a reason.

Tony rubs his eyes until he sees spots. A collective hour of sleep spread over a full night of images and fantasies. A series of What If scenarios, a string of Maybe If I variations. A night of constant imaginary friend reinforcement that nothing in Tony's head makes any sense.

Tony pulls his phone from his pocket, checks if his father has made any moves since the ATM withdraw downstairs.

Nothing.

Tony knocks on the door again.

Mikey says, "Shower. You'll feel better after a shower. And

breakfast. Maybe breakfast pizza?"

Tony says, "Fuck this," takes a few steps down the hall to 405, knocks.

A woman, Tony's age, opens the door a crack, asks if she can help him.

Tony holds up his phone, the picture of his father, says, "Have you seen this man? Maybe going in and out of the room next door?"

The woman contorts her face, says, "No. Sorry," and closes the door.

Tony hears the conversation inside the room. Something about some nut smelling like smoke and sweat.

Tony crosses the hall to 406, knocks.

A man opens this time, says what.

"Have you seen this man?"

"Nope." The door closes.

Before moving to the next door, Tony calls his father. When he's told to leave a message at the beep, he says, "Dad, it's me. I'm in 408 in the Extended Stay America you are staying in. I think you're 407. Open the—"

On the other line, a robot tells Tony his father's inbox is full.

Tony goes to 403.

Then 404.

Then 401.

Two no-answers and a fuck off.

Mikey says Tony's name, tells him to stop, says, "Come on, he's not here. Please stop. Come on."

Tony tells Mikey to shut up, surprises himself with the volume of his voice.

A door opens. The woman from the 405.

Tony waves, says, "Sorry."

Back in their room, Tony calls his mother. He says, "He's here. I know it. I've almost got him. I'll call when I have more to tell you."

His mother says, "Anthony, what's the matter?"

"What do you mean?"

"Are you okay?"

He tells her he's fine, says he'll call again soon.

He calls Karen, says, "I'm pretty sure he's here. I'm working on a way to smoke him out of his hole."

Karen says, "Tony. Do you hear yourself?"

"Literally? Yes."

"That's not what I mean."

"What do you mean?"

"Are you sure he's there?"

"Pretty sure. Right across the hall."

"Tony..."

"Tony what?"

"I think it's time to come home."

Tony ends the call. He winds up, almost throws his phone, but stops drops it into his pocket.

He throws the TV remote instead.

It shatters against the wall. Plastic and batteries clattering against the end table, the headboard, the walls.

Mikey, on the bed, sitting the way Nate was sitting when Tony found him, stares into his lap. Same way Nate was staring.

Tony says, "Stop sitting like that."

"Sorry."

"How many rooms do you think are in the hotel?"

"I don't know. Why?"

"I have an idea."

Tony takes the notepad from the desk next to the TV stand. He sits, starts writing.

He starts with Dear Dad.

He writes about Nate. Scribbles down everything that comes to his head. Hating him. Wanting to be nothing like him. All the times he'd wished Nate had died when they were younger when he felt left out and left behind. How much he regrets wishing that now. How much he wants to miss him for the right reasons but can't figure out what the fuck those right reasons are.

Then he writes about himself. All the horrible things he's done. Maura. Karen. The baby. The trip. The reasons he thought he went after his father. The actual reasons he went after his father.

Then he writes about his father. How fucking furious he is with him for doing this. How tired he is. How he wishes that the next time he calls his mother she'll tell him his father just got home, took a flight out of San Diego.

He writes I'm not sure you deserve me chasing after you.

And, But I chased you anyway. I'm across the hall. You won't open the door. You haven't returned any of my calls.

And, I want to go home. I don't have too much left to go home to, but I want to go home. Hopefully with you.

He signs Love Tony.

Mikey follows him out the door, says, "Where are we going?"

"Do you think the hotel has a Xerox machine they'd let me use?"

In the elevator, Mikey says, "Can we go home after this?"

"He's here. I know it."

"We both know he's not here. If I'm saying it, we both know it."

"That's not true."

Mikey hits the emergency stop button.

The lights dim, a buzzer sounds.

Mikey says, "Who did that, then?"

"You did."

"Stop it. Who did that?"

Tony reads his letter again. Catches some misspellings. Regrets how many times he wrote fuck.

Mikey says, "Who hit that button?"

Tony doesn't say anything for a beat, two. Then, "I did."

"Once you're done with that, let's go home."

"He's here. I know it."

"Then lets leave that for him and go home."

"If I don't go back with him it's like I failed. At another thing."

"Nuh-uh."

"Yuh-huh. I promised."

Mikey taps his finger on the paper in Tony's hand, says, "Did you say what you needed to say in that?"

"Yeah."

"Then let's leave it and go."

"What about Mom?"

"She won't be mad. You'll be back."

Tony reads the letter again. He checks his father's bank records on his phone. He sucks back something wet in his nose.

Mikey says, "Please."

Tony folds the paper in two, nods. Then he hits the emergency stop button.

The lights come back on, the buzzing stops. The elevator jerks to life takes them to the lobby.

***

Karen didn't knock. Just walked in the house like she used to.

She closed the door behind her, hung her purse on the banister. And before she could say anything, Tony's mother was up off the couch saying hello and walking with her arms held out wide.

A hug. A few kisses on the cheek. A series of greeting questions that were more family than guest.

Tony's mother directed Karen to the fridge if she wanted something, told her to take anything she wants. She asked if Karen was hungry, said she could make something.

How was work, life, Sam.

Were there any plans for babies.

Karen cocked an eyebrow at Tony, said she and Sam were working on the baby thing.

Tony made coffee while his mother and Karen talked in the living room. He heard his mother tell Karen the same things she'd said to him about his father's disappearance. "He'll come back when he's ready," and, "He's figuring some things out," and "It's not a surprise, it's—"

"Someone has to go get him," Karen said. "You know that, right?"

Tony walked the coffees into the living room during the silence.

He sat next to Karen.

She scooted herself an inch or two further down the couch from him.

Karen put her hand on Tony's mother's. She said, "You do know that."

Tony's mother lifted her mug from the coffee table with her free hand, blew into it, said, "Of course I know that."

Karen said, "Tony told me he's ready to head out whenever you're okay with him leaving."

Tony's mother sipped her coffee, said, "I won't be okay with it." She points at Tony, still stares into Karen's eyes. "It's him and me now. Without him, it's just me. And what do I do then? I don't want to be the lonely old lady whose family ran from her when things got bad. I don't want to be a Hallmark movie. I don't want people to wonder where I've been. I don't want my neighbors to send police to the house because of the smell of a rotting old corpse sitting in this chair waiting for someone to come home."

Tony and Karen stared, their mouths hanging open.

Tony's mother said, "That was...that was joke, guys."

Karen said, "Think I finally figured out where Tony gets his sense of humor."

Tony laughed, said, "Yeah, morbid stuff's—"

"I didn't say it was funny."

"Okay, then."

Karen sipped from her mug, said, "What if I told you you wouldn't have to be alone while Tony was gone? If you had someone here with you, would you be okay with Tony leaving for a few days to get Nathan back?"

Tony's mother laughed, stood, said, "I sound that pathetic, don't I? This is completely pathetic."

"It's not pathetic to want someone around. Not after everything. Maybe if this happened a year from now, things would be different, but everything's so fresh."

Tony stood, said, "Yeah, Mom. Come on—"

"Will you please?" Karen said. "Just stop for a minute, okay?"

Tony clenched his jaw, said, "Sorry."

Karen stood, said, "What if I make sure you don't feel alone? What if I'm around while Tony's gone?"

Tony's mother cupped Karen's face in her hands, kissed her forehead. "I wouldn't ask you to do something like that."

"I'm not waiting for you to ask. Tony has to do this. And I want to help."

"Karen, stop."

"Mom," Tony said. "Think about—"

Karen said, "Tony. Go upstairs."

And he went. Not without almost cursing. Not without wanting to ask her what her fucking problem was. But he didn't because he already knew.

Mikey reminded him of all that upstairs in his room.

Tony tried to listen to the conversation going on below him from the same spot he would listen to his parents discuss his behavior when he was a teenager. At his desk, door open, leaning forward in his seat.

Mikey stood at the top of the steps, said he couldn't hear any better than Tony could.

Tony shushed him. Listened.

It was talk of family. Love. Repaying kindnesses. All sentiment and sap. Stuff Tony would have said if Karen hadn't sent him to his room. Stuff Tony agrees with but wouldn't be able to say out loud unless getting his way was in jeopardy.

When he heard footsteps on the steps, saw Mikey flagging him away from the door, he got up, jumped onto his bed.

His desk chair was still spinning when Karen walked into the room.

She said, "Listening in?"

"What makes you say that?"

"We spent like a third of our lives pawing at each other in this room. I'm not stupid." She pointed at the chair's slowing spin. "And that."

Tony sat up, said, "What did she say?"

"I'm going to check in during the days. Eat dinner, drink coffee here at night. Watch some TV with her, or go to the mall or the movies. Anything she feels like doing. I'll be on-call."

"What about Sam?"

"I don't know yet. I'll have to make him understand."

"Thank you. I'd hug you if you'd let me."

Karen leans against the doorjamb, purses her lips, says, "We've got to work our way back to handshakes first, Tony."

Tony nodded, crossed his arms over his chest. "So, you want to make your way back to that, then?"

Karen pushed away from the wall, sat on the bed, took a breath. "For whatever reason, I can't seem to get rid of you."

"Do you want to get rid of me?"

"Want the truth?"

"Yeah, I want the truth." Tony sat up.

"Yes. I do want to get rid of you."

Tony flopped back down onto the bed, said, "Yikes."

"But maybe you'll come back different."

Tony sat up, rolled off the bed, stood, said, "Can't make any promises."

Karen stood up, grabbed Tony's arm on his way out the door.

"But that's the point to all this, isn't it?"

"To what? Make promises I can't keep?"

"To start making some you can."

"To who?"

"Yourself. Your Mom. Your Dad. Nate."

"You?"

Karen pushed him out the door.

Tony could hear her walking behind him. Her breathing. Her hand on the railing. Then the thought of the freckles on her hand. The birthmark under her bellybutton.

He turned, said, "Thank you for this."

"Shut up."

Downstairs he made promises to his mother he could only hope to keep. He made promises to himself that he was unsure he could keep. And he made promises to Karen that went unsaid, but he knew were lies no matter how much he wanted them not to be.

He and his mother hugged. His mother got teary-eyed.

Karen stayed for dinner.

They watched *Seinfeld* over dessert.

Then Karen left, said she'd see Tony's mother in the morning. Said she'd see Tony at some point.

Then Tony's mother fell asleep on the couch.

And Tony went upstairs to pack.

***

Tony spends most of the morning and early afternoon sitting in the hotel lobby.

When he's not watching the elevator for his father, he's watching the desk clerk's patterns.

When he's not watching the desk clerk's patterns, he's refreshing the mobile wallet app on his phone.

When he's not refreshing the mobile wallet app on his phone, he's picking at the scabs on his swollen knuckles, or scratching at the red micro cuts on his arms, his neck, his face.

Just after lunch, the desk clerk steps away, walks across the lobby to the public unisex restroom.

Mikey pops his head up from behind the desk, says, "Psst,"

waves Tony over.

Tony's up after he hears the restroom door close. He jumps the desk without looking to see if anyone's watching.

The Xerox machine hums in the back corner.

Tony lifts the lid, places his note on the glass, programs the thing to print a hundred copies, and ducks.

Mikey says, "Why are we hiding?"

"Shh."

"It."

"Swear Jar."

"Hey, you can't—"

Tony presses a finger to his lips, waits.

Once the machine finishes up, Tony stands grabs his copies, the original, turns, jumps back over the desk, and smiles as the desk attendant asks him what he was doing back there.

"Making copies."

"You could've just asked. I would've done it for you."

Mikey laughs the entire elevator ride to the fourth floor.

Tony starts with 407.

He knocks, slips the original note under the door.

He goes down the halls, folding the copies in half, stuffing them under doors.

He does his floor first, goes up to the fifth, down to the third, second, first.

Some people pop their heads out, say what the hell, holding up the note.

Tony apologizes to them, takes the note back, tells them it won't happen again.

Sometimes he forgets which rooms he's already hit, slips the notes inside the same room twice. Once, three times.

He's on the second floor when one of the hotel staff approaches him and tells him of the hotel policy regarding solicitors.

Tony says, "I'm not soliciting anything." Then he hands over one of the notes.

The staff member reads the note, cocks an eyebrow, says, "You can't disturb our guests like this, sir. We've gotten several calls already."

"I'm not disturbing anyone. I'm just sliding these things under people's doors."

"That's disturbing the guests, sir."

That's when Tony turns and sprints down the hallway to the elevator.

Back at the room Tony slides the Do No Disturb sign into the key slot, closes the door, then stares through the peephole at 407.

He laughs. Two rooms staring each other in the face with signage saying they want nothing to do with one another.

He leans his shoulder into the door, forehead above the peephole. Waits.

Mikey talks, but Tony doesn't listen.

The hotel staff member knocks, but Tony doesn't say anything, just watches until the guy walks away.

It's an hour before he legs begin to ache. Before his eyelids start to droop. Before his knees clobber the door, wake him up just before he collapses onto the floor.

This time he listens when Mikey tells him to go to bed despite the sun just starting to set. And he sleeps until he hears paper being slid under his door.

He's up, tripping over blankets that were thrown off the bed overnight, covering his eyes from the morning sunlight.

He's on his knees in front on the door, lifts the sheet that was left for him.

His bill.

A reminder that checkout's at eleven.

He checks the peephole. The Do No Disturb sign across the hall.

Then it's Mikey pulling at his shirt.

Tony turns, leans against the door, slides to the floor.

Mikey grabs his face, said, "You promised."

"I'm promised a lot of things I can't deliver on."

"Then let's go home. That'll be a promise and a half you're keeping."

"Bullshit."

Mikey holds up a hand, puts up a finger, "One, you told me we'd leave once you did everything you could to find your Dad. You did that. We can go now." He puts up another finger, "Two, you'll be going home. You promised your mom you'd be home."

It takes Tony a while to stand. Longer to get in the shower. Almost an hour to bring himself to pack his shit.

When he and Mikey leave the room, Tony knocks on the door across the hall again.

No one answers.

"I'm leaving now," he says.

Still nothing.

He slides another copy of the note under the door and follows Mikey to the elevator.

He gets nasty looks from the hotel staff walking through the lobby.

People he recognizes from yesterday, people who stepped outside to ask him about the note, cock eyebrows, look away, point.

Tony says nothing, keeps walking. Through the sliding doors, past people unloading their cars, across the parking lot to his car.

He throws his duffel in the backseat.

Mikey crosses his fingers, smiles.

The car starts with the first try.

No green arrow. No grinding sounds. No shakes.

He shifts into reverse, pulls out of his spot, then out of the lot, and follows the GPS directions to the highway.

Then he makes three lefts in a row and pulls back into the hotel parking lot, ignores Mikey telling him to stop.

Tony parks, says, "Wait here," and jogs back into the hotel.

He catches the same looks from the same people—more worried now than pissed.

He takes the elevator up to the fourth floor.

He runs to 407, sees the open door, says Dad, walks inside.

A woman wearing a staff shirt jumps spins around, says, "Holy God, you scared me."

Tony says, "When did you get here?"

"What?"

"When did you start cleaning this room?"

"I don't know, couple minutes ago?"

"Did you see the person who left?" He pulls his phone, finds the picture of his father, hands it over.

"I saw someone walking down the hall with a bag, other than that I don't know."

"Which way did he go?"

The woman sticks out her thumb, and points left down the hall.

Tony thanks her, says, "Sorry for scaring you," and takes off in her thumb's direction.

There's no one to see on his entire run around the fourth floor, which circles back to the elevator bank.

He hits the Down button, and Mikey says, "You left the car on."

"What?"

"You left it on."

"I meant to do that."

The elevator doors open, they step inside. Mikey says, "Why?"

"So we wouldn't have any trouble starting it again."

"You're lying."

Most of the people milling around the lobby have cleared out. It's the guy from the first night standing behind the desk, someone flattening out a dollar bill for the vending machine.

Tony asks the both of them if they saw his father walk through the lobby just now, holding his phone up to their faces.

The vending machine guy shrugs. The clerk says, "Sir, I told—"

"Oh, fuck it."

Breathing heavy, sweating, Tony runs out the doors into the heat.

He smells smoke.

Mikey says, "Uh oh."

Tony doesn't ask what. Doesn't look at Mikey at all. He already knows.

His car is in flames.

Glowing orange and smoking, fire eats up the insides. The steering wheel, the seats, his duffel bag in the back.

Then it's the envelope tucked under a windshield wiper.

Tony runs, makes sounds he's never heard himself make. Desperate, panicked, whiney.

The windshield bows inward. The windows blow out. The trash bag melts.

Tony reaches into the flames, finds paper with his fingertips.

The hood pops open when the engine ignites. He's forced onto his ass with the shock, onto gravel, onto glass.

Then it's the pain.

His hand on fire.

The envelope on the blacktop on fire.

Tony writhes on the ground from the burns on his hand and forearm, the heat on his face, but watches the envelope burn away to a letter inside. The letter curls, blackens, sparks and breaks open around a glass cylinder.

Nate.

Tony reaches for the vial of ashes with his good hand.

Then the car's undercarriage bursts. Sends another gust of hot air, fire, and shrapnel at Tony. Knocks him flat to the ground again.

He opens one eye, the other, can't see the vile, the black pile of flakes from the envelope and letter.

He crawls, hand and knees, wrecked arm tucked to his chest. Through the glass, metal, ash. Bleeding, screaming from his burns. Screaming, "Where is it?"

And, "Where did it go?"

And, "Do you see it?"

Until the strength in his good arm gives out, puts him face-down in black chunks of his car.

He rolls onto his back sucking snot back into his nose, wiping his eyes with his shirt.

It's Mikey telling him to get up.

Tony asking if he saw where the vile went. Pushing himself backward with his feet, dragging his ass along the blacktop to a parking block. His arm, black and red most of the way to his elbow.

Mikey sits down next to him, pulls his knees to his chest.

"You see it?" Tony says.

Mikey looks at him, looks away.

People come to Tony, ask what he needs, ask if he's okay. They tell him an ambulance is on the way, tell him the fire company's coming. They hand him water, offer to help him with whatever.

Tony and Mikey nod, say thank you.

Then it's sirens, lights, noise.

And Tony and Mikey sit and stare.

Tony's eyes sifting through the soot for the vial.

Mikey's at Tony covered in blood and ashes.

Someone turned the light off. The boy doesn't remember who did it. Or when it happened.

Sometimes, when he wakes up in the middle of the night, he sees things. Sometimes it's Shredder standing where his closet should be. Or Krang sitting on the TV stand across the room. But everything—after a flipped-on light, or a bit of convincing— turns out to be just a mess of hangers creating sharp angles in the darkness. Or the old television sitting across the room.

But now. Now there is something in the room. And it stands at the end of the bed moving slow, shifting its limbs into familiar shapes the boy has seen before. Has done before.

The boy says, "Raph?"

"Just practicing my moves," the boy's brother says. "Master Splinter told me to."

In the dark, the boy focuses on the shell, the sai, the moves. He says, "I'm sleeping."

"Not if you're talking to me you're not."

"Sleeping."

The boy's brother jumps up onto his bed. He doesn't make much noise aside from the groaning springs under his feet. He says, "I need your help. Shredder erased my games on Super Nintendo. I can't get them back alone."

The boy smiles, rolls himself over, keeps himself from laughing by breathing into his pillow.

His brother says, "I'll be in my room. Remember, if you're going to help? Be ninja."

The boy waits for his bedroom door to close. Then he slips out of bed. He puts his shell on, buckles his father's belt around his waist, tucks his nunchucks between the belt and shell. Then he ties his mask on. He says, "Cowabunga."

He doesn't make a sound in the hallway, steps over the noisy spots in the hardwood. He turns the doorknob to his brother's room slow enough to hear it working, clicking, unlatching.

Inside, his brother sits in front of the TV in his orange mask and shell. He brings his finger to his lips, shushes, then waves the boy over.

The boy sits next to his brother.

Level after level the boy's brother plays through the game.

The boy doesn't ask for a turn or speak at all. He watches while his brother plays. And this goes on for an hour.

Two.

Three.

Until the boy's head is on his brother's shoulder. Until he can't fight his eyelids anymore. Until he lets himself just listen to the game being played.

Until he's asleep. Sitting on the floor, next to his brother, who plays on.

20

Tony smokes sitting on the parking block in front of the black spot left by his car.

He shuffles his feet, makes footprints in the soot, scrapes them away. Wonders if Nate's ashes are mixed somewhere in the melted blacktop. If the vial glowed orange, sank into itself, turned into one of the dried globs catching the soles of his sneakers.

He stubs out his smoke in the black, lights another.

The Extended Stay was nice enough to wash his last set of clothes. But he can still smell his melting car on his skin. The smell of his burning skin is baked into his nose hairs. Mixed with the cigarettes, the burn ointment, the antibiotic gauze. His senses pick up nothing but...whatever he is now.

It's the fourth time he's left his room in as many days. The second time he's been outside that he hasn't dirtied his hands digging through the ashes. The first time the pain meds haven't reminded him of his impressions of Nate.

He still has to squint in the sun, though. Drugs leave funny scars.

When his stitches—where glass had to be dug from his skin—begin to tighten, when the burns on his face feel hotter than usual, that's when Tony knows it's almost time to go back inside.

He stands, stretches, winces and flicks his cigarette into the middle of the lot.

Mikey, standing on the other side of the burn splotch, says, "Hey, watch this." He jumps, kicks, lands, somersaults, ends in a karate stance twirling his nunchucks. "Cool, right? Just learned that one."

Tony clamps his smoke between his lips, claps his good hand on his thigh, says, "Nice one. But how much longer do you think I'm going to put up with this?"

Mikey scratches his head, says, "Um," drags out the M sound. Then, "Oh, yeah. Watch this one." He stands up straight, hurls himself backward and lands on his shell.

Tony says, "That was awful. You good?"

Mikey rolls over, his hand behind him. He says, "Yeah. Got any Turtle Wax?"

They both laugh.

Maybe the medicine is still working its way out of Tony's system. He has to force himself to stop.

But Mikey keeps giggling.

Tony says, "You did see it, right?"

Mikey gets up, brushes himself off. Says nothing.

"If you saw it, I saw it."

Tony's phone goes off in his pocket.

Mikey goes back to karate.

Into the phone, Tony says, "Hey, Mom."

On the other end, "How are you feeling?"

"Good, Mom. I'm fine." He hadn't wanted to worry her, refused to let the hospital call her. But he told her about the car. And the vial. Despite having nothing to show for it.

"Are you sure?" his mother says.

"I'm sure."

"Have you booked your flight yet?"

"Still figuring things out. But I'll call as soon as I know. Talk to you soon."

Tony ends the call, stands, leaves Mikey to his moves.

***

The room stinks. Antiseptic, hydrogen peroxide.

He's kept the Do Not Disturb sign in the door his entire stay, let the bandages pile up in the trashcans, let the empty food cartons rot on top of the mini-fridge, let himself smoke in the room once, twice. He left too little time to clean up between doses of Percocet—before he learned Take As Needed doesn't mean Take When Achy.

He undoes layer after layer of bandages. Removes nonstick pads from the most severe burns. Wraps the bad hand, most of his arm under his elbow, in plastic. Rubber-bands it to healthy skin. Then he gets in the shower. He washes his bloated body, massages hotel shampoo into his smoky hair, cleans his stitched up skin, all one handed. All slow, deliberate, practiced.

After he finishes, he stares at himself naked in the mirror. Black bags under his eyes. Bloated gut with a trail of black fur running down the middle. His wrecked hand almost glowing in comparison to the rest of his pasty body.

Mikey knocks on the door.

"Yeah?"

"Phone's ringing."

"Hold on."

He wraps a towel around himself, heads out of the bathroom, and picks up his phone singing through the chorus of "Ninja Rap."

Karen says, "How are you?"

Tony sits on the bed next to his bag of bandages, creams, and wipes. He tucks the phone between his ear and shoulder, says, "Good. How are you?"

"Your mom's worried about you."

"I'm good, really." He rubs burn ointment into his flaking, red, black skin.

"I'm worried about you."

"We both know that's not true."

There's silence on the other end. Just Karen's faint breathing. Then she says, "Are you coming home?"

He applies medicated pads to the worst sections, says, "Of course I am. Soon as I figure out how I'm going to do it."

"What's that mean?"

"Just..." One end of an Ace bandage between his teeth, the other orbiting his arm, Tony says, "Soon," like Shoon.

"What's that mean? Did you book a flight?"

"Not yet." Another roll of wrapping.

"Tony."

"Karen."

"Are you really coming home?"

"Yes. I am."

"You have a responsibility—"

"Karen, I came all the way out here because I felt responsible. Yeah, I failed at bringing Dad home, but, it's like...Ever feel like you were so close to something, a win, whatever. So close that if you could just hold on for a second, or a minute longer, something'll go your way?"

"I don't know, maybe?"

"Well, I don't know how else to describe it then."

Karen ends the call.

Tony stands, dresses in his old tattered, torn clothes the best he can, and sets his phone to vibrate after calling for a cab.

***

On the ride to the Promenade Temecula, Tony checks his father's bank records. Something he hasn't done for days.

The ATM withdraw posted. Checking is at zero. Nothing on the credit card.

Next to him, Mikey leans over, looks at Tony's phone, says, "Where do you think he is?"

"Could be anywhere really."

Tony watches the cab driver's eyes in the rearview mirror. He says nothing, pulls his phone, opens Facebook, accepts the friend request from Marie that's been waiting there for a week or so. Then he types out a message to her saying he didn't find what he was looking for. But he's pretty sure it can't matter anymore.

Then he takes a picture of his bandaged hand, sends it to Marie with the caption, Ugliness on the Outside.

The cab pulls up to the front entrance of the mall.
Tony says, "Is it cool if I pay with a credit card?"
The cab driver says, "I'd prefer cash."
Tony says, "Sorry. I don't have anything else."

***

Mikey fits in just fine with the customers at Hot Topic.

Tony gets odd looks. He hasn't belonged here since he turned eighteen, but a trip every year or so for new band tees never hurt anybody. Until now. Disheveled at best in tattered clothes and covered in wounds.

He stares up at the wall placards displaying the t-shirts, tries to ignore looks from high schoolers. Tries to ignore Mikey asking for some Ninja Turtles key chains. Lunch boxes. Thermoses. Vintage action figures. The stuff Tony grew up with that's cycled itself out and back in without him noticing.

His whole life in reruns.

Tony looks for a Descendents shirt. Then a Misfits. A Social Distortion. An Operation Ivy. But there's a shirt with a splotch of red oozing from the neckline, and The Devil Wears Prada in jagged typeface in the center of the mess. Another with a teenaged girl looking bored, holding her own guts in her bloody hands, advertising Bring Me the Horizon. Then what looks to be an eye exam, large letters at the top reducing in size until Tony has to squint to see the last few lines that spell Of Mice and Men.

"These are band names?" he says, laughs.

The cashier, a girl with her ears gauged, her eyes painted, feline, says, "Are you looking for someone in particular?"

Tony whips around, says, "What? Was somebody asking for me?"

Eyebrow cocked, upper lip hooked in the corner, the cashier says, "I meant bands, dude. Like, is there a band you're looking for?"

"Is everything you have up on the wall?"

"Pretty much. There's some older stuff in the clearance pile over there, though." She points to a table in back covered in heaps of clothing, a sign that says fifty to seventy-five percent off and Everything Must Go.

Tony shakes his head. One thing to linger somewhere people will stare, another to dig through their garbage hoping to find something to bronze.

He turns, finds Mikey staring at him across the store.

Mikey waves.

Tony smiles. A little one. A nod.

Then Mikey points at a Ninja Turtles figure and asks if Tony can buy it for him.

The cashier girl says, "You know, if you buy five shirts you get a free one."

"No thanks. I thought Of Mice and Men was just a book."

The girl nods, says, "Hemingway, right?"

Tony's eyes widen. He says, "Okay, sure."

Across the room, Mikey says cowabunga, and Michelangelo, please.

Tony steps away from the counter to the Turtles display, picks up a figure, then feels his phone in his pocket.

He answers, says, "Hi, Chris."

"Hey, man. How's it going?"

"Good."

Back at the counter, the cashier scans the box, tells Tony his total.

Tony says, "Holy shit."

Over the phone, Chris says, "What? What's wrong now?"

"These used to be five bucks when I was a kid."

The girl shrugs, bags the figure, puts it on the counter.

Tony looks at Mikey.

Mikey, hands folded, says, "Please, please, please."

Tony rolls his eyes, uses his bandaged hand to keep his phone to his ear. "Still there?"

"Where are you?" Chris says.

"In a store."

"Oh thank God. Thought you were talking to someone else while not, you know, with someone else."

"Thought we were going to talk about that later."

Chris starts to speak, but Tony doesn't hear much while he works through the transaction. Handing over a card, signing a receipt, switching his phone to his good hand, gesturing for the girl to hang the plastic bag from his bad hand, mouthing thank you.

Into the phone, Tony says, "Say again."

"I was saying I think it's time for you to come home."

"My mom call you?"

"Karen."

"Didn't realize you were that close."

"We're not. Meg was pretty pissed."

"Meg? Seriously?"

"She's not so bad. Says she'll kill you if she sees you. Jealous after a second date. But still."

Tony turns around, asks the cashier girl if she knows of anywhere he can get a six pack of undershirts and pair of jeans for under thirty

bucks.

The girl rolls her eyes.

Chris says, "Hello?"

"Sorry."

Mikey asks to hold the toy, says he won't open it until they get back to the hotel, that he just wants to look at the box.

Tony tells him to stop it.

Chris says, "Who are you talking to now?"

"What's that?"

"Come home, dude. People are starting to freak out a little over here."

"No, they're not. Stop it."

"They're worried enough to call people and ask them to call you to convince you to fly home. What are you waiting for?"

Tony takes a breath, says, "I don't think I should be waiting for anything anymore."

"What is it, then?"

Tony doesn't say anything.

"Hello?"

"I think I just want to do something on my own for once."

"What does that mean?"

"Just think I want to figure out what I want to do and do it."

They talk a little longer, but Tony says he's got to go and ends the call before Chris can say anything else.

Mikey says, "When are we going home?"

"Don't know." Tony turns, walks toward the Macy's sign.

"I'll tell you what I saw if we leave right now."

"No, you won't."

"Want to make a dollar bet?"

"Nope."

"Why not?"

Tony stops, turns, says, "Pretty sure, either way, it won't be very good for me."

Mikey puts his fists on his hips, makes a face. "Then can I hold the toy now, please?"

Tony laughs, leaves Mikey where he stands.

***

Back at the hotel, Tony changes into his new clothes. They feel new, smell new. They're not faded, torn. They make the mirror take it easier on him.

He orders Domino's.

He eats while watching movies he charges to his room.

He remembers liking *Teenage Mutant Ninja Turtles III* better when he was a kid. But Mikey loves it, practices his moves during the fight scenes.

Tony silences his phone once, twice, three times.

Then he turns it off for the night.

It's just getting dark when he figures he'd be spending most of his time staring into the vial of Nate's ashes if he had it. Tracing the ridges of the granules with his eyes until the sun comes back up. Using pain meds to sleep though the day with it clutched in his hand.

Without it, he orders Chinese with the hotel phone, has a couple cigarettes outside waiting for the delivery guy to show up. He eats until he's full, watches another movie and a half.

Then he falls asleep just past ten. And sleeps through the night.

***

Tony smokes sitting on a parking block a few spots down from the black spot left by his car.

Cigarette between his lips, phone on his thigh, he scrolls through the texts he missed overnight.

Karen saying he's the same person he was before he left.

Chris saying that there's nothing in California for Tony, so why not just get on a plane, come home.

His mother saying she's worried about him, telling him to come back.

Mikey, sitting next to him, says, "Think your dad will go home?"

Tony laughs, "Thought we weren't going to talk about him anymore."

"Do you think he'd open the front door like he used to when he'd come home from work and say he was sorry for leaving?"

"Probably not," Tony says, lighting another cigarette. "I'm sure he'd find a way to justify everything he's done. Something like, there comes a time in every man's life when he questions just about every single move he's made. And when there are no answers to any of those questions, just sadness and pain, there's nothing else to do but go out looking for some new questions to ask."

"Boring."

Tony laughs, says, "Yeah, well, he never had a way with words."

"What are you going to say?"

"What do you mean?"

"Well, you're ignoring everyone at home. You're not running, but you're not there. Wouldn't going home be the opposite of what he's doing? You always liked that."

Tony stands, says, "I'm not going to go home in spite of Dad."

"Then why go home at all?"

"That's a good question. Maybe I won't. Look, everything I've ever done has been a reaction to one thing or another. A defensive move one day. An aggressive one the next. Or I didn't make a move at all and shut down. I've never done anything for myself. Like, at the core. Everything was a response."

"That sounds like what you said your dad would say."

Tony gives Mikey the finger, arm straight, angled down into the kid's face.

Mikey sticks out his tongue, eyes clenched shut behind his mask.

The sun starts pulling at Tony's stitches, making his burns sting. He says, "Let's go," takes a long last drag, drops the butt, doesn't bother looking over to the black spot.

Mikey stands, brushes off the back of his shell, says, "Can't you do both?"

Tony turns. Mikey the stillest he's been. The sun melts the air above the car burn behind him.

Tony says, "Both what?"

"Can't you go home because it's something you need to do mixed with something you want to do?"

"What makes you think I want to?"

Mikey cocks an eyebrow, crosses his arms.

"Whatever. I'd like to do something for myself. That's all."

"Then do it your way."

Tony almost lights another cigarette but doesn't. He says, "Why are you still here?"

"I'm you, dummy. Just trying to help. My way."

"You mean, my way."

"You're not a dummy all the time, are you?"

Tony tries not to laugh. Shuts his mouth up tight. Looks away. But he gives in, laughs.

Mikey does too.

A woman, walking through the parking lot stares as she passes, walks faster when Tony makes eye contact.

"Sorry," Tony says. "Just thinking out loud."

***

Tony uses the hotel's computers to transfer funds from savings, to pull a high-interest cash advance from his credit card to his checking account.

The cab to San Diego International burns through what little is left in on his credit card.

Plastic-bagged luggage in hand, Tony watches the departure screens, looks for flights to Philadelphia.

He waits in line to buy a ticket, texts.

Chris is going to pick him up from the airport.

Karen's going to kick his ass when he gets to the house.

His mother's going to make a nice dinner for him.

Mikey wanders through the crowds, walks farther and farther away after each time he comes back to tell Tony he's bored waiting.

Tony minds himself, doesn't respond with words. Speaks in cocked eyebrows, head nods.

He shuffles his feet, moves forward in line. A handful of people ahead of him.

He'll laugh when he's asked if he has anything to check. He'll wander around the terminal after getting his ticket, watch people with their families, watch people make business calls. He'll flip through shit books on cardboard displays. Cringe at the prices of headphones and wireless phone chargers.

And if he had it, he'd read his father's letter over and over sitting in the terminal bar waiting for his plane. He'd convince himself it was good enough. Enough of a reason to move on.

He'd hold the vial of Nate's ashes in his good hand. Rub it for good luck before getting on the plane. Hoping somewhere Nate was making up for everything.

They'd get him home. They'd be reasons to go home, start over.

He moves forward again. Two people away from the counter.

He reads the signs hanging above everyone's heads.

The names of airlines. Flight times.

Car rentals.

Then it's his car being dragged onto a tow bed smoking and soaked. The shiny red paint, bubbles of matte black. His iPod a metal lump fused with the melted center console. His duffel, ash. The t-shirts he'd worn since college, smoke. He and Karen in the backseat. He and Maura making out leaning up against the side. He and Chris listening to Lagwagon on CD. His father handing him the keys. His mother driving him to school. Nate passed out in the back.

He steps up to the counter, says hi.

"How can I help you today, sir?" the guy dressed like a pilot who's not really a pilot says, smiling.

Tony takes a breath. Once. Twice. Three times

"Sir?"

"Where can I rent a car?"

The guy behind the counter points, pissed. And Tony gets out of line, starts walking.

Mikey says, "Where are you going?"

"Home."

"Then what are you doing?"

Tony stops, turns, says, "Can't be a dummy all the time, can I?"

"My way?"

"My way."

Mikey smiles, says, "Cowabunga, dude."

***

Karen is pissed.

Tony's mother cries a little but says she understands.

Chris asks him what the fuck.

He tells them all he's on his way. But he won't be flying. He says, "I feel like I need to take my time."

Karen hangs up on him.

His mother says they'll have that meal together when he gets home.

And Chris asks him if he needs any money—which he does.

Tony's walked to a gray sedan. The attendant hands over the keys, a brochure, the insurance policy should Tony change his mind.

Before tossing his bag in the back and getting in the car, Tony looks left, right, behind him, off into the vastness of the garage.

No karate.

No laughing.

He says, "Mikey?"

Nothing.

Just his voice bouncing from the concrete under his feet, off the cement walls, to the metal skeleton roof, and back to his ears.

He takes a breath, gets in the car.

It takes him couple minutes to figure out where everything is. The headlight switch is in the wrong spot. He can't turn the windshield wipers on without spraying fluid onto the glass. The gear shift isn't behind the steering wheel.

He'll be halfway across the country before he figures out how the thing works.

He pulls the Ninja Turtles toy in its box from his bag in the backseat. Opens it, wrestles the figure out of its plastic mold and sets it on the dashboard with its back to him. If he gets tired, at least Michelangelo can watch the road for him.

He opens the GPS app on his phone, taps the Home button.

A tinny female voice tells him he's all set, to drive safely.

He breathes deep, says, "Ready?"

He pulls out of the rental lot garage, checks for Mikey in the rearview mirror.

Checks again on Airport Terminal Road.

And again on North Harbor Drive.

On West Grape Street.

Interstate 5.

Merging onto 163, he readies himself, expects Mikey to pop his head between the seats, to yell cowabunga, something stupid.

Tony would scream, high pitched and sustained for effect, swerve the car a little.

Mikey would laugh.

Tony would say, "Fuck you."

Mikey would say, "Swear Jar."

But nothing happens. No Mikey. No laughing.

Just the GPS telling him to merge onto I-15

So he does.

Tony has to remember not to use his bad hand. Has to work against his instincts. Otherwise it's pain. Enough to make everything that's not hurting that second more sensitive.

It takes a while to figure out what hurts and what doesn't. He can't rely on his burned up fingers for much. He has to use his knee to help with the steering. Has to keep his good hand on top of the wheel, ready.

It gets a little easier after a hundred or so miles. But still, easy is relative.

Nothing would've hurt on the plane. He wouldn't have had to do anything. Sip free drinks. Buy doubles of the good stuff. He would've put his seat back, tried falling asleep. Would've stared out the windows at the clouds. Would've read his father's letter, held onto Nate's ashes.

Luxuries.

Fantasies.

Simple.

But now, he drives until he can't. Until his eyes won't stay open.

He stops, sleeps a while. Then gets back on the road when he's ready.

It'll take him a while to get home. He tells his mother, Karen,

Chris so. He can't give them an ETA, or even name a day. He says he can't because there's a lot out of his control. Weather. Traffic. Whatever.

"I'll get there," he says.

"I'm on my way," he says.

"I'll see you soon," he says.

And he's not lying. Or stalling.

He's driving at his own pace.

Doing what he needs to do to make sure he gets there when he's ready. Learning to live with how bad his body hurts.

When his mother, Karen, Chris ask what he means by soon, Tony answers with what he knows for certain. It may be all he has to offer right now, but it's a start. And it's the first promise he's sure he can keep.

He'll get there.

Acknowledgments

My wife Lizz is the most optimistic person I've ever met. Considering I'm the exact opposite, the happy, encouraging, and creative environment she created allowed this book to be written. In keeping with our nightly tradition of falling asleep to Nick at Nite, I'll borrow Full House's DJ Tanner's words to thank Lizz: "Thankyouthankyouthankyou!" Literally wouldn't be here without you.

I wrote a Power Rangers "novel" when I was a kid, handed it over to my mother and told her it would make us rich. It didn't. Neither will Good Grief. Regardless, my mom and dad let me figure out what I wanted to do with a soft hand and an open mind. For that freedom and support—and my hundreds of quirks—thank you.

Thank you, Mallory Smart, Bulent Mourad, and Maudlin House for having faith in this weird, sad, funny book. And me as a weird, sad, funny writer. As you read above, I've been writing a while. This is dream come true. Thank you.

Thank you to Joshua Isard, Katherine Hill, Paul Elwork, and my Arcadia University MFA cohort, especially Maddie Anthes, Nate Drenner, Andy Mark, Greg Oldfield, and Chad Towarnicki. You guys taught me to write. Can't thank you enough for scaring the hell out of me and ripping me a well-deserved new one whenever my stories weren't up to snuff.

I learned I could maybe give this writing thing a go at Chestnut Hill College. Dr. Barbara Lonnquist, Dr. Karen Getzen, Dr. Suzanne del Gizzo, and Sister Rita Michael told me so, each in their own way. Very uncharacteristically of me at the time, I believed them. Well, here we are. Thank you.

My first writing group was with Dean Steckel and Zach Smith. Over cigars, beers, power metal, and heaps of foul language, we had ridiculous amounts of fun savagely berating one another for our shit writing. It was the best.

Every Monday night I drink beer with a merry band of wondrous scoundrels at a bar called Pizza Time Saloon in Lansdale, Pennsylvania. Michael Zakrzewski, Michael Mintzer, Jerred Snow, Josie Nagurney, Dave Bauer, Aaron Trieu, Dr. Joseph

"Dr. Candy F. Mang" Candelore, David Boe, Todd Schatz, and Kyle Rodden are all supportive, and they're also all smart enough to verbally slap me off my proverbial high horse whenever I catch my own scent.

To all my in-laws, cousins, aunts, uncles, and grandparents, you are legion, and you are many. As such, if I'd attempted to write each of your names here, two things would've happened: 1.) Longest acknowledgments section ever, and 2.) I would have left someone out because I'm just about as scatterbrained as a person can get. So, to each and every one of you, thank you. Truly. Your support means everything.

To everyone I've played punk rock with over the last sixteen years especially Eric Jaen, Bob Maiden, Rory Staub (who read an early, early draft of Good Grief), and Danny Herb. We've probably had enough fun to fill ten lifetimes. How about ten more?

Thank you to the book.record.beer guys, Nick Mehalick, Daniel DiFranco, and Michael Mehalick. Writers, artists, and scholars alike.

The second, third, and fourth drafts of this novel were revised, edited, and scrutinized to the music of Explosions in the Sky. Mostly The Earth Is Not a Cold Dead Place, and Take Care, Take Care, Take Care. Occasionally The Rescue. The rest were involved too. Just trying to be specific here, people.

And finally, thank you for reading.

Thank you.

-Nick Gregorio, 6/11/17

Nick Gregorio writes, teaches, and lives just outside of Philadelphia with his wife and dog. His fiction has appeared in Crack the Spine, Hypertrophic Literary, Driftwood Press and many more. After graduating from Arcadia University with his MFA in Creative Writing in 2015, he went on to become a fiction editor for Driftwood Press, contributing editor for Spectrum Culture, and cohost for the monthly podcast book.record.beer. Good Grief is his first novel.

For news, updates, and other assorted silliness, please visit: www.nickgregorio.com